BURNING EMBERS

L.S. PULLEN

Copyright © 2020 by L.S. Pullen

Burning Embers

Text copyright © 2020 L. S. Pullen

All Rights Reserved

Published by: L. S. Pullen

Beta Read by: Kirsten Moore

Edited by: Cassie Sharp

Proofread by: Crystal Blanton

Formatted by: Leila Pullen

The right of L.S. Pullen to be identified as the author of the work has been asserted by her in accordance with the copyright, Designs and patents act 1988

No part of this book may be reproduced in any form or by any electronic or mechanical means, including information storage and retrieval systems, without written permission from the author, except for the use of brief quotations in a book review.

All characters in this publication are fictional and any resemblance to real persons, living or dead is purely coincidental.

Dedication

To those fighting an invisible battle, who feel unseen and unheard, you are not alone. I see you, and I hear you, don't give up. You've got this.

"I am alone and miserable. Only someone as ugly as I am could love me."
—Mary Shelley, *Frankenstein*

Chapter One

Rachel

The bar is buzzing tonight; apparently, Thursday is the new Friday. I glance at my Rolex and want to swear. He's late and by more than what's socially acceptable. Why did I agree to this? I blow out a breath, trying not to look at my watch again. Because I miss intimacy, miss being cherished. And I'm getting bored with my vibrator.

Olly eyes me suspiciously from behind the bar, and I can't help but exaggerate an eye roll back so he knows that *I* know he's been watching me. I would be embarrassed at how long I've been waiting for my date if I thought the cocky bartender cared. He probably finds me pathetic. Though we share mutual friends, and he's nothing but amicable, I've always gotten this…vibe from Olly. Like he'd prefer us *not* run in the same circles.

I want to refuse to admit that I've been stood up…again, but I have. I'm sick of it, and I know I'm too stubborn for my own good to get up and leave right now. Picking at the corner of a cardboard coaster, I continue to make a mental list of who to avoid in the messed-up dating pool.

Men who are married.
Men in relationships.
Men whose mum still panders to their every need.
Men who are still in love with their ex.
Men who run when they find out I'm a mother.

I break off from my list when I sense his presence. We barely talk, and yet I've always felt him. Olly, who is carefree with everyone else, isn't like that with me. He's always kept me at an arm's length. I've seen him flirt with other patrons… even my friends, Felicity and Sophie—and surprisingly once even Simon—but never me.

"Been stood up?" he asks, not even attempting to sugar coat it.

"Oliver," I reply. His name drips off my tongue with a trace of venom. Truth is, I don't even know if he's an Oliver; he could be just Olly, but any excuse to get under his skin… I let out a heavy sigh before turning my face up to meet his eyes. Blue-violet orbs stare back. And for a split second, I'm ensnared, forgetting what he just said. Does he manage to do this to all the girls?

"You okay?" he asks, his gaze darting over my face.

I look away and concentrate on the perspiration as it works its way down my almost empty glass of soda. "I'm fine, thank you, Oliver. Just fine," I lie.

He hesitates, ready to rebut my comment no doubt, but surprises me when he doesn't. "Well, you know where I am if you need me."

He walks away, leaving an earthy scent of sandalwood in his wake that has me wanting to trail after him. This only fuels my irritation with him, my no-show date, and every male currently on the planet. I'll wait a little longer, and then I'm out of here.

Olly

Rachel's been sitting there for the best part of forty-five minutes, and I feel sorry for her—almost. I thought she would've given up on waiting by now, but she appears to have been more irritated by my intrusion when, like a fool, I called her out on it. I never meant to embarrass her, but it just kind of slipped out.

I pause while mixing a mocktail when someone arrives, tapping her on the shoulder. She grins, but it's guarded as the guy leans down and kisses her cheek before he sits opposite.

Her lips move, but I can't read what she's saying. I slide the cocktail glass to the patron and smile as I pass her change. My eyes dart back to Rachel to see she's now up and walking towards me, purse in hand.

She looks around the bar for the other servers, but I'm the only one free. Resigned, she leans on her elbows, ash blonde locks falling over her shoulder, teasing the wooden surface below. She clears her throat. "Can I get a bourbon and another soda water with lime please?" she asks.

I quirk my eyebrows but nod. He couldn't even get her a drink after keeping her waiting? She pulls out her card and fiddles with it while I prepare the drinks. I slide them over in front of her and enter the amount owed into the card reader. She taps her card, the machine taking its time, thinking, before finally delivering the bad news. Her eyes glance to the reader and back to the card in her hand. Sighing, she digs through her purse for another. It's declined, too.

"Fuck," she curses under her breath, cheeks glowing red.

Something shifts in my gut. "I got this," I say, but she leans away, shaking her head. It's not hard to see when she pulls a twenty-pound note from her purse that it's the only money she has in there.

"I insist," I say, then call out to Mavis, "What happens when we serve our hundredth patron of the night, Mave?"

She smirks, her eyes dancing between Rachel and me. "They get their round on the house," she hollers back.

I turn back to Rachel and wink. An almost inaudible gasp escapes her plump lips, and I'm hit with the reminder that I've never flirted with her before. The soft scent of raspberries slithers along my senses, and between that sexy sound and the smell of fresh summer, I'm not sure which one is hotter.

Her eyes dart to her purse where she busies herself organising, placing everything back in its place. Just on the inside, staring up at me, is a picture of a toothless Molly-Mae, her daughter. My heart clenches. Lottie was around the same age the last time I saw her.

"I'll bring them over," I say, averting my eyes.

"Thank you," she replies. I know how sour those words must taste passing her lips, and I can't help but beam at her confusion.

Her hips sway as she returns to their table, and I stare at that voluptuous arse of hers. Mavis saddles up beside me, the smell of liquorice replacing the faint scent Rachel left in her wake. "Here you go." She passes me a tray, her eyes probing.

"What?" I ask

She shakes her head. "I thought we only do that on a Monday?"

I adjust the drinks on the tray. "Yeah, we do, but…I made an exception. Thanks for not outing me, by the way."

She nods, her expression amused, but I don't like it. "Well, you didn't ask me what day, did you?" Her hip bumps against mine before she returns to the other end of the bar.

I take the drinks over and place them between Rachel and the douche who dared to show up almost an hour late—who is now tapping away at his phone. I catch enough to see he's messaging someone about getting lucky. I clear my throat, and he puts it face down next to him.

"Do you want nachos with this?" I ask, addressing Rachel.

The corner of her mouth twitches, but it's the moron who answers, "Yes, and don't be stingy with the jalapeños."

I look at him but say nothing as I walk away until I hear Rachel's voice call out, "Thank you." I glance back over my shoulder, and her eyes are cast down. *How did she end up on a date with him?*

Continuing with the bar service, I keep my ears open for the buzzer indicating the nachos are ready, and then wave Mavis away before she grabs them. I place the large plate in the middle of their table along with two smaller ones and a pile of napkins.

"Hey, are you deaf?" asks the moron as I walk away.

"Excuse me?" I reply, turning back to him, stifling a glare.

"I said extra jalapeños."

His arrogant fucking demeanour rubs me the wrong way, but I keep my cool. "I heard you, but your date here," I say, gesturing to Rachel, "—is allergic. So how about you be a gentleman and go without."

His nostrils flare ever so slightly, ready to retort, but he must see something in my expression. His Adam's apple bobs ever so slightly, though he remains quiet.

"Thank you, Olly," Rachel says.

I turn and give her another wink. It's the first time she's ever called me *Olly*, the syllables dripping off her tongue as smooth as melted caramel. I step away, tossing her one last wink and watch as her lips twitch and eyebrows raise in appreciation. She deserves so much better than this knob of a date.

I'm distracted while making drinks, and I had to actually force myself to go to the back, a pile of dishes needing loaded. It took no time before I was back in my place at the bar, my thoughts betraying me. I don't know why I continue to glance in their direction, but I swear he keeps reaching his hand under the table. My fingers tingle with a charge of frustration.

She stands abruptly, grabbing her purse before she dashes to the ladies'.

I head over to clear the plates, and he's on his phone again. He sets it down, screen face up, still lit up on the message—something about his date being an easy lay. My heart hammers in my chest. It's none of your business, I tell myself.

"So, you know her?" he asks. Does this jerk not have any manners whatsoever? I nod, dropping the plates on top of each other a tad aggressively. "An ex or something?"

I ungracefully drop the plates back on the table with a heavy clunk, causing the prick to flinch.

"Nope, she's a regular here," I reply, and then want to kick myself. It sounded wrong, even to me. His mouth slides into a sleazy slant. I am just about to correct the terminology when Rachel returns, looking between the two of us.

But she doesn't sit back down. "I'm afraid I have to call it a night. I need to get home to my daughter," she says.

The moron dares to look inconvenienced by this but stands anyway. "Let me walk you out," he says.

She nods, but I notice her posture—rigid. She'd prefer it if they parted ways in here.

Without looking me in the eye, she grumbles goodbye and begins to walk towards the exit. His hand grazes her arse, and she sidesteps him. He doesn't take the hint, crowding her as they leave. I have to force myself not to grab him by the collar and sling him away from her.

Chapter Two

Olly

I've always been good at reading people—except with Rachel, who appears to have built her walls even higher than mine—and even those barriers weren't high enough to disguise the truth: she wasn't comfortable just now. I get this sinking sensation in the pit of my stomach and suck in a deep breath.

Leaving the plates, I wave at Mavis, holding up my palm and mouthing—*I'll be five minutes*. She nods, and I follow the path Rachel just took.

Jase, our head of security, smiles when I walk through the doors, my head turning left and right around the punters smoking outside.

I don't see her.

The hairs on the back of my neck rise. I choose to go left—there's a space between our building and the one next door where the streetlights don't quite reach.

"I'm not interested." Her voice catches my attention, but it's his back I see, crowding her against the wall.

She shoves at his chest, but he doesn't budge.

I place my hand over his shoulder and yank him away.

"What the fuck?" he groans.

"Yes, *what the fuck*, exactly. I suggest you make yourself scarce."

He looks to Rachel, then to me and shrugs. "It's not like she's worth my time, anyway."

Stepping around me—I don't leave him much room to pass—he scurries away like the rat he is. Rachel stands in place against the wall, her mouth slightly agape, eyes wide.

"Where are you parked?" I ask. She clears her throat and nods her head in the direction of her car. "I'll walk you."

Finding her voice, she says, "Okay, thanks."

I'm not sure what she's thanking me for, but I nod, stuffing my hands into the pockets of my jeans. She strides out and into the dim streetlight, and I fall into step beside her, our feet smacking into the concrete the only sound apart from an occasional car passing by.

Coming to a stop at what I presume is her car, I cock my head. It's not what I thought she'd drive. And I can't help shaking my head.

"What?" she asks, fidgeting. "If you're going to give me a lecture, you can leave it. Why do you think I only meet my dates *here*? Because it's a safe space. How was I to know he'd turn into a complete prick as soon as we walked outside?"

I raise my eyebrow at her. "Like he was such a great bloke inside?" I ask, deadpan. She squints at me, crossing her arms. I step in a little closer. She doesn't budge, raising her chin in defiance; I struggle to hold back a smile. "I was surprised this was your car," I say.

Her nostrils flare ever so slightly, jaw hardening. If I'm not mistaken, she appears more annoyed by *me* than she did with *what's-his-face* back there.

"Oliver, there is nothing wrong with Betty. So, you'll do well to keep your opinions to yourself."

I can't contain it as the laugh bubbles from my lips. "Betty," I wheeze out. "Who did you name your car after? Your grammy?" Her face goes slack, crestfallen, and I swallow my laugh, scrubbing my hand over my jaw.

"Yes, as a matter of fact, I did."

We stare at each other for what may only be for a few seconds, but it's enough to make me squirm. I'm such a fucking *tool*. I reach out and touch her arm. Heat radiates from her; I drop my hand. "Sorry."

"It's fine, Oliver, I know what you think of me. Spoilt little rich girl, right?"

I don't get the opportunity to answer as she continues, "Yes, my parents are minted. Yes, they piled me with gifts growing up, but I'd rather they had spent more time with me instead—" She stops abruptly, her eyes darting everywhere as she tries to cool her outburst. "Anyway, thanks for walking me to my car," she says, then hurries around to the driver's side and climbs in.

I tap my knuckle on the passenger window. She leans over and lowers it using the handle.

"For the record, I happen to think *Betty* suits her," I say.

I have no idea why I felt compelled to say this, but when the corners of her mouth rise in a small smile, I'm glad I did. I straighten and tap the roof of her VW Beetle. The squeak of the window being wound up makes me grin.

I head back in the direction of the bar, but I can't resist the urge to peer over my shoulder. My eyes connect with hers in her rear-view mirror as she drives away.

She's right.

I've always thought of her that way…up until she had Molly-Mae, anyway. But then she started working at the deli for Sophie—my boss, Charlie's, girlfriend—and I guess I saw glimpses of her I hadn't seen before. I definitely pretend otherwise, but I go out of my way on occasion to drop by and grab a sandwich or a cake in the hopes Rachel will be there. I always manage to get a rise out of her without even trying, and I can't deny I secretly enjoy I have some sort of effect on her.

"Jase, if you see the bloke who left with Rachel again, make sure to let him know he's barred."

"You got it," he replies.

I should leave her well alone, but truth is, she's piqued my interest and my curiosity. The more I see glimpses of a side to her that she tries so hard to conceal, the harder it's becoming to stay away as I should. She always seems irritated by me when I'm around, and damnit, I'm finding myself wanting to remedy her animosity towards me.

Chapter Three

Rachel

I was mortified last night with Olly's eyes staring after me as I drove away from the bar. But it made me think I need to consider a self-defence class. I hate that I even found myself cornered by Neal. He has to be one of the sleaziest guys I've met. I was shaken, and yet at the same time, so grateful Olly turned up when he did…though I was a little surprised, too.

It was one of the first things I googled when I returned home to a sleeping Molly after seeing the babysitter out. I booked a self-defence class for tomorrow, which works perfectly for me. Marcus said he'd take Molly, fingers crossed he doesn't bail out. Again. Being a single parent is bloody hard, and it makes dating that much more difficult to wade through. Marcus and I are more-or-less on friendly terms for Molly's sake. The break-up was hard, but it was doomed from the start—we were paired off as infants, our parents pushing for the relationship that never actually ended in real love…just a mixture of hormones and intrigue. And a beautiful little girl.

I enter *Sofia's* to find Sophie mixing up some butter icing, singing along to the radio. She waves the wooden spoon in the air, spinning on the spot when her eyes collide with mine.

"Hey, lovely," she says, turning the volume down.

"Hey, yourself, Hot Mumma."

She laughs off my comment, propping a hand on her hip. "Well?"

"Well, what?" I ask, dropping my bag onto one of the stools.

She rolls her eyes. "Your date—how was it?"

I eye the icing in the bowl and lean on the counter. Without asking, Soph grabs another spoon and scoops some mixture onto it before holding it out to me. I'm weak when it comes to sweet things, so I gladly take it from her. Sticking it into my mouth, I allow it to soak on my tongue—butterscotch. Smiling, I lick the spoon clean and place it in the dishwasher. "*Dreadful*. He was an absolute arsehole."

"What happened?"

I take a seat and give her the low down. When I'm finished regaling her, a look of mischief crosses her face.

"What is that look all about?"

She shakes the spoon in my direction. "Oh, you know… Olly being your knight in shining armour."

I scoff, but I don't have a retort. Sophie and her boyfriend, Charlie, are friends with Olly. He's worked for Charlie at the bar for years. Her suspicious smile makes me wonder if Olly has ever mentioned me… I shake the thought from my head. She's right, though, about him. I hate to think what might have happened if Olly hadn't come along when he did last night.

"I don't care what you say. I think he likes you," she says.

I hop off the stool and turn my back to her to hide my smile while I wash my hands. Guys like Olly and girls like me aren't a good match. Besides, he hasn't made the slightest notion—not even an inkling—that he's attracted to me.

I think of what he told Neal about jalapeños. How he knows they make me break out in hives…

I shake it off. I need to stop overthinking it, and maybe I should give up on dating for a while. Having a daughter seems to have one of the following reactions: run for the hills in case I'm trying to find Molly another daddy, or even better, they think I am an easy lay.

"I think it's easier to swear off guys for the foreseeable future."

Sophie's shoes squeak as she comes towards me, and I face her as I dry my hands.

"Let's not be too hasty now," she says, wiggling her eyebrows.

"Some days I wonder if I should've stayed with Marcus—at least the sex was good." But I wanted to set a good example for Molly; I don't want her ever settling.

Sex was never the issue between Marcus and me—trust was. And it wasn't all Marcus's fault. I pursued Sophie's best friend's now-husband, Nate, while Marcus and I were still dating. Mostly because Marcus was already fooling around, and I was young and reckless. Felicity wasn't in the picture at the time, and I relished Nate's ability to stroke my broken ego. I'm glad that didn't last. And that Felicity never held our past against me when they finally settled down. She and Sophie are now two of my closest friends.

"You are all talk Rachel-Mae, you know that?"

I poke out my tongue. I only get called that by my mother. "I know. Damn it, why can't I do *no-strings-attached* sex?"

She scrunches her nose. "Believe me. It's not all it's cracked up to be." Her cheeks blossom a cute shade of pink. I can't envision her having an occasional hook-up—not when I've seen how she is with Charlie. He dotes on her and their daughter, Selene; it's quite beautiful to watch. My heart squeezes in my chest. Once upon a time, I dreamed I'd have a family like that, adamant I didn't want to become a carbon copy of either one of my parents.

I came from a workaholic father and a distant mother. When I told them I was breaking off the engagement and pregnant, my mum was beyond bereft. *What would her friends think?* The whole ordeal, along with my anxiety over being a single parent, made me question who was in my life.

"I'm starting self-defence classes," I blurt out, not wanting her to feel awkward about her confession.

Sophie raises a perfectly plucked eyebrow. "Oh?"

I nod. "Yeah," I say, smiling while I don my apron to begin my shift. "Maybe my trainer will be hot."

She gives me a wicked grin, and I head in back to start cleaning.

Chapter Four

Olly

I quickly tie my laces and begin pulling out the mats, making sure everything is ready for my next appointment. I haven't been able to get a blonde haired, green-eyed beauty off my mind since I watched her drive away from the bar the other night. I shake off thoughts of her fresh summer scent, needing to get focused for my next client.

I grab some extra towels from the array of oak cabinets that take up one wall, the rest a seamless sea of mirrors. The ceiling is open to the rafters height above, yet the space is cosy, comfortable. This room works perfectly for one-on-ones, and my clients are less self-conscious without the sometimes-ogling bodybuilders from downstairs watching them train. Private and away from the main gym. It's easy to become intimidated by what everyone else is doing. This is secluded without being claustrophobic.

Majority of my clientele are women, and the money I

earn from giving these lessons goes straight to the charity I support.

Kneeling to wipe a spot off the mat, I hear the creak of the door opening and closing behind me. "Just a moment," I call out, but the sound of footsteps moves closer, and a familiar scent invades my senses.

Impossible.

My eyes dart to the reflection in the mirror. Rachel.

I stand and turn to face her. She's in yoga pants and a tight-fitted top, and I strain to keep my eyes focused on her face.

"Have I got the right room?" she asks, looking around, not even a *hello*.

I bridge the gap between us. "If you're here for the self-defence class, then yes."

She points at me. "You're the instructor?" she asks, the skin along her throat blotching slightly.

"That would be correct." She's fidgeting, and I don't know whether to grin or grimace. "Listen, if you're not comfortable, I can see about getting one of the other guys to teach you."

Her eyes spring to mine and go wide. "God, no, I was surprised to see you. I didn't know you worked *here*, too."

I take her bag from her hands and walk it over to the bench. "I work out here and run a class from time to time." I also have a share in the gym, but it's neither here nor there. I point to her hands. "You need to remove your jewellery," I say, glancing at her necklace. She slips off her ring and unclasps her chain before striding back to her bag.

"And your watch," I say as she comes back towards me.

She shakes her head, her ponytail whipping around. Something stirs, and I think of what it would be like to wrap it around my fist. *Shit.* I cough.

"Oh, no. I never take it off," she says, covering it with her other hand.

I look heavenward. *Please give me strength.* "Rachel, it's health and safety. I don't make the rules."

She taps her foot, and just when I think she's going to give me shit, she unclips the strap. I hold out my hand. "I can put it in the office."

She bites into the pink plump flesh of her lower lip, and I almost groan out loud. "Please be careful. It was from my grandmother."

I nod, turning away from her, heading for the door by the full-length mirror. The links are warm from her skin. I turn it over to have a look before I lock it in the safe, letting out a low whistle—easily a good four grand for this watch.

I notice an engraving just as I put it down. *You are stronger than you realise.*

When I come back out, she's eying the room, wringing her hands together.

"So, I take it after the other night, you want to know how to get yourself out of a situation like that."

Her cheeks redden. "Yeah, I was mortified."

I walk towards her and put my hands on her shoulders. "Well, you shouldn't. He had no right to corner you like that."

A shiver rolls through her. "So much for him being a gentleman, hey?" she says, trying to make light of it.

I drop my hands and smile. "Believe it or not, I've met worse."

She studies me for a few seconds, and I don't know what she sees, but her eyes soften. "I'm sorry to hear that," she replies, her words sincere.

I clap my hands together. "Okay, tell me, what's the best form of self-defence?"

She puts her hand on her hip, drawing my line of sight to her voluptuous figure. "Isn't that what I'm paying you for?"

I can't help but laugh—she's sassy, and she knows it. "Very funny, Princess. I do need to gauge where your head is at."

She grumbles under her breath, her posture rigid. "Don't call me *princess*."

"Then answer my question. Best self-defence?"

Screwing up her nose, she nibbles on her lip. "Strength?"

I shake my head. "Not quite. *Prevention* is the best self-defence."

"What?"

I sit down, motioning for her to come join me in the middle of the mat. "Attackers will always go looking for the unsuspecting, vulnerable targets. It's why we teach you to be aware of your surroundings—sticking to well-lit areas when walking or parking your car; having your keys in your hand, ready when you approach your car or your front door—"

She holds up her hand to interrupt. "Hold up. Don't you think we know that? Every time we leave the house, we have to think of shit like this." She waves her palms around for emphasis. "Like not having our hair in a goddamn ponytail or listening to music when we're on public transport. For crying out loud, *how about men stop assaulting women?*" She clamps her mouth closed as if she's said too much.

I hold up my palm. "I one hundred percent agree. You shouldn't have to consider any of those factors when you leave your house. But unfortunately, it happens. Why do you think I teach these classes? I want women and children to have a chance of getting away or at least defending themselves."

Her lips part, her eyes wide. "Wow, okay, point taken. Sorry, it's just infuriating—a never-ending cycle. You don't understand. You don't know what's it's like to be in a situation…knowing that if a man wanted to—I couldn't stop it."

I take her hand in mine and give it one firm squeeze. "That is where you're wrong. I do understand."

Rachel nods in silent acknowledgement but doesn't push. "Shall we continue?" I ask, releasing her hand.

She tucks some stray hair behind her ear. "Of course, it's why I'm here," she says with a small smirk.

"Okay, good. So, if you find yourself in a situation where you're unable to avoid confrontation, what would you do?"

She doesn't come back at me with sass this time as she chews on her lower lip, eyes cast up, mulling it over. "Try and defuse the situation?" she asks.

"Yes. But remember, not everyone can be talked down. If they want your purse or your fancy Rolex, you hand them over. *Nothing* is worth your life or your health."

Rachel's hand moves to the white tan line where her watch should be, nodding in understanding.

"And now this is where I come in. If violence is unavoidable, I want you to know how to defend yourself, how to fight back effectively." I push myself up and hold out my hands. Pulling her to her feet, I notice she's not that much shorter than me—her chin comes to my shoulder. "I want you to know it's possible to defend yourself against someone bigger or stronger than you."

She raises her eyebrows in question.

"Okay, so imagine I'm coming at you. I'm backing you into a corner, what do you do?"

"I push back. Like with Neal, but he didn't budge."

"Firstly, yes, you did the right thing, but I would suggest getting loud and *then* pushing back. You shout, *'BACK OFF'!*" She flinches as my voice echoes off the walls. "And then you push him." I show a pushing gesture. "Let's try it," I say.

I move towards her, crowding her space, and she instinctively steps back, so I move closer. We do this until her back meets the mirror. I place my hands on her shoulders. "Now, what do you do?" I ask.

She tries to look past me for an escape, but then she surprises me. *"BACK OFF!"* she shouts, louder than I would've expected, and then shoves me hard. I stumble.

She's blushing from the exertion and reaches out as if to apologise. But I wave her off. "Well done. By being loud, you're signalling for help, and it also lets your attacker know you aren't an easy target."

She looks pleased with herself, and a jolt of pride shoots through me, knowing I had a part to play in her reaction.

"Now, unfortunately, it won't dissuade all attackers, but it will at least ward off those who are looking for an easy target." I bring her back into the middle of the mat. I want her to feel strong, powerful, so even if she were to find herself in an uncompromising position, she'd have a chance.

I flinch as a glimmer of the past flashes in my mind. The memories I have of my dad are that of him being a monster. My mother suffered; she took the brunt of the beatings, but as I got older, his attention also wavered towards me. I didn't care as long as he left Lottie alone.

Chapter Five

Rachel

I can't believe I did it. I know this is role-playing, but I found being firm and shouting to be quite liberating. And with Olly as the trainer... What are the chances?

"When you're in a confrontation, you only have a few seconds before the fight is decided." He is so serious as he explains, and I can't help but be in awe of his passion for something so important. "The aim is for you to do everything you can before an attacker gains full control." He turns me, so our bodies are square as he continues. "You must do everything you can to inflict injury whilst conserving as much energy as possible to get away."

I nod as my adrenaline begins to spike.

"This is where it's the case of you or them; it's hurt or be hurt." He points to himself. "I want you to show me the parts of my body where you can do the most damage." My eyes scan down to his private parts. He gives me a knowing smile. "Come on, Princess, tell me where you'd aim for."

I shake out my hands which I had clenched into fists. "Your groin, knees, and your face?" I say, but it comes out a question, my voice rising.

"Excellent, but it also depends on the position of the attacker." His voice is thick, masculine. "This will help you choose where to strike and which part of your body to use." He crowds me again; I step back. "Never move *closer* to your attacker. If you think you can aim for his nose, but this involves you moving towards him, *you don't do it*."

He shows me an example, coming close to my face with his hand and then mime-reaching my knee with a kick.

"If you're going for the upper body, use your hand." He takes hold of mine and adjusts it, bringing it towards him. "You could strike me using the outer edge of your hand —like so."

Curling my hand into a fist, he adjusts us so we're facing the mirror, then leads me through a punching motion.

"I'll give you a leaflet before you leave today's session. It has examples of highly sensitive pressure points." His breath tickles my ear as he leans over my shoulder ever so slightly, causing a tightening in my lower stomach. I stare at our reflection in the mirror, my cheeks are growing redder by the second.

"Eyes," he says, pointing out mine in the mirror.

"Why eyes?" I ask.

"Because it can cause maximum pain. Have you ever accidentally poked yourself in the eye? It hurts like a mofo, right?"

I cringe. "Yeah, and so does a mascara wand to the eyeball. I'm pretty sure that shit is more painful than childbirth."

His laugh vibrates through my upper body, making me smile. There's something about seeing him like this, in his element, eyes sparkling—captivating me. It's *almost* easy to forget that this man—when he wasn't deliberately trying to irritate me—has mostly ignored me since the day we met. Almost.

"I wouldn't know on either count, but I take your word for it. If you can mess with their vision, even if it's only temporary, it can mean the difference in making your escape easier."

He goes into detail, pretending to gouge, poke and scratch. If he ever needs work, I think he could join the theatre—the way he explains this has me imagining a female version of Fight Club.

"Nose," he says, tapping the tip of mine gently. "Using the heel of your palm, you can strike up under his nose, throwing your whole-body weight into the move. Believe me, this will cause pain."

He re-positions himself until he's standing behind me, the heat from his body enveloping.

I turn my head slightly to eye him over my shoulder. "Olly, why does it sound like you're speaking from experience?"

He laughs, and damn, the sound makes me tingle. "I used to get into a lot of scrapes in my late teens. Boxing helped me harness my excess energy."

His hands slide to my hips, and he tightens his grip, not enough to hurt but enough to keep me rooted in place. "If your attacker is behind, you can strike the nose with your elbow. Always aim for nasal bones. Go on, give it a try," he says.

So I do. Even though this isn't the real thing, he isn't making it easy on me. I have to work hard out of his grasp to swing my elbow behind me. The thud of it connecting with his cheek causes him to let out an *oomph*.

"Shit, sorry, Olly," I say, turning to try and get a look, grabbing his chin between my fingers to scan his face.

His hand covers mine. "It's fine. I wasn't concentrating." His feather-light touch strokes down to the pulse in my neck. Then, opening his fingers, he cups the back of my neck. His eyes lock with mine, and I'm caught in a web—unable to look away.

Something is lodged in my throat, and I swallow roughly. A strange noise escapes my lips; his fingers loosen.

He clears his throat. "The side of the neck is the bigger target, with both the carotid artery and jugular vein."

He lets go, then holds up his hand, all fingers straight and tight together, his thumb tucked in and slightly bent at the knuckle. "This is a knife-hand strike. With your hand like this, you aim at the side of the neck." He shows me the motion on my own. "Or if you wanted to cause more of an injury, you could thrust your elbow into their throat while pitching the weight of your body forward. Kind of like when you went for my nose but landed on my cheek," he says, humour in his voice.

I let out an unamused laugh, crossing my arms and rolling my eyes.

"But all jokes aside, remember, if you can cause them an injury and give yourself a couple of seconds to get away, it can make all the difference."

I've already learnt so much from him; this is the kind of class I wish I had growing up. I wish my daughter could grow up in a world where women didn't have to be on guard, looking over their shoulder constantly, but this is reality. My worry is that my strength will always let me down.

Chapter Six

Rachel

I never expected to get so much from an hour and a half self-defence class, but I'm already looking forward to the next one.

Olly is in his element when he's teaching, and there's something I can't help but be mesmerised by—his eyes. All I want to do is paint them to canvas. Maybe my sketch pad will do until I have enough money to buy more art supplies.

I can't remember ever aching this much and am desperate for a long hot bath. It's a rare night I don't have Molly—Marcus takes her on Wednesdays—and as much as I miss her, it gives me extra time to do all the things I need to get done.

I plug the drain and start running my bath, thinking about my dinner options. It's strange how my eating habits work around being a mum—I know I need to be better, but it's hard juggling everything. And I find I'm a lonely eater; I like the company of dining with others. It was one of the nicer sides of being in a relationship with Marcus.

I pour in a fair amount of bubble bath, strip out of my

clothes, and step in while the water is still running. I let out a satisfied sigh as I sink into the water.

I look at my wrist—the water splashes up and over the edge as I sit up too fast.

Fuck, my watch.

How did I not notice sooner?

I turn off the tap and make quick work lathering up, washing my body and my hair. After pulling out the plug, I rinse under the shower hose, the water peppering my skin, and I groan, not ready to get out.

Wrapping myself in a towel, I cover my hair in a smaller one and grab my phone from my bag. I text Sophie, asking for Oliver's number. She replies with his number and an aubergine emoji.

I hit dial.

"Hello?" His voice is deep and rich, and I almost forget I need to speak.

"Oliver?"

"Yes…Rachel?"

I pull the phone from my ear, making sure I haven't video-called him.

"Hello?" he asks again.

"Sorry, yes, it's me. I forgot my watch. Don't suppose there is any chance anyone is still there so I can come and pick it up?"

I pull open a drawer and grab some clean clothes.

"Well, yeah I'm still here, but… I could also pass it along to Charlie for Soph to give it to you."

I shake my head. "No, it's like missing a limb, I feel practically naked without it," I reply and then my face heats when I hear him stifle a laugh.

"Okay, well, I'm here if you want to come by and grab it."

I thank him and hang up, promising to be there within a half-hour.

When I pull up to the gym, the car park is dark and almost

empty. I stare at my phone—nearly nine o'clock. I look around before I exit my car, then jog to the metal staircase on the side of the building.

I get to the door, and it opens, startling me. Olly stands in the threshold, the expanse of the room behind him empty.

"Sorry, did you stay because of me?" I ask and brush past him as I walk in.

He shakes his head. "No, I had to work on the books. I was waiting for my dinner."

I spin to look at him. "Shit, Oliver. I'm sorry."

He laughs it off. When there's a tap on the door, he holds up his finger.

"Hey, thanks man," he says and takes a bag, passing the delivery guy some money. "Keep the change." I don't hear what the delivery guy says as his feet clatter back down the metal steps.

Olly nods his head to me. I follow him up to the same room we were training in earlier. He holds open the door, allowing me to enter first. "It's in the safe," he says in the way of explanation.

I step inside. It's not just an office; it has a kitchenette, sofa and glass coffee table. Very cosy.

Chapter Seven

Olly

She's gripping the strap of her bag tightly, and I wonder if this is making her feel uncomfortable—being alone with me.

"This is a nice setup," she says.

"Yeah, I like it. When I bought into the gym, I had it renovated."

Her eyes spring to mine. "Oh, I just thought you worked here and at the bar," she says, almost embarrassed.

I wave to her to take a seat on the sofa and place the takeaway on the counter. "I do, and I'm a partner here. I do a lot of charity fights, so it just came about. And getting this office kitted out was one of the first things I did."

She nods and sits on the edge of the sofa. I walk over to the safe and type in the code. There's heavy clang as I open it and reach for her watch. Her eyes light up when I pass it to her. She slips it over her hand and fastens it back onto her wrist, giving it a quick shake.

Staring at it wistfully, she smiles. "My nan got this for my twenty-first birthday. I'm surprised it took me as long as it did to notice I'd forgotten it."

I nod in understanding. The smell of dinner assails my senses. "Where's Molly-Mae?"

"I left her in the car," she says, deadpan.

"Ha, very funny." I'm unable to hide my smile.

"With her dad tonight."

I nod and pull out the containers from the bag. "Hey, have you eaten?" I ask, glancing over my shoulder. She shakes her head. "Want some Chinese? There's plenty."

I reach in the cabinet to pull out some plates. When she doesn't answer, I turn back to face her. I think she's going to say no, but she looks at her watch and then back to me. "Are you sure there's enough?"

"Absolutely," I reply. "Choose what you want."

I hear the air leave the soft leather as she gets up to check out the options. "I'll just have a bit of everything," she says, her stomach growling loud enough to hear.

"Girl, you *are* hungry."

She covers her belly with her hand and her cheeks heat. "It's been a busy day."

I load up our plates, and she takes them back over to the table. I follow behind her with napkins and two cans of coke, which I place on coasters. "Sorry, do you want a glass?" I ask.

"No, this is good." She taps the top of the can with her fingernail and pulls the tab open, taking a small sip as I struggle to take my eyes off her lips. I clear my throat and sit beside her.

It's not a small sofa by any account, but something about being this close to her and alone…the room feels smaller than it is, heat radiates off her. I open my can and take a huge gulp, fidgeting in my seat.

She groans as she takes a bite of her noodles, and I've never been jealous of food before now. *What the hell?*

"Oh my god, Olly, this is delicious," she says, around a mouthful of food.

I can't help but smile in satisfaction over the fact not only did she call me *Olly*, she's enjoying my favourite Chinese as much as me. "I train one of their daughters. They have the best takeout and restaurant for miles. I'll give you a menu to take home," I say.

"*Please*. Chinese is only my favourite food group."

"So, how did this come about—you teaching self-defence?" she asks.

I turn slightly, so my body is angled towards her. "I wanted to make sure women had a way of defending themselves."

She takes another bite of her food, and I can't help but watch her. It's like she's awakening something in me I didn't know was dormant.

"So, did you know that guy was a jerk? Is that why you swooped in and saved me?" she asks.

"Something like that." The picture of Rachel cornered against the wall with that prick has sprung to mind more than once since that night. And it earned Henry, my sparring partner, a few over aggressive punches.

We eat the rest of our food in comfortable silence except for the sound of our chopsticks.

"Thank you for letting me crash your dinner," she says before sipping her coke.

I shrug. "It was nice to have the company." I pick up our plates; she stands, grabbing the empty cans and following me over to the sink. I run the tap, ready to wash them.

"Here, let me do that," she says, her shoulder brushing mine.

I bump her with my hip. "Nope. Why don't you go open your fortune cookie," I say, nodding to the side where I left them. "Oh, and take that menu, too."

"So bossy, Oliver."

I leave the plates in the drainer and dry my hands as she

passes me a cookie. "What does yours say?" I ask, ripping open my wrapper.

"I can't tell you—it won't come true," she says, holding the thin piece of paper towards her chest.

I let out a laugh. "I think you'll find that's not the case with fortune cookies," I say, snapping mine in half and pulling out my fortune. I cock an eyebrow.

"Well, what does it say?" she asks.

"Oh, you want to know mine, but won't tell me yours?"

She looks to hers and then back to mine. "Fine." she holds hers out to me, and we exchange fortunes.

I read hers and can't help but laugh. *Love is on the horizon. The stars predict he will be tall dark and handsome.*

"If you love something, set it free. If it returns, keep it and love it forever," she says, reading mine aloud. She peers up at me and sighs like it's a powerful sonnet.

"Tall, dark and handsome, huh?"

She blushes, snatches it back and slips it into her bag. After she passes me mine, I go to chuck it in the bin. "You can't throw it away. You have to keep it."

I shake my head and stuff in my pocket. "Satisfied?" She nods. "Come on, let me lock up, and I'll walk you to your car."

She plays with her watch. "You don't need to do that."

"Yes, I do. The lighting is crap out there."

She follows me through the gym, then waits as I set the code for the alarm. Neither of us speak as our feet crunch on the gravel. When we get to Betty, I can't help but smile.

"Thank you, Olly, that was unexpected but nice."

"Any time. So I'll see you again on Wednesday?"

She nods and smiles before climbing into her car. I wait for her to start the engine and watch as she drives away.

Reaching into my pocket for my keys, I feel the fortune and pull it out. Inside my car, I tug down the sun visor and stick it under the elastic before closing the flap back into place.

Chapter Eight

Olly

It's been a busy week between the bar, the gym and my training schedule. My mum always worries I take on too much, but I like to keep busy. I've just finished one of my classes when Charlie, my buddy and owner of the bar, comes by the gym.

"Hey mate, you up for sparring?" he asks.

I smile. "Always. Let me just get this sorted, and I'll be down."

He leaves me to it, and when I join him downstairs, he's speaking with Henry and Nathan.

"Hey, Henry, how did the competition go?" Charlie asks.

He shrugs with a soft smile. "It was okay."

Nathan punches him on the shoulder. "H, you are so modest. He completely smashed it—he's through to the semi-finals."

I reach out and connect my knuckles with Henry's. "Well done, man." He smiles wide.

Nathan says under his breath, "On your six."

Meghan, one of our badass trainers, comes up to our group, smiling. "Hi, what's going on?" she asks, eying Henry. He looks away quickly, and the ever-present smile he harbours slips.

"Just catching up," Nathan says. He seems a little uncomfortable, which is unlike him. He nods his head towards the weights, then he and Henry flee.

"What was all that about?" I ask Meghan.

She shakes her head, dropping her eyes. "You don't want to know. I need to get going—catch you later, guys."

Once she's out of earshot, Charlie leans in. "Was it me, or was that a bit of a frosty reception?"

I nod, a little dumbfounded myself. Henry and Nathan are not usually like that at all. "Ready to spar?"

"That's why I'm here."

I park at Sofia's deli.

I frequent here at the best of times, but today... I can't get Rachel out of my head. The bell chimes when I enter, and it's quiet this time of the day when they're getting ready to close.

"Olly," says Soph with a huge smile.

"Hey, beautiful," I say. She blushes but rolls her eyes, and I can't help but smile. "Don't suppose you have any of that lemon drizzle cake left, do you?" I ask, approaching the counter. My eyes do a sweep of its contents, and then I look around for Rachel.

"I do, as it happens."

"Thank you."

"To go?"

"Yes, please." It will go down with a cup of tea once I get off work tonight.

"Soph, do we need any cartons of milk for the front fridge?" Rachel asks, breezing out of the kitchen.

"Hmm, let me check."

Rachel sees me, and for the first time since I've been coming here, she greets me with a genuine smile. "Hi, Olly. Couldn't stay away?" I almost choke on my saliva, my face heats. "Sophie's cakes are to die for," she says with a wink.

I nod and find myself momentarily stuck for words.

"Rachel, can you finish serving Olly? I just need to take this," she says, holding up her vibrating phone.

Rachel washes her hands and then comes over to the counter. I watch, transfixed, as she adds two huge slices of cake to the carton. "One's fine," I say.

"It's on the house, Olly. Besides...you're our *fiftieth customer*, and if you don't take it, that means I'll end up having the rest all to myself," she says with a wink.

I cock an eyebrow. "Touché." I kind of hate that she knows that round wasn't on the house, but to be fair, she's taking it in her stride, and I quite like seeing this...carefree side of her.

"Thank you," I say, reaching for the box.

"How's your fortune coming along?"

I laugh and lean my hip against the counter. "Nothing to report as of yet, but it's only been a few days. What about you? You found Mr. Right?"

She throws a wooden stirrer at me. "Ha ha, very funny. Are you trying to imply something?"

I shake my head and back away from the counter holding my cake box close in case she tries to steal it back. "Never would I ever. So...I'll see you tomorrow?"

"Of course."

I'm reluctant to leave, but I'm conscious of the fact I'm standing here, grinning like a fool. "Bye, Princess."

"It's Rachel to you, pretty boy."

I laugh over the noise of the door chiming and smile all the way to my car. Tonight's shift couldn't finish quick enough—I've never looked so forward to a morning training session in my life.

Chapter Nine

Rachel

This is my fourth class with Olly, and I'm finding it's the day of the week I look forward to the most—even with everything going on, I need this outlet.

"Well, aren't you a sight for sore eyes?"

I drop the leg I was stretching and turn to Olly. "Do you always greet your clients like that?" I ask, cocking an eyebrow.

"Only the pretty ones who are out of my league," he replies with a wink.

I can't stop the blush from creeping over my face. He's just flirting, I'm sure, but there is something in the way he stares at me that has my pulse racing, my stomach squirming.

"Are you ready?" His breath tickles the back of my neck, causing a flush of goosebumps to break out over my skin. I rub at my arm absentmindedly and turn back toward his voice. He's so close, I almost bump into his chest. He grabs my shoulders, gently, to steady me.

"Sorry," I say, but the word comes out breathy.

His violet-blue eyes wander over my face, and for some reason, I feel wholly exposed. But I can't move or look away. His thumbs rub small circles over my skin; tingles shoot through my entire body, releasing me from his spell.

I take a step back.

He clears his throat and shakes his head. "Okay, right." He claps his hands and then rubs them together. "Are you ready to show me what you've learned?" I nod, hoping to impress him with how much he's taught me in such short amount of time.

Almost an hour later, I'm struggling to catch my breath. He never eased up on me today—not once. My body is already suffering, and I know I'm going to feel it when I get home.

"You did well. You're a fast learner—already building your stamina." He's flushed from our workout, but if I didn't know better, I'd say there was a slight blush on his cheeks.

"Stamina, huh?" I tease, smiling.

He lets out a rumble of laughter. The sound vibrates straight to my stomach. *What is wrong with me?* I've always found Olly attractive, but his personality…not so much—well, up until recently. He always seemed to enjoy getting under my skin, but lately his manner has become…friendlier.

Before, when he'd come to *Sofia's*, I'd make a point of busying myself with something else so Sophie had to serve him. Now, I can't ignore the flutter of excitement coursing through me by his presence.

This is dangerous, very dangerous.

He's a flirtatious bartender—a player, even. I've seen the way he is with the girls who seek him out when they approach him at work. He laps it up, clearly he loves the attention. I mean what would he see in a single mum like me, anyway? But when he said I was out of his league earlier… I felt disappointed by his comment, but worse—he genuinely believes it. And I hate that.

"Are you working today?" he asks.

I grab the towel and wipe my sweaty face, nodding. "Yep."

"Okay, make sure you save me some cake. I'll be stopping by on my way to work."

I let out a laugh and pat his stomach. "Where do you put it all?"

"Hollow legs," he replies with a wink.

"If only we were all so lucky." Since having Molly, my body has changed. Stretch marks, extra weight I don't think I'll ever be able to shift.

"Are you implying that you don't like your figure?"

"Well, it's not that I don't like it…" And that's not a lie. I'm more than grateful for the extra boob and arse. I wish, however, they were more to the north and less to the south.

"Rachel, you're beautiful," he says, his face serious as he steps closer to me.

The air in the room thickens. I'm not used to this version of Olly, and I'm not sure how to respond. I glance to my wrist, but of course, my watch is in the locker he assigned me on my second lesson. "I bet you say that to all the girls," I whisper, because it's the easy comeback.

"I don't." My eyes spring to his face—his expression holds only truth.

An almighty *bang* followed by screaming and shouting echoes from somewhere down below. And without even a flicker of hesitation, Olly sprints off through the door and down the stairs, me dashing after him.

By the time I'm at the bottom of the stairs, he's already lifting a weight off of someone's chest and shouting orders.

I stand, watching in complete awe; everyone else is panicking—except for him. I'd offer to help, but there's already a crowd of spectators, and he's told them to move back while he talks to the guy on the floor.

"Call an ambulance," Olly barks to one of the employees who is already on the phone.

Olly continues to speak to the gym member on the ground, and everyone else disperses, talking in small groups until the paramedics arrive.

They ask Olly a few questions, and then their sole concentration is on the injured man. It's not long before he's strapped to a gurney. Olly shows them to a lift I never knew was there, and they leave with the man.

He jogs over to me after talking to the other employees for a moment, wearing a half-smile. "Are you okay?" I ask, noticing the slight tremble in his hands.

"Better than that guy," he says, wincing.

I give his arm a firm squeeze before letting go. "Will he be all right?"

"I hope so. I don't know how many times those guys have been told to have spotters. It's no joke lifting those kinds of weights. Henry has been doing this for years, and even *he* would never without someone spotting him." He runs his fingers through his hair.

"You were amazing—how quickly you reacted," I say.

He smiles. "Careful, it kinda sounded like a compliment."

I laugh, turning to head back upstairs before glancing over my shoulder. "It was meant to."

He smiles, but it's not the cock sure one I've seen him use on women at the bar…or when he's flirting. I force myself to look where I'm going before I embarrass myself by falling up the stairs.

Chapter Ten

Rachel

"What do you mean, you're moving to Dubai?"

Molly fidgets in my hold; I let her get down. Barely through the door to drop her off to Marcus, and he launches into a speech about moving out of the bloody country—*what the hell?*

"As I said, it's a great opportunity."

I shake my head, struggling to digest his words. "Molly, go put your bag in your room." She spins in a circle, showing off her tutu before doing as she's told. "You are positively crazy, Marcus. You don't just decide—not without talking it through with me."

He crosses his arms. "Last I checked, I was free to do what I wanted."

I cannot believe him. "Yes, as a single guy. But as the father to our daughter? Not so much. What about Molly—have you even considered her?" I ask, waving my hands in front of me.

"Of course, I have."

I lean back, incredulous. "How so?"

"For fuck's sake, Rach."

"Fuck," repeats Molly. I gasp and spin around to crouch down in front of her. "You do not repeat that word, Molly. It's naughty."

She pokes out her chest in defiance. *Great,* here we go. "*Daddy* did."

"And Daddy is sorry, aren't you, Marcus?"

He at least has the good grace to seem apologetic as he nods. "I am. I shouldn't have said it, and you shouldn't repeat it."

"We need to discuss this, but now is not the time."

"I don't know why you can't be happy for me, Rach…"

I squeeze my eyes closed and take a deep breath before I open them. "Marcus, my priority, in case you haven't noticed, is our daughter—not another one of your whims."

His phone vibrates, and I know his attention is now lost.

"Molly, come give me a kiss goodbye." I give her a big squeeze and a kiss on the top of her head; she's already wriggling to get free.

"Hey, Pumpkin, shall we have pizza?"

Does he ever cook?

"I'm not a pumpkin," she says, annoyance lacing her voice.

"Oh? Then what are you?" he asks, amused.

"I'm a flamingo princess." Marcus and I share a laugh.

"My bad, Flamingo Princess."

Molly stuffs her thumb into her mouth. And Marcus quickly pulls it free, a little too harshly. "Marcus," I scold.

"What?"

"You know *what*."

"Don't tell me how to parent, and I won't tell you how to parent."

"I will when I don't agree with it." I grip my bag tighter.

"Co-parenting. That was our agreement, Marcus, but I'm not doing this in front of her. We need to arrange a more suitable place and time to talk."

"Fine, I'll let you know *when*."

I can't be bothered to entertain him any longer. *He'll let me know when*—*arsehole*. Rummaging through my bag, I find my car keys and don't stop moving until I'm behind the wheel. Betty doesn't start on the first go. I let out a string of curse words and bite my lip. *I will not fucking cry.* She starts after two more attempts.

Exhausted when I get home, I run myself a bath and pour a large glass of wine. It would be even better if I didn't have to run into work tomorrow, but Charlie is taking Soph away for the evening, so I offered to open for a delivery—

"*Shit!*" Wine swooshes over the rim of the glass, and I quickly lick up the spill on my hand as I rush to my bag. "Please let them be there." I hunt through, but sure enough, no shop keys.

I thought my bag was light.

I check the time, wondering if Soph has already left. I send her a quick text, but her response tells me I'm too late. With that, I down the contents of the glass and shudder.

She lets me know there is a spare set at the bar, and Olly can get them from the safe. I can grab them in the morning, she says. Before I have a chance to reply, she sends me his address. "Great—fucking excellent."

Done with this day, I grab the wine bottle, my empty glass, and head to the bathroom. I sink into the bathtub—the hot water welcome—and take a huge sip of wine.

This is how my Saturday nights are now: me, a bath, and a lonely bottle of wine for one. But the truth is, I don't think I'd have the energy for much else, anyway. Well, that's a lie. If my supplies hadn't run out, I would most definitely paint. Olly's eyes would be the first, the colour so vibrant, I can't get them out of my head. I have this urge to paint the intricate shade of his irises. My body begins to heat at the thought; I push it aside.

"I so need to get laid," I groan.

Once the water cools, and I am pruned to shrimp-like status, I get out. The wine has me loose and relaxed. I think of my Rabbit in my bottom drawer and shrug. It's why I went out of my way and overindulged when I bought batteries.

Chapter Eleven

Rachel

I don't know what I expected when I walked into Olly's home, but this was not it. He has a small bookcase, and I can't help but tiptoe over to take a peek, my forefinger rolling over the spines—some worn, some pristine, like they've never been read. But what has my mouth gaping is they are all different editions of the same book. I pull one out to take a better look.

Mary Shelley's, *Frankenstein.*

"Caught you!"

I don't even realise what I've done until it's too late—my reaction happens on instinct as my arm swings up and behind me, whacking Olly square on the jaw.

I drop the book, scrambling to make sure he's okay.

I kneel to pick it up at the same time as him; his forehead smashes into mine, causing my teeth to crash together. It takes me a moment to catch my breath.

"Fuck!" groans Olly.

"I am so sorry, Olly. Shit," I say, trying to turn his face

towards me to see what damage I've done. His eyes are sparkling with surprise and something akin to pride.

"It's fine. Good reflexes," he says, appreciatively. He turns the book over in his hands. "So, I see you found my odd obsession."

Busted, I chew on my lip as he leans towards me, his hand moving to my face. "You have an egg on your head," he says.

"Excuse me, what?" I ask, perplexed, lost in the violet-indigo speckles around his irises. When we are this close, it's hard not to get drawn in.

He reaches out his hand, and his feather-light touch zings through me. The tender skin where he brushes his fingers is enough to let me know my forehead is going to bruise. A small hiss escapes me as I sit back on my heels.

"Let's get some ice," he says, standing and placing the book back where I found it. Then he takes me by the hand and leads me to the kitchen.

"Wow." I spin to take in the expanse of the room.

"It's nice, isn't it?"

"No, it's gorgeous," I reply. This kitchen is stunning, the skylight streaming early morning light in all the right places. I skim my hand over the black quartz worktop. One day I want something like this for Molly and me.

"I'm glad you like it."

I shake my head, the pain reminding me why we came in here in the first place, and grimace as I answer, "No, I love it. Who did this?"

"I did," he replies and again I'm fucking floored. I point to him and then open my hand to the room in front of me. "Oh, don't look so surprised. I studied architecture."

"Damn, Olly. I want you to pencil me in for some time in the next five years or so."

He cocks his head. "That's way off," he replies, walking over with ice he's packed inside a dish towel. Reaching out, he gently holds it up to my head.

"Olly, you're quite the anomaly, aren't you?"

He quirks his eyebrow. "What? Not your typical stereotype, you mean?"

I scoff. "*Please*. I learnt my lesson about judging people a long time ago. I'm trying to be a better person. What I mean is—you take something ordinary and made it extraordinary. And you teach people how to protect themselves. I'm struggling to find any flaws where you're concerned, and I'm in awe to be perfectly honest…"

What's wrong with me? Too much information.

He laughs, and it spreads this warmth through my entire body—one I don't think I've ever felt before. "Believe me, I'm no saint. I have my flaws. I am a *man* after all."

Yes, he is. I almost forget why I'm here and have to shake my head to clear the fog. "Did you get the keys?" I ask, desperate to divert my wandering thoughts.

He nods, and they jingle as he pulls them out of his pocket before passing them to me.

"Thank you." I turn my wrist and sigh. "I need to get going." I don't want to be late for the delivery guy.

The air thickens, and swallowing isn't quite as easy—not while I'm this close to him. Which is weird since he has his hands all over me while we train, but this seems…more intimate, standing alone in his kitchen.

I need to get out of here.

"No worries, any time," he says, putting some space between us as he stuffs his hand into his pocket, drawing my line of sight to his crotch. *Fuck me.* I avert my eyes and take in the kitchen while I stumble my way towards his front door, hoping my embarrassment isn't written all over my face.

I sense his presence behind me, followed by the patter of his bare feet as he pads along the wooden floor, heightening all my nerves. Why is a man barefoot suddenly so appealing? It's not like I have a foot fetish, but damn, Olly in jeans with no socks is sexy. My skin heats again from my wayward thoughts, and I thank God I made it to the door without tripping over my tongue.

He reaches over my shoulder and unlatches the lock. I move back a little to make room for him to pull it open and step into his body, his chest now flush against my back. My breathing audibly hitches, and I hate that he affects me. I squeeze my eyes closed, unable to move. His breath breezes over my ear. When he leans in closer, my skin prickles with anticipation.

"Rachel?"

"Hmm?"

"Are you sure you're okay?"

My eyes snap open. "Fine, thank you." I grapple for my car keys, then make an unceremonious exit, his echoing chuckle only making me more flustered. Unable to look back, I climb into Betty and take a deep breath, my hands shaking that it takes me more than one attempt to get my key in the ignition.

I turn it over and nothing. Taking a deep breath, I try again—nothing. "What the fuck?"

I close my eyes and lean against the headrest, trying to remember if I still have recovery on my insurance plan, knowing full well I don't. It was too much of an added cost, so I opted out upon renewal. I don't often have the urge to cry, but try telling my eyes as they betray me and begin leaking.

Chapter Twelve

Rachel

A tap on the glass causes me to sit up straight. I let out a huff and get out of the car. Over the roof, those violet orbs that haunt my dreams stare back at me. "Car trouble?" he asks, tapping the roof.

"Yes, Oliver, you would be correct."

"Do you want me to take a quick look?" He moves around to the bonnet.

I shake my head. I already know what's wrong—it's the case of what isn't. "It's the alternator, the battery…amongst other things. How long have you got?" I ask.

Olly shrugs with a small smile, something very boyish in the gesture. "Well, it's not worth getting upset over. I'll grab my keys and give you a lift."

I don't get to respond before he jogs back inside. When he returns, he's wearing a pair of pristine white trainers, donning sunglasses, and swinging his keys on his finger. He angles his head for me to follow, so I do. His car is…well, blimey.

"Climb in," he says.

"Thank you," I say and clip on my seatbelt.

"Couldn't have you all stranded, could I, Princess?" I cross my arms and huff. "Oh, come on, you're offended when I call you Princess?"

I look out of the window, giving a non-comital shrug, on the verge of tears again.

His fingers tap my thigh, and I turn my face towards him. "Hey, I'm sorry. I don't mean it in a bad way," he says, scanning between me and the road.

"It's fine, Olly, I've just had a rough couple of days," I reply. And that's putting it mildly. I have so much pressure from my parents, never living up to their expectations. Not to mention Marcus dropping the bombshell about him and Dubai. I have no idea how to make this work for Molly.

"Anything I can help with?" he asks, sincerity in his voice.

I chew on my bottom lip, deliberating his question. "Maybe some other time," I reply.

His eyes dart to mine and back to the road. "Well, I'm a good listener. I've even been known to give good advice a time or two. Offer is open whenever."

I try to hide my smile as I stare out the window. Apart from Soph and Felicity, my circle of friends shrank when I had Molly, and then when my Nan died, it pretty much diminished. "I'll bear that in mind," I reply quietly, fingering my watch. I have no idea how I am going to pay to have my car fixed. Even with mate's-rate—if Nate can fit me in—it's still more money than I can afford.

We pull up outside *Sofia's*. "Coffee?" I ask. It's the least I can do. He nods and parks.

I'm grateful he's not invading my space as I raise the shutters and walk out back to enter the code to the alarm system. Sophie is working on always having someone open and close with us—safety in numbers.

I switch on the lights and wash my hands before turning to

the Barista machine. His eyes are on me, burning into my back, causing my fingers to fumble, not quite as agile as they usually are. I open the fridge to pull out the carton of milk. It slips from my grasp, and to my horror, explodes everywhere.

Milk drips from my face and hands, patches on my clothes, and the rest pools around my feet. It's insignificant in the grand scheme of things, but try telling my hormones that—I burst into a flood of tears.

Olly rounds the counter, his eyes darting between my sorry state and the milk tsunami. He moves around the mess, and in one move, picks me up by my waist. He sits me down on a stool in the kitchen, and then he's in the supply cupboard pulling out the mop and bucket.

"Oliver," I hiccup.

He walks back towards me, grabbing a tea towel. Instead of handing it to me as I anticipate, he lifts my head, two fingers probing gently under my chin as he wipes me clean. His eyes, almost magenta in colour today, are so open—clear, yet full of questions I don't know how to answer…answers I don't know myself.

When another tear escapes down my cheek, he swipes it away with his thumb and then leans in close to my ear, whispering, "No use crying over spilt milk." A giggle breaks free from my chest until it's cut off by his lips pressed into my cheek at the corner of my eye. "I meant what I said in the car—"

A hammering at the backdoor cuts him off before he can finish.

"Delivery," I say, trying to sniff back my tears without snotting all over myself.

"Keys?" he asks, holding out his palm. I shake my head but pass them to him before he slips out the back door. I hear murmurs followed by laughter. I peek my head around the door frame as he talks to Ron, our usual delivery guy, like they are old pals.

He peers over his shoulder and gives me a wink. I pull back and rush into the toilets to try and sort myself out.

When I come back, he's already mopped up the spill, and the boxes from the delivery are lined up on the far wall. "Oliver…" I begin but have no idea what to say.

"Sit," he says, pointing to the stool. I do as he says, and he pulls one up so he's sitting opposite, his knees brushing mine. "Talk."

I look up and shake my head. "I wouldn't even know where to begin," I say in answer. And then a fresh wave of tears assaults me.

"Okay…then start with why you can't stop crying." He leans forward and strokes away the hair that's stuck to my temple. I'm not an ugly crier per se, but I always end up sweaty and puffy.

There is something about the way he's staring at me… It makes me want to confide in him. So, I do. I tell him all about Marcus and his plans to move to Dubai with no consideration for Molly whatsoever.

Chapter Thirteen

Olly

I listen to her as she tells me about the bombshell her ex dropped on her when she was dropping off Molly. What an inconsiderate bastard. Even I can see what a dick move that would be. "Is it set in stone?"

She shakes her head, trying to sniff back her tears. Her vulnerability at this moment softens her in a way rarely seen, and maybe I'm an arsehole—because I find it quite endearing. "So, you still have time to sort it all out?"

"Maybe," she replies. Standing, she crosses her arms like she's cold. Her sweatshirt took the brunt of the milk, and now she's only wearing a thin t-shirt.

"Here," I unzip my hoody and slip it off, passing it to her.

"Thank you."

I watch as she pulls her arms through and have to keep my groan at bay while she rolls up the sleeves, looking positively sexy in my clothes. Thankfully, my phone rings the opening line of Bohemian Rhapsody, and Rachel raises an eyebrow with a smile.

"Hi, ya," I say when I answer. I look back to Rachel, an idea popping in my head, and I can't hold back my smile. "I'm bringing someone over for lunch," I tell my mum. I laugh. "Yeah, she is," I reply before saying bye and disconnecting the call.

Rachel turns to grab her bag. "I can get home from here. Thanks again, Olly, I appreciate…well, everything," she says.

I shake my head. "You busy?" I ask.

"Nope." She fidgets on the spot.

"Good, because you're coming to my parents' for lunch."

She backs away from me, looking down at herself. "Umm, no way, I don't think so."

"Why? You said you weren't busy."

Her cheeks heat. "I look a mess, and I probably smell like gone-off milk," she declares. I can't hide my laugh as I step into her personal space and lean in. Her breath catches. "What are you doing?" she whispers.

"Seeing if you smell." Swatting my arm, she pushes my chest, and I step back. "Come on, don't make me let my mum down." I give her what I hope is my best pouty face, which always works on Mum. "You smell fine, honest. And remember, I did do you a favour—it's only fair you reciprocate."

Her jaw drops. "Are you bribing me?"

"No, more like coercion." I take her by the shoulder. "Rachel, we're friends. Come on, you know you enjoy spending time with me." All I know is I'm not ready to let her go just yet, and I think she needs cheering up.

"Fine, but only because you got me out of a tight spot."

I wink and head for the door, glancing over my shoulder. "Hurry up then, slowpoke."

Rachel

We pull up outside a lovely, detached house. The front garden is full of wildflowers on one side and rose bushes on the other, and I scan them as we trail a path winding up to the front door. He uses his key and ushers me inside, his warm palm on the small of my back.

We walk through the hallway and into a big open kitchen, and I wonder if he designed this, too. "These are my parents for all intent and purposes," Olly says waving between us. "This is Rachel."

His mum walks straight over and pulls me in for a hug, I freeze. "Sorry, love, we're huggers. I'm Lily, and this is Joshua." He reaches for my hand and shakes it as Lily steps away.

"They're my foster parents, in case you're confused," Olly drawls. My cheeks begin to burn, and I want to elbow him in the ribs. Joshua is dark, with hazel eyes, and Lily is light blonde—not bleach, but naturally so—with porcelain skin. I don't know how I found myself standing in Olly's parents' home. This is so surreal.

"So, how long have you two been courting?" Lily asks with a bright smile.

My voice gets lodged in my throat, and my eyes fly to Olly, who laughs and shakes his head. "Mum, behave," he says, but doesn't correct her.

I cross my arms, wanting to be anywhere but here. Joshua slings his arm over Lily's shoulder. "Yes, wife, behave." She swats his chest as they turn and walk out the back door.

"She's winding you up," Olly says with a smile. I cover my face with my hand and let out a breath. "Come on. I'm not that bad," he whispers and pulls my hand away, linking our fingers before leading me the way his parents just headed.

I take in their back garden. It's beautiful, almost in three tiers, with a summer house right at the very end. Guilt consumes me. I want Molly to have a garden like this. Living in a flat has been an adjustment for me, and now that she's getting older...soon, she'll notice all of the things her dad can give her that I can't. "Sorry, can I use the bathroom?" I croak.

Olly raises an eyebrow and hooks his thumb over his shoulder. "There's one just back through there and to the right."

I avoid eye contact and dart off. Inside, I lock the door and cover my face with my hands before sitting on the closed toilet lid, willing the tears away. Ever since Marcus dropped the bomb on me about Dubai, I've been a mess. I take in a few deep breaths and flush the toilet, trying to sort out my face.

When I open the door, Olly is standing opposite, arms crossed, staring at the floor. His eyes move up when I walk out. "Weird much?" I say.

He pushes off the wall and steps into my space. "You all right?" he asks.

I nod and look away—anything to avoid his probing eyes. But his finger hooks under my chin, bringing my face up to meet them anyway. "I'm fine, Oliver," I say.

"I think you're lying, Princess, but I won't push. Are you hungry?" he asks.

I can't hide my smile. I hate being called Princess, and he bloody-well knows it… But when he says it, there's nothing facetious in his meaning. "I am."

"Good, because my parents kind of went overboard when I told them I was bringing someone over for lunch."

"Why would they do that?"

"I don't bring people home, and then when they found out you were the opposite sex, my mum practically started naming our babies." My mouth gapes open, and he laughs, his finger tapping my nose. "Don't worry. I told them I'm not good enough for you, but this is my mum we're talking about, and she kind of gets a little kooky."

"Why would you say that?" I ask.

"What? She *is* kooky," he replies with a lopsided grin.

"No, before that?" His lips pull into a straight line, his

Adam's apple bobbing as he swallows and shrugs. "You're a good guy, Olly," I say, reaching up, tugging on his wrist. "Come on, let's go eat before she thinks we're back here making babies." I smirk and walk past him, heading back into the garden.

"And she's back," he says, his laugh echoing behind me as I make my way to join his parents.

I can't remember the last time I ate so much barbecue, or had so much fun, for that matter. My face and sides hurt from smiling and laughing. His parents are so down to earth. They told me about the number of children they've fostered; they have hearts of saints to see that many children through their doors.

"Next time you come, be sure to bring your gorgeous little girl," says Lily as she kisses me on the cheek goodbye.

"Mum," Olly groans, grabbing my elbow and ushering me out of the front door. "Are you trying to scare her off?" he says, kissing her on the forehead as he passes. What does he mean by scaring me off? We're just friends…

He doesn't let go of my arm until we round his car and he's opening the door, giving his mum one final wave. "Quick, get in before she changes her mind and makes you go back inside."

I begin to climb in when he leans down and grazes my ear with his soft lips, his breath warm. "Thank you for coming," he says. I peer up, caught in the violet hues of his stare, and then without forethought, I lean up and press my lips softly against his.

I pull back just as fast and fumble with the seat belt. When he gets in, I pretend to be overly interested in my phone.

Chapter Fourteen

Rachel

Olly pulls up outside the entrance to my flat. I notice all the workman milling around, unsure what's going on and why it seems so dark. Olly turns the engine off, peering through the windscreen, no doubt thinking the same thing.

I jog over to one of the guys in a hi-vis jacket. "Excuse me... I live in the flats here. Is everything okay?"

He shakes his head. "Power outage. Doesn't look good—we don't think we can get it back up until the morning. We're doing everything we can, miss."

"Oh, thanks," I reply, turning away. Squeezing my eyes shut, I tilt my head up to take a deep breath and exhale. "*Shit.*"

"Everything all right?"

"Nope," I reply, digging my phone free to type out a quick text. His fingers wrap around my elbow. "Power's cut, and it *would* be the day after I did a freezer shop." My lips tremble, but I refuse to get upset over this.

"Do you want to go empty your freezer and bring it to mine?" I'm taken aback. "Oh, come on, we're friends. You've met my parents—I'm not a psycho," he says, flat.

I smile. "Are you sure?"

At his nod, we walk to the main door and up the three flights of stairs to my flat. I pause, my key in the lock. I've never had anyone in here except for Marcus.

"Excuse any mess," I say, my unease surfacing. I may not have much, but I'm house-proud nonetheless.

My hallway is dark when we enter. I hear the sound of the door click shut behind me, and then his footsteps as he follows me into the kitchen. After clicking the torch on my phone, I look around in a drawer that holds anything and everything from hair bands to bin liners. Then I pull out some of the heavy-duty freezer bags.

When I turn around, he's gazing into the living room, and that's when I see the space where my TV used to be. I swallow down the lump in my throat and open the freezer to pull out frozen vegetables and meat.

His phone torch joins mine as we work in silence.

"Where are you and Molly going to stay tonight?" he asks.

"Molly's staying at her dad's. I'll stay here. I have plenty of candles, and the fridge stuff should keep until morning."

"No, I don't think that's a good idea."

"What?" I ask, standing up, bags at my feet.

"It's not safe—all those naked flames." He looks around, shining his phone around as he takes in all my candles; I may have a bit of a collection.

"I'll be fine, Oliver."

"You can stay at mine," he says in a rush.

"No, it's fine, but thank you."

"Come on, you've been to my house. I don't live like a pig. And it's one night. There's even a lock in the spare room, in case you're worried I can't keep my hands to myself."

I audibly sigh. "I never implied any of the above. Why do

you do that? I'm not the stuck-up cow people make me out to be." He's starting to piss me off.

He scrubs his hand over his face. "I know, and I'm sorry… But I do have a thing against candles—it's a long story—but I'd feel better if you just stayed somewhere else until the power is back up."

I don't have anywhere else to go. I refuse to go to my parents', and if I went to Marcus, it would only confuse things more. My fingers fiddle with my watch. "Only if you're sure."

He nods, and I move past him to grab a few necessities. I hear him moving about while I rummage and want to cringe. I forgot to close the door to the box room. I stuff clothes into a bag and make quick work of snatching what I need from the bathroom.

"Did you paint this?" he calls out.

I stop and stand in the threshold as he studies my canvas. "Yeah."

He turns to me, but I can't see his eyes in this light. "It is phenomenal," he says, and I'm glad it's dark—my cheeks burn from his compliment.

"Thanks," I croak out. It's my last love and my favourite, but I refuse to let it go for anything less than the asking price. And since I'm out of art supplies until it sells, I can't paint anything else.

"You should sell it," he says, turning back and flashing a photograph of it.

"Oi, copyright much," I say, laughing. "And I'm planning on selling it. It's my last piece."

"Wow. Do you have an online store or something?" he asks, joining me as I make my way back to the kitchen.

"Just on eBay and Facebook." I don't tell him I couldn't afford to renew the hosting for my website.

"Who knows? I've never heard anyone talk about it," he says, grabbing both freezer bags.

"No one knows." I grab my keys. "Are you sure about this?

You could barely tolerate me not so long ago, and now you're offering me a room for the night?" I turn, and he's standing over me. I tilt my head and look up while he shuffles the bags in his hands.

"Why do you think I couldn't tolerate you?" he asks, raising his eyebrow.

I roll my eyes and wave my hands for him to get moving. "Well, you've always been kind of *off* with me. I've seen how friendly you are with everyone else."

He stops abruptly, and I slam into his back. He turns and looks down, his eyes so dark in this light. "You're mistaken. It was never because I couldn't tolerate you—the opposite, in fact. Now, come on, let's get your frozen goods back on ice," he says, spinning on his heels, leaving me speechless.

Chapter Fifteen

Rachel

I should have said I'd stay with a friend, let him be none the wiser, but I didn't, and now I'm standing in the middle of his kitchen while he packs all my food into his freezer.

An excessive buzzing hums through my bag. I dig around and pull it free—Marcus. "What's wrong? Is Molly okay?"

"Calm down, she's fine, but—"

"What, Marcus?" I turn and head into the living room, eyeing the bookcase, wondering what his fascination is with the same book.

"I need to bring Molly back."

I close my eyes; he has got to be shitting me. "Back where, Marcus? I told you there's no power."

"Sweetheart, I have to go to a work thing." *I can't believe him.* "And before you swear, you're on speakerphone."

I shake my head and spin around. Olly's leaning on the doorframe, one leg crossed over the other.

"Where are you?" I sigh into the phone.

I hear the sound of him flicking the indicator before he answers. "About ten minutes from yours."

"I'll call you back." I hang up before he can say another word.

"I need to go home. Marcus needs to bring Molly back," I say to Olly, unable to keep my irritation at bay.

"Get him to drop her off here." I shake my head. "I'm good with kids—*hello*, foster kid," he says as if it's enough of an explanation.

"Oliver, I can't impose on you like that. We'll be fine at mine."

He walks towards me in purposeful strides. "No, not happening. Don't make me call my mum." He crosses his arms over his chest, and I'm momentarily speechless.

"Okay, fine."

I swipe my phone and call him back. "You'll need to drop her where I'm staying."

"Cool where?" I roll my eyes and look at Olly who mouths the address I can't remember off the top of my head.

"He won't be long," I tell Olly when I get off the phone.

He nods and then turns back to the kitchen. I don't know why I'm so nervous, but I am.

My phone vibrates with a text. *Outside*

I let myself out and approach the car just as Marcus unbuckles Molly and helps her down, handing me her bags. He kisses her on top of the head, and no sooner has he arrived, he's calling out *bye* and getting back in his car. And then he's gone.

"Mummy." Molly tugs on my hand.

"Yes, baby girl, come on." I grab her bags and walk back into Olly's. He's standing just in the hallway and takes the bags from me. My heart turns to goo when I see him holding her tiny flamingo backpack, and I can't help but stifle my giggle.

"Who that?" Molly asks, wiggling to get down.

"Molly-Mae, this is Oliver. Oliver, Molly," I say.

She walks over and stares up at him, putting her arms out. He doesn't miss a beat. He scoops her up and pops her on his hip. "Hi, Molly, nice to meet you," he says and taps the tip of her nose.

She wiggles, wanting to get down, and when he obliges, she runs into his living room.

"Molly, what are you doing?"

"Looking for the puppy," she replies.

She's obsessed with dogs. Even if we had a garden, I couldn't afford to get her a dog at the moment. I couldn't afford one even if I wanted to.

"Oh, sweetie, Olly doesn't have a puppy," I say, following behind her. She stops and peers up at me with her big, soft eyes, and I want to slap myself for disappointing her.

"Well," Olly replies from behind me. "I don't have a puppy, but I do have a dog, and he's almost two."

"What?" I ask, confused, looking around.

It doesn't even smell like he has pets, and now I sound like a stuck-up bitch, like pet owner's homes smell or something.

"Yeah, he's with the dog walker—should be back any time."

I swear it's like he's a white witch or some shit. There's a knock followed by a rattle of keys, and then a commotion of padded paws and feet in the hallway.

"Olly?" A female voice calls out as she rounds the doorway.

"Hey, Judy," he says.

A dog runs circles around him, wagging its tail like a maniac, and then it spots us and rushes to Molly. I tense, but as soon as he gets in front of her, he rolls over on his back, tongue hanging out. She crouches down and tickles his belly.

"Sorry, I didn't realise you had company," she says, and I remember the woman and turn around. Wow, she's stunning for someone only wearing a pair of hunters over leggings and a loose, baggy jumper, her perfectly straight hair under a beanie. My stomach drops, my back bristles, but I don't know why.

"This is Rachel and her little girl, Molly."

"Judy," she says, reaching out her hand. A gorgeous engagement ring sparkles as I shake her hand in mine. And it instantly distinguishes the unwanted weight which nestled in my gut the moment I saw her.

"And this, here, is Buster," Olly says, joining Molly on the floor. I take a good look at the dog, at his gangly limbs, but what stands out is the scar on the right side of his face and a missing eye—poor dog.

"He's a rescue. I fostered him for the shelter, but he kind of stuck and I've had him ever since," he says with a shrug.

"I've got to run. Be by again tomorrow," Judy says, waving to us all.

"Come on, boy, let's get your dinner." Buster is gone in an instant and sitting in the kitchen as we trail behind him.

It's then I notice the cubby area under the sink with a huge fluffy bed and toys sticking out that I didn't see before.

"Want to help me, Molly?" Olly asks, and she drops her toy and rushes to his side.

What am I even watching? She's never taken to anyone as easily, and how did she know he had a dog in the first place?

Chapter Sixteen

Rachel

After Buster has eaten, I check the time, knowing if Molly doesn't get to bed soon, she'll be a villain tomorrow. "I need to get her settled," I say.

Olly nods and leads us upstairs. The room we enter is larger than my living room. "Here you go, make yourselves at home," he says, slipping out of the door.

I settle on the bed with her and can't help but slink into the plush mattress. I miss having a bed.

When my reading puts her to sleep, I slip out to search for Olly. He's perched on a stool in front of the kitchen counter with Buster at his feet, mouthing on a soft toy.

"She's asleep," I say, and he turns to me with a smile.

"Drink?" he asks, slipping off the stool.

"Yes, please."

He looks around in the fridge, then waves around a bottle of unopened Moscato. I nod—it's a glass of wine kind of day.

He pours me one and nudges his head in the direction of the living room.

Nothing about his home screams *bachelor*, but I'm starting to realise that nothing about him surprises me anymore.

"Thanks for this," I say.

"No worries."

We settle into a strange kind of silence, and I'm not sure if it's welcome or not. "So, how's the dating going?" he enquires, and now I think the silence wasn't so bad after all.

"Ha ha, you know full well it's *not*," I reply, hiding behind my glass and taking a huge sip. Truth is, since the last guy, and taking up self-defence classes, I haven't bothered.

"What about you? Any conquests?"

"I don't have conquests," he says, bringing his beer to his lips before taking a swig. I watch as he swallows—the veins of his throat pronounced—and my fingers itch to trace the lines, then paint them to canvas. "I only have *a* conquest," he says with a wink. Surely he doesn't mean me.

I stand and find my way over to his books to run my fingers over their spines. "I've never read it," I ponder out loud. "Why do you have so many editions?" I ask, scanning over the different sizes and colours.

"That's for me to know and you to find out," he whispers over my shoulder. My heartbeat accelerates. He reaches out, pulls one free. I squeeze my eyes closed as the heat from his body causes me to sway slightly. "Here, read this." He places it in my empty hand, his chin just shy of resting on my shoulder.

"I have quite a bad attention span. I'm fine when I read to Molly, but other than that, I struggle to stay focused." I turn the book over and read the back.

"But it's a classic. Listen—" He flips open the book and reads aloud, "So much has been done, exclaimed the soul of Frankenstein,—more, far more, will I achieve: treading in the steps already marked, I will pioneer a new way, explore unknown powers, and unfold to the world the deepest mysteries of creation."

I peer up over my shoulder, his voice thick like warm honey. He moves back to the sofa. "Come sit," he says, patting the space next to him.

Sinking into the deep filled cushions, I do as he says. He opens the book and begins reading. "What are you doing?" I ask.

"I'm going to read it to you," he says, like it's obvious. I shake my head but go with it, pulling my legs up underneath me. "Ready?" he asks with a cock of his eyebrow. I nod and trace the condensation on the outside of my glass while he starts from the beginning, pulling me into the extraordinary world of Mary Shelley.

I roll over, the softness of the sheets like heaven against my skin. I sigh and blink a couple of times, my surroundings too dark. It takes me a moment to remember where I am. I put out my arm for Molly, but the space beside me is cold.

Sitting bolt upright, I check to see if she's migrated to the other end of the bed—she's always been such a fidgety sleeper.

My heartbeat picks up speed.

I jump out of bed to switch on the light, and it takes a moment for my eyes to adjust. "Fuck."

I pad out of the room, the house unfamiliar as I look in the bathroom, switching on lights as I go, my insides squirming as raw panic sets in.

Without thinking, I swing open Olly's bedroom door. He sits up, blinking at me, confused.

"I can't find Molly," I say, looking around in case she wandered in here.

"What?" He springs from the bed in one swift movement.

"Did you check the bathroom?" he asks, pushing past me—bare-chested and in low slung pyjama bottoms.

"Yes," I say, frantically moving past him to run downstairs. "Oh, my god, this is all my fault. It's been so long since I slept in a bed. I didn't hear her." I run to the front door to see if its bolted.

"They're all locked," he says from somewhere behind me, an air of worry laced behind his words.

I need to check it for myself, and sure enough, it's locked. I'm spinning back around as he rushes to the kitchen, stopping so suddenly, I collide into his hard back.

"What?" I ask in a strangled panic, then push him to the side, my eyes darting over the room. He grabs my arm, stilling me, and points.

Small feet poke out from under the countertop. I leap forward and crouch down, putting my hand to my chest. She's curled up next to Buster, sleeping. I fall back on my haunches and cry.

Olly kneels beside me. "She's okay," he says, rubbing my back. I nod and wipe my face. "What did you mean? About sleeping in a bed…"

I fall to my bottom and bring my knees to my chest, keeping my eyes on Molly, her chest rising and falling with each breath. "I sleep on my sofa. I wanted her to have her own room and the spare room—well, box room—you've seen it. Harry Potter had more space under the stairs. And it's the space I use to paint."

He doesn't say anything as he crawls forward, and in one swift movement, he scoops Molly into his arms and stands, Buster wagging his tail.

"Good boy, stay," he says, and the dog lies back down, his eyes watching as Olly heads towards the stairs. I scramble up and follow him.

She hasn't even stirred. I watch Olly from the doorway as he carefully lays her down and steps back.

"I'm so sorry for waking you," I say, feeling like an absolute fool. He gently takes me by the elbow and pulls me back out onto the landing.

He scrubs his hand down his face. "Don't be ridiculous, and of course you should've woken me."

I cross my arms and can't help my roaming eyes as they take in his torso. He has tattoos all over—almost a full sleeve on one arm, some others just over his ribs—a kaleidoscope of colour and intricate artwork. My fingers move of their own accord and trace the lines, names, scars.

"What happened?" I meet his gaze. "Sorry it's none of my business," I say, pulling my hand away, but his fingers wrap around my wrist.

"It's okay. I don't mind you asking. At least you didn't look repulsed," he says. "I was burnt in a house fire trying to get my little sister out."

I suck in a breath, my eyes darting to his, no longer surveying his upper body. My hearts clenches.

"She was fine," he replies. "But me—not so much." He let's go of my wrist, and I place my palm on his chest. He shivers.

"Olly, I happen to think you're perfectly fine as you are." I go up onto my tiptoes, place a soft kiss to the corner of his mouth, and step back. "Goodnight. Thank you," I say and turn back to Molly. When I look over my shoulder to close the door, he's standing still, watching, his eyes sparkling with a lopsided smile on his face.

The door closes with a soft click.

Chapter Seventeen

Rachel

I glare at my latest pile of bills and sink in the chair at the table. I have one piece of art left to sell, but with my website being out of commission, and eBay being so hit and miss, it's not making it any easier to find a buyer.

If I can't get my car fixed, I can't get to work, can't get Molly to and from school. It will be near impossible. I already sold the TV but made sure to keep the tablet for Molly so she could at least still watch her programmes.

All the expensive bags and shoes I purchased over the years, I've since sold. And now this—my last resort. I finger the watch on my wrist, knowing what I need to do.

I only have to wait six more months until my twenty-fifth birthday, then the money my Nan left me will be released. Marcus doesn't get it. He's swanning around like a bachelor. He treats Molly with outfits here or there, and toys, but no help financially with our cost of living. He's never given me maintenance, and the last thing I want is for her to appear like she's some kind of transaction. But he is her father, and maybe it's time he understood the full extent of his responsibilities.

I send him a quick text. *Call me as soon as you're free.*

Which means if I'm lucky, he'll ring me on Sunday.

Resigned, I grab my bag and keys. I could get the bus to the high street, but I'd rather keep that money to treat Molly to a Happy Meal. She never asks me for anything, but I know how much she loves them.

It takes me just under an hour to walk to the pawnbrokers. I ring the bell, wait for the click release of the automatic lock, and then push my way into the air-conditioned shop.

I walk up to the counter and smile when I see Ralf. "Hi," I say, plastering on a fake smile.

"Hey, love. What brings you back so soon?"

"Unexpected expenses," I say, forgoing any pretence.

He nods in understanding. "What can I do for you today?"

I unclasp my Rolex. It slides from my wrist, and I hold it out to him. A whistle escapes his lips. It's the most valuable item I own. "I have the certificate of authentication," I say.

He nods, eying me. "You sure you want to pawn it?"

"I don't have a choice."

"How much did you want?"

I know these sell well, even used, but I want to be able to get it back. "Ten percent of the value," I reply, my mouth dry.

He asks to see the documentation I brought with me, and after nearly an hour, I have a bank transfer of two grand. Should be enough to cover the costs I need for my car, Molly's childcare fees, rent, and other amenities. If I'm lucky enough —more art supplies.

I have to make a payment each fortnight to get it back. I hope like hell I'll be able to. This is the one treasured gift my Nan ever gave me, and not because of its value, but its sentiment. Yes, she had money, but she wasn't frivolous. For my eighteenth, she purchased my car; my twenty-first, my watch.

I finger my bare wrist, missing the weight of it already.

I pull out my phone and type out a quick text to Nate. I need to find out if he can fix my car. It will require a tow from Olly's, and that's all going to add up. Truth is, by the time I've forked out for the repairs, I might have well just bought a runaround. But I love my car, and hopefully, once she's fixed, she'll be good for a while yet.

Nate replies almost straight away. He's just finished a job, so he can fit me in as soon as I want. Finally—something going my way. I tell him the sooner the better, but I will need to have it towed to him.

He rings me. "Hello?"

"Rach, have you broken down?"

I smile and walk as I talk. "No—I mean yes, I did over the weekend. Betty is currently taking up residence outside Olly's house."

"Oh yeah? Something you want to share?"

I pause to check the road and dash across. "Not particularly. Anyway, I appreciate you being able to take a look at it. I'll need to arrange recovery to get it to you."

"No, I'll sort that out, don't worry about it. I just need your keys."

"Shit, yeah, of course. I'm just picking up Molly now. I can try and get them to you later."

I hear a rattling in the background. "No, I'll come by to grab them. How are you going to do that with Molly and no car?"

He's right, of course. "Are you sure you don't mind?"

"Of course not. Anything for a friend."

I agree to call him in an hour after I've gotten myself together. I could almost cry. It's not lost on me how I pretty much came between him and Felicity. It wasn't my proudest moment, and everything turned out as it should. I flick my gaze to my wrist, cringe, then check the time on my phone.

Thankfully I make the bus in time and get to Molly before they charge me for being late.

"How would you like a Happy Meal for dinner?" I ask, swooping her up onto my hip. She's growing so fast.

"Yes," she squeals.

I smile and tweak her nose before putting her back on her feet. We make our way to the bus stop. "Did you have a nice day?"

"Yeah, I did a drawing." She pulls out a crinkled piece of paper from her book bag.

"That's amazing," I say, holding it up to examine.

I quickly tuck it back into her bag as the bus approaches, and after a twenty-minute game of eye spy, we arrive at our stop. I get her dinner to go, and we take a five-minute walk back home.

"Go sit at the table to eat, Molly." She doesn't argue, excited to see what toy she has. Two treats in one.

Nate rings while I'm putting in a wash load.

"Hi."

"Hey Rach, so I'm coming by with Felicity to grab your keys and drop you off a car to use until yours is sorted."

"What? No, I can't let you do that."

"Yes, you can, and you will. I've already made sure you are covered on the insurance."

"I don't know what to say," I reply, my nose tingling, and I hate that again, for the second time today, I might cry.

"You don't have to say anything. We'll pop by in the next twenty minutes, is that okay?"

"Perfect, thank you."

I end the call, not having to worry about how to juggle getting Molly to school and me to work without a car. I know I made poor choices before she was here, but I hope, more than anything, I can atone for them and prove my friendship is valid.

Chapter Eighteen

Olly

I look forward to Wednesday's—not only does it break the back of the week, I also have a class with Rachel.

Henry comes over and slaps me heavy on the back. "Hey man, how's it going?" he asks, always with the smile. It's contagious; like yawning, you can't help but return it.

"Good man, how's the training going?"

"It's going," he says, staring out over the open expanse of the gym as the hum of the air-con clicks up a notch.

I raise my eyebrow. "Looking for someone?" I say with a lazy grin. He shrugs it off, but I swear the dude is blushing. I lean into him, fluttering my eyelashes and pursing my lips in a mock kiss.

And that's when I feel her.

I go stock-still and flick my eyes towards the door. Rachel is standing there, head tilted, watching. I wiggle my fingers in a wave, and she comes towards us.

"Henry, this is Rachel." I wave between them, "Rachel, Henry."

"Boyfriend?" she asks, holding out her hand.

I almost choke on air as he busts out laughing. "Only in his dreams," Henry replies, and she smiles, eyes roaming over his body. Can't blame her—his physique is fierce.

"You ready?" I ask, nodding my head in the direction of the metal staircase.

"That's why I'm here," she sing-songs.

"Later man," I say to Henry. He salutes me, turning to the weights laid out in front of the mirrored wall.

Rachel looks over her shoulder as we make our way upstairs. "Like what you see?" I tease. She turns back, and as I peer back over my shoulder, I see her gaze on my arse.

"Yeah, it's not too bad," she says.

I let out a laugh. "Don't you need to put your watch in your locker?" I ask, dropping her bag onto the bench.

She touches her wrist. "Oh, no. I left it at home this morning," she replies and looks away. She once said it's like missing a limb when she's not wearing it, but it's none of my business.

I walk over to the mats, and she follows, mirroring me as we begin to warm up.

"I just wanted to say thank you again for the other day. It was appreciated." She turns, pulling her leg up behind her, and now I'm the one zoning in on her backside. I shake my head, I need to stop thinking like that—especially here.

"What are friends for?" I say and mean it. Molly is ridiculously cute and tenacious; so much like Rachel in her mannerisms. She turns, her eyes flashing with something I can't decipher, then just as quick, it's gone. "Nate came by to pick up your car. I was going to hold on to Molly's car seat so I could offer to come pick you up, but he said he was loaning you a car."

She drops her other leg having stretched enough. "You were?"

I nod. Damn if the rubescent colour creeping up her neck and over her cheeks doesn't distract me. I clear my throat and clap my hands together. "Right, you ready?" She nods. "I want you to use some of the techniques I've taught you." And I realise how gutted I'll be when her class is over.

I circle her and grab her in a bear hug from behind. She wriggles, so I tighten my hold. Grunting, I whisper in her ear, "Come on, you've got this."

Her whole body tenses. She peers at me over her shoulder, and I'm trapped. Her pupils dilate, she licks her bottom lip, and I'm a goner—my dick hardens.

Fuck.

Never has that happened to me before—not while doing this. "Sorry," I say and pull away from her luscious body.

Then out of nowhere, she dips, hooking her ankle behind my leg, and I go down, pulling her with me. The air whooshes out of me with an oomph. "Shit!"

"Got you," she says, half on top of me.

"Yeah, you do," I say, swallowing hard, watching her eyes dance with satisfaction. I groan when her elbow digs into my ribs.

"Sorry, did I hurt you?"

"No, just wounded my pride. Well played, young Jedi." She laughs, and I tighten my grip on her waist. I fucking *love* that sound from her lips.

She rolls away from me. If I can't keep my emotions in check, I need to get one of the other guys to finish her sessions for me. The thought riles me the wrong way.

I push myself up and hold my hand out to her; she waves it away and stands in front of me. Her scent is beginning to drive me crazy. Even when she's sweating, she smells sweet, like vanilla icing sugar.

"Be right back," I say and turn to rush for the changing room off to the side. Once in one of the cubicles, I lean my forehead against the cold tiled wall and close my eyes. She's under my skin and has no bloody idea. I shake out my hands and count to ten.

Pulling myself together, I return to find her chatting to Meghan. "Hey, Smeggy," I say as I approach them.

She swats my arm. "Are you not bored with that nickname yet?" she asks.

"Never," I reply with a wink.

Rachel is staring between the two of us, an unspoken question on her face; she raises an eyebrow. I shake my head. Meghan bursts out laughing—we've known each other since secondary school.

"Olly and I go way back," she tells Rachel, who nods but has gone quiet. "Anyway, I didn't mean to interrupt, I just wanted to see if you'd be up for sparring sometime?" she asks.

Rachel points to herself and shakes her head. "I wouldn't even know where to start," she says. Her ponytail whips back and forth, vanilla hits me again, and I let out a groan.

"I'll give you some pointers," I say, wanting to take it back immediately.

"You would?"

"It's settled then," Meghan says as she walks away.

I need to catch up with Meg. I've been distracted lately, but I've noticed she's been acting strange, and I feel bad I haven't had much time for her recently.

Chapter Nineteen

Rachel

I thought things were on the up, but I should have known better. I've gone and broken the heel of my favourite boots—my only boots—and I can't afford to replace them any time soon. Marcus is going to have to come up with some money for Molly. I usually don't ask, but he's living the life of a carefree single guy. He's a father first—anything else second.

"Is everything all right?" asks Sophie while rinsing the mixer attachments.

I nod once and turn to her with a smile. "Yeah, fine," I reply.

She tilts her head. "Why don't I believe you?" I shrug and continue filling up the sugar containers. "You know what we need? A *girls' night* out." She claps her hands together; I can't suppress my laugh. There's something infectious about her excitement.

"I'd have to wait until payday," I admit.

She slaps the counter. "I don't think so. It's my treat. You helped me so much leading up to Selene being born."

I shake my head, ready to argue with her, but she's not taking no for an answer. Hand on her hip, her eyes bore into mine. "Okay, fine. As long as Marcus will have Molly tomorrow, it sounds lovely. Will you ask Felicity to come?"

She smiles wide. "Of course, this is going to be so good. I can't wait."

"Don't you need to clear it with Charlie?" I ask.

She shakes her head. "No, he won't mind. He'll be pleased I'm doing stuff again."

She struggled when Selene came along, opened up to me when she returned to work. She blamed herself for their little girl's early arrival. But it was out of her control. I couldn't imagine being in a relationship like theirs; they are lucky.

I can't remember the last time I had a night out, but I'm grateful for Sophie, I needed this. "So, how are the classes going with Olly?" Sophie asks over the brim of a margarita glass.

"It's okay. I was apprehensive at first, but he's a great teacher," I reply, unable to hide my smile.

"I bet he is," she says with a wink.

"Who is what?" asks Felicity, looking up from her phone before slipping it back into her bag.

"Olly—he's a good teacher. He's giving Rach self-defence lessons."

Felicity stares at me, a warm smile gracing her lips. "How does that not surprise me?"

"You know, Charlie thought maybe there was something between Olly and me," Sophie says on a light chuckle. I almost choke on my drink. "Yeah, he asked me once, but I told him I thought he liked you."

I cough to clear my throat. "Who—Charlie?"

She shakes her head, laughing. "No, Olly. I think he likes you."

I stutter as I try to come up with a response. "He—what no way—he doesn't. I mean…not like that." He acts like he's not good enough for me, he's even said as much, but I've found myself disagreeing.

"Really? Because if my sources are correct… Did he or did he not have you and Molly-Mae stay over at his house?"

I am so glad my glass is on the table and not in my hands. "It is, but nothing happened. He was just being a friend."

They both laugh in unison.

"Listen, friend or not, there is no way he would go out of his way for you like that if there wasn't more to it."

I cover my warm face with my hand, hoping to hide my embarrassment. I'm a grown woman, and yet I feel like a giddy teenager.

"Well…do you like him?" asks Felicity, sipping on her cocktail.

I'm just about to answer when someone clears their throat from behind us, and the girls' eyes go wide. I turn to peer over my shoulder.

"Rachel, I thought that was you."

I quickly stand and grab him in a hug. "Harris, oh my god. How are you?" I step back. He looks good, a little less awkward than the kid I knew from school.

"I'm good. Blimey, this is a blast from the past," he says, his eyes dancing all over my face.

I quickly turn back to my table. "I'm so sorry. Harris, this is Felicity and Sophie."

They wave at him; he nods back. "Sorry, I didn't mean to interrupt, but I had to come over and say hello."

I grab hold of his forearm. "Of course, I'm glad you did." I can't stop beaming at him.

"You look good," he says.

My face heats from his compliment. Felicity shuffles past. "Sorry, we're just going to use the ladies'. You good to watch our drinks?" she asks.

I nod, letting Sophie out. When I sit back down, Harris takes Felicity's seat. "It's been what? About five years? So, what's new with you?"

"Has it? Wow. I've been good. I have a daughter," I say, unable to keep the pride out of my voice.

"I heard. You and Marcus, right?" I nod, retrieve my phone from my clutch, and then lean over the table to show him. "She's beautiful, just like her momma," he says.

The hairs on the back of my neck stand up, and I scan the room until they come to a stop.

Olly is behind the bar, arms crossed, and he looks kind of pissed. I tilt my head and raise a smile in his direction. He completely blows me off, turning his back towards me. Weird.

"So, where's Marcus?" asks Harris.

"Oh, it's his turn to have Molly tonight."

"I did hear you split up," he says, strangling his bottle of beer.

"Good to know gossip isn't dead," I reply, trying to hide my annoyance.

"You know, I wanted to contact you…"

I sit back in my chair. "You did?"

He nods just as the girls return. He stands to let Felicity sit back down as I stand to let Sophie in beside me. We brush together and laugh at the same time.

"Here, let me give you my number." He takes my phone and types in his number, and then his phone pings in his pocket.

"I'll let you ladies get back to your evening." He reaches for my hand and gives it a tight squeeze before leaning in and kissing me on the cheek. "I'll give you a call," he says and turns towards the bar.

I sit back down and wave my hand in front of my face. "What?" I ask as Felicity and Soph both stare at me.

"Oh, nothing much, just watching you get hit on was priceless."

"He was not," I say.

Felicity nods. "He most definitely was."

My eyes flee to the bar—he's talking to Olly, who does not look impressed. "He was a boyfriend, but we didn't go out for long. It was when I was going through an off stage with Marcus."

"Looks to me like he might have some unfinished business with you," says Sophie, finishing off her drink.

"We were seventeen. He barely got to cop a feel," I reply as a shadow falls over us.

"Here. With compliments from Harris," Olly says, passing us each a drink. I try to catch his gaze, but he avoids making eye contact.

"Thanks," they say, clinking their glasses.

I look past Olly to Harris and smile. He nods before making his exit. Olly turns to walk away, and I'm left a bit bewildered by his mood.

"Two secs," I call to the girls, quickly getting up to catch him. "Olly," I say to his back. His shoulders tense, but he doesn't turn around, so I move around him. "Everything all right?" I ask.

His dark violet eyes connect with mine, and he shrugs. "Yeah, why wouldn't it be?"

I cross my arms. "Because you seem off with me."

"Just thought you were over the stereotypes."

"Excuse me?"

"Your man, Harris, whipping out his AMEX to buy you a drink—little cliché, don't you think?"

What is his problem? "Olly, he's an old friend from school."

He laughs. "From the way he was peering down at your cleavage, I think he wants to be more than just friends."

Did he just say that?

"Very mature, Oliver," I reply, dumbfounded by his hostility. "And just an FYI—*who* I choose to be friends with is *none of your business*." I step past him and hurry back to my table just as he's called back to the bar.

"You okay?" asks Sophie.

"Of course," I reply and hold my glass up in salute before downing the contents.

Chapter Twenty

Rachel

I tried not to allow Olly's outburst at the bar get to me. I managed to ignore him for the rest of the night and found myself enjoying being out with the girls, but after I returned home to my empty flat, I couldn't help but feel melancholy.

Harris messaged me on Sunday, and we've texted back and forth, but it feels...wrong, somehow. It wasn't until he asked me to go out with him that I finally told him I wasn't dating. It's not technically a lie—since the last fiasco, I haven't found myself wanting to. And besides, if I'm honest with myself, Harris doesn't evoke the same feelings in me as Olly does. Before he was a jackass on Saturday, anyway.

"You all right?" asks Sophie from somewhere behind me.

"Yeah, fine," I reply, wiping down the last table.

"Really? Because I saw a little hostility between you and Olly on Saturday. I didn't want to bring it up at the time, but it's been a few days, and you haven't mentioned anything..."

I shrug. "Nothing to say. He was a bit of a jerk."

She laughs, ducking out from behind the counter. "I think you know he was *jealous*." I shake my head. "Deny it all you want, but Charlie said he's been in a mood since then, and he never gets like that."

"Isn't Charlie going against boy-code gossiping about his friend to his girlfriend?"

She waves her hand around, dismissing my comment. "Hardly. Besides, I was asking questions, and Charlie answered. It's not the same thing."

"If you say so."

"Anyway, as I said, he was jealous."

My body is heavy with fatigue from the past couple of days; the weight of whatever transpired between us has been at the forefront of my mind. I shrug. "It doesn't matter, Soph. I don't have the time or energy for any more drama."

She eyes me, contemplating her next words, tucking her hair behind her ears. "Don't take this the wrong way—and believe me when I say this is coming from someone who knows all too well about self-sabotage—Olly is a good guy, and if he was jealous, it's because he likes you." I go to interrupt, but she holds up her hand. "All I'm saying is, talk to him. Find out what that was all about. Don't you have a class with him this week?"

I let out a frustrated groan. "It was this morning, but I didn't go."

She frowns. "Why not?"

"Because I'm pissed about his attitude on Saturday, and I don't know…maybe I'm just scared."

Sophie walks right up to me and takes my hands in hers. "Rach, fear and I are old acquaintances, and I assure you, taking a risk is sometimes the only way to kick fear up the arse."

I pull back and laugh. "Did you just say *arse?*"

Her cheeks flame, and she smiles. "I did, but I only reserve curse words for when I feel like they are warranted."

Coming from a woman who rarely swears, it's refreshing to hear it from her lips. I smile. "Duly noted."

"Anyway, I think you should just talk to him. You've been happier these past few weeks, and whether you care to admit it or not, he has a part to play." She squeezes my hands, then leaves me to finish up as she heads back to the kitchen. Her words are ringing in my ears. *Have* I been happier?

Maybe… I mean, he has come through without me even asking. Not that I would, but still, he's become a friend. I let out a frustrated groan. Why does it always have to be so complicated?

I'm tempted to text him back from his message earlier, but I don't. Maybe I'll do it later once I'm home, and perhaps he won't see it until tomorrow.

Chapter Twenty-One

Olly

She didn't show up for her lesson.

I sent her a message—she didn't reply.

So, here I am, stalking about outside Sofia's deli like a tosser, contemplating whether I should go in and call her out on it.

Fuck it.

I peer through the window. Her back is to me—no customers. I pull open the door, and it chimes my intrusion. Rachel spins at the sound, her smile ready to greet a customer. It falls away when she sees me.

"Oh."

"Rachel?"

She turns her back to me and continues wiping down the —already clean—table. "What do you want, Oliver?"

Is she fucking kidding me? I scrub my hand through my hair. "You missed your class," I reply.

She spins around, and I take a step back. "What? You thought I'd come back?"

I hold up my hands. "Princess."

Her eyes go wide. "Don't call me that," she says through gritted teeth.

I feel my jaw tick—a smile trying to break free—but I tamper it back down. "Why? You are…" I can't stop myself as the words pass my lips.

She takes a step towards me, clutching the cloth in her hand so tight, her knuckles go white. "You're an arsehole," she replies.

"Come on, we had a disagreement. No need to get your panties in a twist." I don't know why I'm trying to downplay what happened. The truth is, I was a complete prick.

She crosses her arms, and my eyes are drawn to her chest. "My eyes are up here," she says, her nostrils flaring.

"Oh, I know," I reply, taking a step towards her.

"Olly, will you please just go?" Her eyes cast down, her chin dips, and she bites her bottom lip.

My stomach sinks. "I'm sorry," I say and reach for her arm. But she won't look at me.

I move my finger under her chin and tilt her face towards mine. "Rachel, I'm sorry," I say again, my eyes trained on her as her tongue darts out over her bottom lip. "Please don't forfeit the classes because I'm a prick."

Her lip twitches and her eyes soften. "Okay, fine," she breathes out.

I don't know who makes up the distance, but before I can stop myself, I lower my mouth to hers. She gasps, her lips parting, allowing my tongue access. It meets with hers. She tastes like vanilla frosting. I cup the back of her head to pull her closer; she reaches out and grips my shirt.

Her kiss is intoxicating. My dick throbs against the fly of my jeans—too confining—and I pull her tighter against me. I need her to feel what she does to me. She groans into my mouth, our mutual desire and attraction palpable.

Someone coughs and clears their throat.

Rachel is the first to pull back, pupils dilated, her skin a deep shade of crimson. I look around, suddenly aware of my surroundings.

Shit!

We both take a step back.

"I'll see you tomorrow, Rachel," says Sophie with her bag in hand, keys out, before greeting me.

"I was just leaving," I reply, moving to open the door. I usher for Sophie to go first and don't look back as I follow her out.

Rachel

He didn't even say bye when he made a hasty getaway. What the fuck just happened?

I slump into a chair and cover my face with my hands. My skin is hot against my palms. I've never been kissed so thoroughly in my life, and then he couldn't get out of here quick enough. Why do I always do this—get mixed up with the wrong guys? I let out a frustrated moan just as the bell rings at the door.

I quickly look up, expecting to see Michael from next door. Charlie wanted to make sure Soph and me had someone else present when we were locking up, and since Michael closes later than us, he agreed.

But it's not him staring back at me—it's Olly. I stand, my legs heavy underfoot. He crowds the doorway, and I continue to stare at him.

"That shouldn't have happened," he blurts out. And I

want the ground to swallow me whole. "I mean, it should have but not like that."

I can't keep up with him. "Let's just forget about it, Oliver," I say and turn away from him. I don't back down to anyone, but for him, I find myself breaking my own rules.

I hear him approach. "Don't act like it was nothing."

I turn, surprised to find him mere inches from me. Whatever rebuke on the tip of my tongue now forgotten, I tilt my head back to meet his eyes.

His hand reaches for my face, and his fingers caress my cheek. My stomach flips over. "What I meant was, that isn't how I wanted the first time I kissed you to go." His hand moves to the back of my neck, holding me soft and yet firm. "Not in the middle of your workplace. Don't get me wrong— it was kaleidoscopic. But I at least want to take you out first. Show you what a real date should be like."

I'm breathy when I find a response. "You want to take me out?"

He nods, leaning down, his lips so close. "Yes," he breathes.

"Okay." His lips cover mine, but just as quickly, they're gone.

"Just tell me when."

"Tonight," I reply before I can think better of it. Molly is at Marcus's.

"What time shall I pick you up?"

"Seven-thirty."

His lips transform into a huge smile, and I can't help but mirror it. He walks backwards without taking his eyes off me until he reaches the door. "I look forward to it," he says, leaving me in equal parts excitement and shock.

Chapter Twenty-Two

Rachel

I'm pissed off.

Marcus was meant to have Molly tonight, but no. He's let her down—again. "Molly, you're not seeing Daddy. He has work tonight," I lie.

She smiles, picks up her stuffed toy, and carries on playing. It worries me that she doesn't seem phased anymore. She shouldn't be used to it—her father disappointing her—not at four. "Bath, book and bed," I say walking over to scoop her up. She giggles when I tickle her.

By the time she's in bed, and I go to tidy up the bathroom, I realise I haven't messaged Olly. "Shit."

I run to the kitchen, grab my phone, send him a text. It's already quarter past seven.

Bubbles appear straight away, and I have a moment of relief—maybe he was running late and hasn't left yet. *I'm outside.*

My palms are sweaty as I try to type back a response when

the phone flashes with his name. Taking a deep breath, I answer. "Hi, I am so sorry—"

"Don't be silly, do you still want to have our date? I could come up, and we could order takeaway?"

I scan around my flat; it's not too messy. "Hmmm."

"You don't have to if you aren't comfortable. We can do it another time."

"No, you're here. Come on up, I'll buzz you in."

We hang up, and I sniff at my armpit. "Eww."

I open the door, waiting after buzzing him in. When he rounds the corner, my breath catches at the sight of him in dark jeans, tight against his thighs, and a white shirt with the cuffs rolled up.

"Hi," he says, smiling when he sees me.

"Hi, I am so sorry. Marcus let Molly down again." He pulls his arm out from behind his back and holds out a small bunch of carnations and a bottle of Moscato. "Thank you," I reply, sheepishly and realise I still haven't invited him in. I move to the side and push myself up against the wall when he enters, hoping he can't smell how ripe I am.

"Would you mind if I quickly jumped in the shower? I'm still in my work clothes and would rather not petrify you on our first date."

"Not possible—I've seen you sweaty already," he says with a wink. I close the door, trying to suppress my grin from his comment. "Go on, have a shower. I'll order dinner. Is Chinese okay?"

"Perfect."

He takes the flowers and wine from me, then turns to the kitchen, completely at ease while I stare as his arse. I shake my head and quickly duck into the box room to grab what I would have worn tonight before rushing into the bathroom.

I'm used to having quick showers, so I am in and out within ten minutes, pulling on jeggings and one of my favourite off-the-shoulder tops. I pull my hair up into a messy bun and let a few strands fall around my face but forgo make-up. I swipe some powdered blush over my cheeks, slick on some tinted lip balm, and then finish off with a quick spray of deodorant.

Already beginning to feel sweaty again, I have to take a few deep breaths before I walk out.

I find Olly in the kitchen, leaning against the counter, waiting, his arms crossed but relaxed.

"Sorry," I say.

"Don't be. Wine?"

I nod and watch as he unscrews the bottle to pour us each a glass. I also notice he has put the flowers in the only vase I have.

"Thank you for the flowers and the wine," I say, taking the glass from him.

He clinks our glasses before taking a small sip. "They said about thirty minutes."

Glancing around, at a loss of what to do with myself. "Do you want to go sit down?"

I turn to the living room and take a seat on the sofa where he joins me at the other end. It's only a two-seater, so we are practically touching.

I can't even offer to put on the TV. Embarrassment begins to creep in, and suddenly this doesn't seem like the best idea. I'm not ashamed of where I live, or how much I do or don't have. Molly is and always will be my main priority.

"I have a question."

I smile. "Then ask, but please don't ever start a question by saying you have a question."

He grins and sucks in his bottom lip between his teeth, and I struggle to ignore the buzz it sends to my lower stomach as I remember the feel of his lips on mine. "Fair enough. Okay, so the self-defence class…could you keep coming to them? Or would you rather Henry take over?"

I shake my head. "No, I'm happy for you to carry on teaching me. We can keep it professional, right?"

"I can." He pauses and looks back towards Molly's door, and his voice drops to a husky whisper, "But I can't say the same for my…you know what?"

I almost snort out the sip of wine through my nose as his eyes dart to his crotch. "Oliver, you're such a playboy."

He puts down his wine and reaches for my hand. "Hardly. I've been single for the past year."

I study his expression, but all I see is honesty. "What…not even hook-ups? Oh, my god. Don't answer that. I didn't mean to be so rude."

He's trying to suppress a laugh. "No, no hook-ups, and isn't this what people do on a date—get to know each other?"

I nod. "Well yes, but the truth is, if you asked me about my sex life, I know I wouldn't have been as easy going as you just were."

He nods. "Duly noted."

I can't believe my mouth when I'm around him. I was at least raised with more manners than this. "I am sorry, I just seem to forget myself when I'm around you."

"No, apology necessary. And I kind of like that you do." He leans towards me, his hand reaching for my face. My pulse races and then the buzzer sounds, and I let out a squeal, barely managing not to spill my wine all over us.

I clutch my chest. "Jesus, it's probably the food," I say, unable to hide my nervous laughter.

He stands. "I'll go buzz him up."

I take a moment to inhale and exhale, shaking out my hands. The flat is small but with him here, it seems tiny. Maybe it's how he makes me feel everything when he's near me—I have the open space of the gym to keep my wits about me there—but him here, like this, in my space, is both terrifying and exhilarating.

Chapter Twenty-Three

Olly

I take a moment to collect myself. I don't want to ruin this. If we were out on this date, I would've waited until I was saying goodbye to kiss her. But the pull in such a confined space has my nerve endings heightened.

I hand the delivery guy a couple of notes from my wallet and take the bag from him. "Keep the change. Thanks, man," I say, closing the door quietly and then walking through to the kitchen where Rachel has plates out on the small table, the flowers I gave her in the centre.

"You hungry?" I hold up the bag.

"Starving." She reaches for the handles, her fingers brushing mine, and there's that spark. I never believed a person could give me such a physical response until now.

I drop my hand once she has the handles securely in her hold. She opens the containers and fills both plates. "Come sit," she says, motioning for the chair as she sits opposite.

The air is still charged from the almost-kiss, and I want to punch myself.

"You okay?"

I look up from my plate. "Yeah. I'm sorry I almost kissed you," I say. Dropping my chopsticks, I smack myself on my forehead, leaning on my elbow. "Shit, I didn't mean that, I mean—" I shake my head.

She swallows, licks her lips, and stands. Making up the small distance between us, she crouches down so we're eye-level. She takes my face between her warm hands, vanilla envelopes me, and then her face inches towards mine.

Her lips mould to mine—it's slow and soft, different to the one earlier, but also the same, familiar.

I pull her closer, wrapping my hand around the back of her head. Rachel hums in satisfaction, exploring my lips and mouth. When she pulls away, her lips are plump from our impromptu make-out session, and she giggles. I kiss the tip of her nose.

"Well, that was unexpected," I say, stroking her cheek.

"In a good or bad way?" she asks, vulnerability evident in her eyes.

"A very good way. Let's eat before it gets too cold," I say.

She gets up and walks back over to her chair, and I don't know if us kissing like that was a good idea because my appetite is no longer for food.

Rachel

I hadn't felt that confident since before Molly came along, but I just knew I had to kiss him. Even if it was to see if the one we shared earlier was a fluke, which it was not. He kisses with raw honesty, want, desire. I've never felt that before.

I tuck the loose strands of hair behind my ears as he clears his throat. "How about we have a quick round of questions, taking turns?"

"Okay, you can ask first."

He taps his glass with his index finger. "Oh, I have one. What colour best describes your personality?"

I laugh. "That's a good one." I bite my lip and think. "Purple," I reply.

He nods. "Stability of blue and the fierceness of red, I can see that."

"Is your given name Olly or Oliver?"

"Oliver."

Taking a bite of food, he ponders his next question for me. "What is one thing that you would like to accomplish in your lifetime?"

I swallow my food and take a sip of my wine. "Wow, this got deep fast," I say.

"You don't have to answer anything you don't want to."

His eyes hold mine, and I know I'll answer every question he throws at me. "I'd like to have an art studio." He is one of the only people outside of my immediate family and Marcus who knows about my art, so I don't see the point in holding back from him.

"I'd love to see that," he replies, sipping his wine.

We both eat some more, and then my question comes to me. "What is your biggest fear?"

He clears his throat, his shoulders tense. His fingers on the glass tighten, and I worry he might break it. "Becoming a monster like my biological father."

I gasp. "Not possible. I don't know him. But what I do know about you...it's impossible. You are a good man, Olly."

His cheeks redden ever so slightly, and he shrugs it off. "It's up for interpretation."

"No. It's not. Do you think I would have you around my daughter or me if I had even the faintest suspicion you weren't? Anyway, it's your turn to ask me." I don't want to linger.

He finishes his last mouthful of food; I still have half a plate left, but I'm full. I push it away and pick up my glass to wait.

"How did you celebrate your last birthday?"

I clear my throat. "I didn't."

His eyes go wide. "What do you mean, you didn't? When was it?"

"The day I came to the gym for my first self-defence class."

He stands up and walks towards me, holding out his hand. I take it, and he pulls me to my feet and into his body. Bending his knees, he brings his lips to my ear and whispers, "Happy belated Birthday, Princess." And then his lips move to my cheek where he plants a soft kiss.

"Let's go sit," I say.

"What about clearing this up?"

I shake my head. "I can do it later." I take his hand with my free one, and he reaches for his glass as we make the short distance to the living room.

"What's the best thing you've ever tasted?"

"Apart from you?" he asks, and I swear I have to squeeze my thighs together. He winks but this flirty is not the same kind I've seen him use at the bar; this is a whole other side to him, and the more I get to see, the more I crave. "Lemon drizzle cake my mum made for me the year I went to live with them."

I smile. "You are quite impartial to lemon, aren't you?"

"Yep. Okay, my turn. What is the one possession you treasure the most and why?"

My fingers automatically go to my bare wrist. "My watch." I don't even have to think about it. "My nan gave it to me for my twenty-first birthday. She had it engraved. It's priceless."

He dips his head, his eyes scanning the tan line where my

watch usually sits. Before he can question it, I take his glass and put it down next to mine. Gripping him by his shirt, I pull him until we're inches apart. "Kiss me?"

Without a word, he obliges, and I'm lost in his embrace, giddy from his touch. I've never wanted to be kissed by someone so badly before.

Chapter Twenty-Four

Olly

Meghan followed through with her request to spar with Rachel, and I think this will be a good confidence builder, too.

Henry stops lifting to sidle up to Rachel when I reach the bottom of the stairs to greet her before her session with Meg. He teases her; she doesn't miss a beat. "I don't think you could handle me," Rachel drawls.

I whip my head in their direction. He's clutching his chest as though she's wounded his ego. Meghan stops next to me, her eyes fixated on them, her jaw set. "You okay?"

"Of course, I'm fine," she replies, turning to me with a smile, her palm going to my arm.

I catch Henry staring from the corner of my eye. He shakes his head before turning his attention back to Rachel—full-on flirting. I'd be concerned if I thought she was taking him seriously, however from the expression on her face, it's obvious she's not interested. "Listen, Megs, you know I'm here if you ever need to talk."

"I know, but it's complicated." She continues to stare over at Henry with a longing I've never seen from her before. I've seen her flirt with him, that's nothing new, but this is…something else.

"Hold on a sec, rewind. You and H?"

Her gaze travels back to me. "There is no me and Henry, and you know that. I mean, how could there be?"

I always thought they'd eventually get together, but I guess fate had other plans. And she's right, there's a tether that ties them, and I can see why she would think that.

"We should hang out. You could come over for nachos," I say, nudging her. But her attention is back on Henry and Rachel.

"Maybe," she mumbles under her breath.

I clear my throat loudly and clap my hands together. "Okay, Rachel, you ready?" I call out.

She slaps Henry on the bicep and comes over. "I'm ready," she says, smiling but I hear the apprehension in her voice.

"Okay, it's only light sparring, so no headgear today." She visibly swallows.

"It'll be fine," Henry says, touching her shoulder, his signature smile on display.

"Are we doing this or what?" asks Meg, bouncing on the balls of feet.

"Easy, Rocky," I reply, giving her what I hope is a warning look. The whole point is to build Rachel's confidence—not scare her into submission.

I help Rachel with her gloves, and then Henry and I move off the mat, giving the girls space. "Okay, so today you'll be working on technique." I signal my hand to Meg for emphasis. "Meg will show you a couple of moves, and then you copy them."

Rachel nods and Meghan gets to work, throwing light punches and kicks. Rachel mirrors her, and the light sparring continues. Henry and I call out a few instructions; Meg obliges.

"Olly, Henry?"

We both turn as Melissa approaches us; it's hard to ignore the way she pokes out her chest.

"What's up," I say.

"Just been to my yoga class," she says, eyes fixated on Henry.

He peers over his shoulder towards Meg and Rachel before turning his attention back to Melissa. She grabs his arm and leans in, whispering something into his ear. I look back to the girls, giving them privacy. "Well, think about it," she says before she saunters off.

I laugh and eye him; he shakes his head.

My attention moves back to the girls the exact moment Meg extends her arm, and before she even makes contact, I know Rachel isn't going to be quick enough to block her attack.

With an oomph and a punch to the side of her head, Rachel goes down.

I help Rachel to her feet; she tries to shoo me away, but there is no way I'm letting her go. She was knocked out for at least twenty seconds. I usher her to sit on the bench and help remove her gloves before taking her face between my hands.

"You probably have a concussion," I say, trying to calm my breathing.

"Yeah, well, I'm not surprised. That hurt like a motherfu—"

Meghan appears with an ice pack and gingerly holds it out to me. Snatching it, I turn back to Rachel. "Oliver, give me a second with Meghan," she says.

Reluctantly, I walk over to Henry. He's not smiling, his face unreadable—the look is alien to me—and I'm at a loss for words. "She didn't mean it," he says. I'm about to disagree when he continues, "I was trying to get a rise out of her, and I guess it worked. Never meant for Rachel to get caught in the crossfire."

His posture is rigid, expression forlorn. "What the fuck is going on with you two?"

He shakes his head, pinching his nose. "Honestly, I have no fucking clue."

I look back over to Rachel as she speaks to Meghan, her head hanging low. That's enough—I'm ready to get her back to mine or the walk-in centre if she needs it. "Sort it out, mate."

I hear him grumble under his breath as I march towards Rachel.

She looks up, and I cringe. Fuck me, she's going to have a shiner. I pull the ice pack away while she grimaces. "That bad, huh?"

"I am sorry, Rachel," Meghan says as she walks away.

"Walk-in centre or mine?"

Rachel crosses her arms. "Fine, yours."

Chapter Twenty-Five

Olly

Buster goes berserk when he sees Rachel, practically drooling at her feet. Yeah boy, I know the feeling.

"Sit," I say, ushering her to the sofa. She looks at me, mouth agape, her hair hanging loose from her braid.

I jog upstairs and turn on the taps to run her a bath, then head back down to the kitchen to grab a fresh ice pack from the freezer. When I round the door, her head is leaning back against the sofa, her eyes closed.

"Rachel?"

She flinches, hand rising to her chest. "Oliver?"

"You might have a concussion." I pass her the pack, but she only swaps it between her hands.

"It was an accident, you know?" she says, her voice strained. I plop down beside her, raising an eyebrow. "It *was*. It happened in the heat of the moment. Come on, we've all done things we're not proud of."

I close my eyes and lean my head back. I know she's right, but seeing her knocked out like that scared the shit out of me. Fingers brush my hand, and instinctively I turn it over and wrap my fingers between hers. "Yeah, but you didn't see it."

I sit forward and pull her hand with mine. "Come on," I say, and she follows me to the stairs, her eyes questioning.

"Thought you'd like a bath," I reply.

She leans her face into her underarm and sniffs loudly. "Do I smell?"

I groan, because yes she does, but in the best kind of way, making me want to bend her over and wrap her hair in my hand. She steps closer—it's too much. I can't keep fighting this current between us. I lean down, my mouth skimming her earlobe. "In a way that makes me want you, yes."

She gasps, her head moves at the same time as mine, and then we're kissing. I reach around her waist, grab onto her arse, and squeeze. I collide with the stairs, and then she's straddling me.

She breaks the kiss, her eyes unfocused. "Woah," she says, and I sit up, lifting her off me.

"Sorry." I shouldn't be kissing her, not when it's likely she has concussion. Gently, I move the hair away from her face. She looks beat up. "Bath?" I ask

"Hmm, I guess, but it's odd," she replies.

She follows me upstairs, hand gripped in mine, I only let go to turn off the tap when we reach the bathroom. "Not really, I thought it might help. You may not feel it now, but come tomorrow morning, you'll feel like you were run over by a herd of cattle."

She bites on her lip, shuffling from foot to foot.

"I'll stay close in case you need me," I say, and I don't know if that only adds to her unease. "Or I can take you home, and you can have a bath there…" I don't want her to feel uncomfortable.

"It's not that," she says, sitting on the closed toilet lid, eying the tiles with a precision inspection. "I'm confused. What are we exactly? I mean—what's going on between us?"

"Well, we are two consenting adults who like each other."

"I get that. But what I mean is, I'm not casual. I'm not just out for..." She doesn't finish her sentence as she picks at some lint on her yoga pants.

I crouch down in front of her. "I like you, Rachel, and whatever this is between us, it's not casual—not to me."

"I haven't been with anyone since falling pregnant with Molly, and I've only been with two people," she says in a rush.

I physically lean back on my haunches. She's fucking killing me. "Princess, look at me."

When her eyes meet mine, they have so many doubts, questions, uncertainty. I almost want to laugh. "We can take it as slow as you want. If you want to see where this can go, there's no hurry." I wave my hand between us for emphasis. Her lips curve into the cutest smile.

I jump up and dash to my room. "Here," I say when I pop back in with joggers and a t-shirt. "There are some towels and toiletries under the sink." She quirks her eyebrow and then winces—yep, shiner. "My sister comes to visit," I reply, and it causes my heart to lurch.

I love my foster family, but I miss my biological sister. We were young when we were separated, but my fondest childhood memories are with her. I don't remember what happened after the fire; there was so much commotion, so many strangers, paramedics, firefighters...and then there was the police. I was taken straight to a children's burn unit.

"What's wrong?" she asks, standing up, searching my face.

"I miss my other sister," I reply honestly.

"Then have her come visit."

"I can't. I mean, I don't know where Lottie is. After the fire, we were separated, and I haven't seen her since." The ball forming in my throat makes swallowing an effort. I clear it and point over my shoulder. "I'll be in my room. If you need anything, just holler," I say, closing the door behind me.

Rachel

I'm left entirely at a loss for words.

His eyes were full of a deep-rooted hurt, an ache he buries deep at the forefront. It's the same ache I've had in my chest ever since I lost my Nan. She was the best of us, held my family together with an invisible thread.

As soon as she was gone, it severed. All the family cared about was what they were entitled to inherit. Like they all had some claim over her possessions. I strip out of my clothes and stand in my sports bra and knickers, looking at my reflection.

I double-take. Damn, my eye has seen better days.

Olly has the power to break me; my feelings for him are already so much stronger than they ever were for Marcus. Is this what Olly wants? A single mum with a sketchy future at best?

He's nothing like the guy behind the bar. Everything I thought about him was what he *wants* people to see. He does so much for charity, it puts me to shame. And don't even get me started on his eye for design—his kitchen is a determinate to how talented he is.

I don't know why he doesn't pursue architecture or design. Maybe he's just a free spirit at heart. He cares for people by giving them hope, showing them they are stronger than they realise.

When I've bathed and changed into the entirely-too-big bottoms—which I had to roll at the waist twice—and in his oversized t-shirt that has me inhaling his scent like a psycho, I step out into the hallway and hesitate at his open door. I peek inside—he's lying on his bed, staring at his phone.

When he sees me, he drops it to his chest, his eyes working over my body, making me squirm.

"Come here," he says, and I gingerly walk around the bed until I'm level with him. He holds up his arm, ushering for me to join him. I do, curling into the crook of his neck.

"Want me to read some more Frankenstein?"

"What if I fall asleep?"

"I'll wake you." He reaches for the book, fingers through some pages, and then picks up where we left off.

His voice is a rich baritone—one I don't think I'd ever get tired of, and so I listen as he reads. He never stumbles once, and I wonder out loud, "How many times have you read this book?"

His small chuckle vibrates through his chest, then through me, and I smile. "I don't know…I've lost count."

His shoulder moves with a shrug, and I lean up to rest my chin in my hand. "But why? What is it about this book in particular?"

He lays it down on the other side of him, worrying his lip before his finger traces my arm. "After the fire… When I finally went back to school, I got a lot of shit because of my scars." I'm angry on little Olly's behalf. Kids can be cruel. He continues, stroking my arm as he speaks, "Anyway, they started calling me Frankenstein—saying I was a monster. I remember the day I broke down at home, crying about it after I popped the boy in the nose at school. My mum, well, she shook her head and told me to help her look for something. After digging through some boxes, she pulled out a book—Frankenstein. She said we were going to read it every night after dinner, and we did." He taps my nose and my cheeks warm when his hand comes to rest on my thigh, his thumb circling the fabric of my bottoms.

The air has an edge to it now. I lean up and give him a chaste kiss on the lips, but pull back, wanting him to continue.

The side of his mouth turns into half a smile. "Anyway, it turned out Frankenstein was the doctor—not the monster—and the monster was more human than the doctor ever could be."

Chapter Twenty-Six

Rachel

When I rouse from a foggy sleep, a feather-like caress is moving up and down my arm. First thing I notice is the ache in my body and the pain around my eye.

"Let's get you fed, and then you can take something for the pain. I'm sure you're hurting," Olly says, soft.

I go to look at my wrist to see what the time is but keep forgetting I don't have it anymore. I reach for Olly's. *Shit.* I conked out for almost two hours.

"Where's your watch?" he asks, tracing the tan line over my wrist, causing the fine hairs on my arms to stand to attention.

"In the shop," I reply—it's not a lie, technically. I swallow, hoping he doesn't pry. He tilts my chin up and checks over my face.

But instead of speaking, he leans over and kisses me with familiarity and a softness I've never felt before. My entire body on high alert as his fingers grip my head, deepening the kiss.

At this moment, I'm lost to him, floating between reality and hope, of possibilities, of what's to come.

He groans, and the sound causes my lower stomach to tighten. A deep longing pools between my thighs. Easing myself over him, I half straddle his lap, my hand roaming up and under his t-shirt.

He pulls back, his eyelids heavy. "You're so beautiful." His words steal my breath away because I know he means it, and the knowledge that he believes it has me believing, too.

"You are," I reply, which sounds so corny, but he must like my response because I'm rewarded with his mouth on mine again.

When our lips separate, our breathing is heavy, and my lips are swollen and tender. I whisper into his chest, "I like you, Olly."

His fingers trail over the length of my back, hand coming to a stop on my arse as he gives it a tight squeeze. "Good, because the feeling is mutual, Princess."

My stomach grumbles in response, and he laughs.

After we've eaten, there's a hammering on the front door. Olly follows Buster out to answer it, and I hear a familiar voice —Marcus.

"Is she here?"

I hear the annoyance in his tone and jump to my feet, headed for the hallway. When he looks over Olly's shoulder and sees my face, he shoves past him and rushes me, grabbing the tops of my arms, his eyes accessing my face.

"What the fuck?" He bares his teeth, and his eyes protrude as he lets go, spinning back towards Olly. "What the fuck happened? Did you do this?"

I cup Marcus's shoulder. "Of course, he didn't. It was an accident," I say, trying to get his attention.

"That's what they all say. *It was an accident.*" He mimics my words with a higher pitch to his voice.

Olly raises an eyebrow, but apart from that, he's calm… considering Marcus's intrusion. "Dude, you need to get out of my house."

"What are you even doing here? And where's Molly?" I demand.

Marcus pulls me by the arm a bit too roughly, and Olly, seeing my grimace, steps between us. "I'm only going to say this once—let go of her now." I don't know if it's the menacing way he said it, but Marcus drops his grip immediately and physically takes a step backwards.

"She's at my parents'. I tried calling you, went to your place, and then I thought I'd try here, seeing as I knew you weren't at work."

I wipe my palm over my face and wince remembering my eye and then take a deep breath. "Is Molly okay or not, Marcus?"

"She's fine, but we have things to talk about that can't wait. I want you and Molly to come to Dubai with me."

I'm unsteady on my feet all of a sudden. I reach out. Olly takes my arm and ushers me into his side, his eyes dancing between Marcus and me.

"Are you fucking serious?" I seethe.

"Deadly. We can all be together as a family."

Olly lets out an almost inaudible gasp, but I'm leaning my weight into him, so it wasn't hard to miss. I'm speechless.

Marcus must be out of his damn mind. We would have to get married for that to happen, and *there is no fucking way.*

"Marcus, go wait for me in the car," I tell him.

With a smug grin, he juts out his chin and walks back out the front door. Leaving what feels like a tsunami in his wake.

I plop myself on the bottom of Olly's stairs and put my head between my legs.

"Fuck," Olly grumbles.

I suck it up and peer up at him. "I need to go talk to him," I say to Olly who nods. "Do you want me to go home or can I come back in?" I ask, worrying my lip.

He lets out a breath. "I want you to come back in," he says leaning down and kissing the top of my head. I look around and slip into a pair of his trainers—too big by far, but I need to go see Marcus and have him on his way.

"I'll try and make it quick," I reply and head out to the car idling in front of his driveway.

Olly

The guy has some balls, I'll give him that.

I'd be lying if I said I wasn't worried she might take him up on it. But who even does something like that? He might as well of pissed his scent all over her. I leave the door on the latch and go out in the back garden to throw Buster his ball. Anything to stop me from curtain twitching at my bay window. My gut is jerky as fuck.

I don't know how long I've been running the ball when I'm tapped on the shoulder. I spin to look at Rachel and reach down, brushing her cheek with my thumb, her bruise now prominent.

"Everything all right?" I ask.

She wraps her arms around her waist. "No, not really."

"Do you want me to take you home?" It's the last thing I want to do, but I want her to know I'll do or be whatever she needs. "I'll stay with you there," I say with a wink, hoping to ease some of the tension.

"Can I stay here?"

I nod and breathe a little lighter. I pull her towards me, wrapping her in my arms. "It's more than all right."

Her arms wrap around my neck, and she tilts her head up,

eyes meeting mine. "I'm so embarrassed. I can't believe he did that."

I pull her closer. "Don't be. It's not your fault."

The wind picks up, the already grey sky grows darker and grumbles, followed by a big clap of thunder.

She flinches. Raindrops fall, hitting my cheek, her nose, and before we can move, it has turned into a heavy downpour. Her mouth opens from the onslaught of droplets, and she blinks up at me. My stomach tightens.

I squeeze her hips, leaning down as she's reaching up, and our mouths collide. I reach around, cup her arse, and then pull her up; she wraps her legs around me. Without breaking the kiss, I walk us back into the kitchen, sitting her on top of the counter.

And then I allow myself to get lost in her taste.

Chapter Twenty-Seven

Rachel

It takes me two trips from the car to get all my new art supplies into my flat. I'm desperate to paint—it's therapy for me, and it's been too long. A sketch pad will scratch the itch, but not numb it.

Olly was the perfect gentleman last weekend. He held me in his bed all night, even after what happened with Marcus. I didn't have my class with him Wednesday. Everything has been full-on between our shifts and Molly. But she's with Marcus this weekend, so we have a date later. Sophie couldn't believe it when I told her what happened, and to be honest, neither can I. It's a lot to try to process.

I set up my easel, not even bothering to change before unscrewing the cap of the oil paint on an inhale. Instant relaxation. Grabbing my palette, I dollop on a pea-size amount and add all the colours I need before reaching for my brush.

The colours come alive before me. Every stroke relieves

some of the stress I've been under the past couple of days, weeks.

A buzzing catches my attention, and I startle before jumping up and jogging out to the intercom. "Hello?"

"Hey, it's me."

"Shit!" Olly.

"Everything okay?"

I shake my head. "Sorry, I'll buzz you up."

I unlatch the door and wait as Olly comes into view. He looks strapping in his tight fitted jeans and shirt rolled up to the elbows. I let out a contented sigh, and he looks up, smiling when he sees me, cocking an eyebrow.

"I'm so sorry. I was painting and lost track of time." I wave over my dishevelled appearance with my paintbrush in hand.

He approaches me, though it's more like a strut, and stops barely an inch from my chest. I have to tilt my head back to look up at him. "Don't apologise," he says, leaning in for a kiss, which quickly becomes more than a hello kiss. When he pulls back, I blink a few times and bite my lip.

"Come in, let me quickly go get ready," I say as he steps into the hallway.

"What are you working on?" he asks, sounding genuinely interested.

I wave my hand about, forgetting I have the paintbrush in my hand, and swipe him across the chest with it, covering him with a line of oil paint.

"Oh, fuck, shit damn!"

I quickly rush around him and drop the damned brush on top of my palette, then dash back to unbutton his shirt.

His eyes skirt to mine, his hands covering my trembling fingers. "It's fine, don't worry about it," he says, finishing unbuttoning his shirt before slipping it over his shoulders.

I can hardly swallow as he stands before me bare-chested.

I've seen him like this before, but back then, my mind wasn't consumed with lustful thoughts. My cheeks heat, probably giving me away. I rip the shirt from his fingers, then jog into the kitchen for a bottle of rubbing alcohol. I rub it into the stain before shoving it into the washing machine and switching it on.

Strong, bare arms wrap around me from behind. My heart beats wildly. "I've never been stripped of my clothes so fast before," he says, chuckling into my ear. His lips skim down my throat and a whimper escapes me.

"I'm sorry," I reply, but there is no remorse in my words with his lips caressing my skin.

I feel his hardness and push myself back, into him. He groans, and I turn in his arms. He lowers his head, captures my mouth with his, and I am lost. When he lifts me, I wrap my legs around his waist. He sets me on the counter, but I grip him tighter, not wanting to lose the friction between us.

"Ahh, Olly," I sigh into his mouth as he grinds into the exact spot I want him the most.

I don't know if he's getting harder or I'm becoming more sensitive, but with every movement, my body is building into a climax, and I know it's coming. Still, I can't seem to stop myself as I rock into him, desperate for there to be no clothes between us. "Don't stop," I say on a sigh as he continues to devour my mouth and rock into me.

"I won't," he says before sucking my tongue into his mouth.

The climax builds until I can't hold back any longer.

My release comes hard and fast. I scream out his name on a drawn-out moan. When I start to come back to reality, I look up at him, wide-eyed, then hide my face into his chest.

"Oi, don't shy away from me," he says, leaning back and reaching for my chin.

"I don't know what came over me," I say.

"Well, I'd say you came over me," he says with a small chuckle.

"*Oliver.*"

He kisses the tip of my nose. "It was beautiful to watch," he says, lust in his eyes.

I can't help but smile. "Looks like we'll be staying in tonight," he says, eying the washing machine.

I nod. "Sorry."

"Don't be. That was the best greeting I've ever had," he says, his grin wicked.

"Bet you say that to all the girls," I reply, trailing the ink of his tattoo with my finger.

"Nope, only you."

I can't stop the grin which spreads across my face. We've not slept together yet, but I think tonight will change that. "Do you mind if I jump in the shower?"

"Depends…can I join you?" he asks, wiggling his eyebrows.

My smile drops—not at the thought of taking a shower with him—but the idea of him seeing all my imperfections.

"What's wrong? I was only half-joking…"

I sigh and shake my head. "Olly, I've had a baby—my body, it's well, it's…"

He hooks his finger under my chin until I make eye contact with him. "Your body, just like you, is gorgeous, Rachel. Don't be so hard to judge. You don't see what I see. You are beautiful."

I almost want to cry. What is wrong with me? He tickles my sides, and I let out an un-ladylike squawk as I slip off the counter and wriggle, pushing him away from me. He smiles. "I'll order takeaway. You go have that shower."

I nod and head for the bathroom, peering back over my shoulder. "You have something else to do first."

He looks up from his phone, half a smile. "Oh, yeah and what's that?"

"Come and wash my back," I say, hoping I sound more confident than I feel.

I look ahead and walk to the bathroom, the sound of his footsteps close behind me.

Chapter Twenty-Eight

Olly

I follow her and inhale as we enter her small bathroom. She reaches into the bath, turns on the shower head, and pulls the shower curtain half-closed.

"Rachel," I say. Her shoulders move up and down before she turns towards me. "I don't want you doing anything you're not ready for." I stroke her cheek.

She bites her lip. "I want to, but ..." She wraps her arms around herself. "It's been a while," she says, looking up at me.

"And that's a problem because?"

"I'm nervous...it's been a while," she repeats, her cheeks glowing.

I reach for her hands and pull her towards me. "I'm nervous, too," I reply, honestly.

"You are?"

Nodding, I bend my knees, so we're eye level. "Of course." And it's the truth; I don't think I was ever this nervous, except for when I lost my virginity. "Listen, you don't have to do anything you're not ready for."

I'm ready to turn around and leave her alone to shower when her trembling hands reach for the fly of my jeans. Speechless, I stand frozen, afraid to move as I watch her fingers slide the zip and unhook the button. Then she pushes them down enough for my dick to spring free. She lets out an, "Oh."

I clear my throat. "Yeah, sorry, I don't usually wear underwear with these jeans."

Licking her lips, she reaches out and touches the tip, causing me to shiver. I try to stifle my groan, but it's impossible.

The mirror has already begun to steam up, and as I reach for the hem of her t-shirt, she raises her arms and pulls it off over her head. She's in a white lace bra, and my breath catches. "Beautiful," I whisper.

She goes to cover her stomach with her arms, but I grab them gently and shake my head. "Please don't hide from me."

She swallows, the nerves present, but doesn't try to cover up again. I lean in for a kiss and pull her into my body, flesh on flesh, a low mewling sound leaving her mouth.

I step back, pushing my jeans the rest of the way down, and kick them out of the way. Her hands go to the waist of her leggings. She pauses, swallows, and then slides them down. They join mine over to the side.

I reach my hand in and let it settle under the spray to test the temperature before stepping into the bath and beneath the showerhead.

When she joins me, I step back, then pull her close, kissing her before my eyes roam her luscious curves, my fingers trailing all over her skin. I gently usher her under the water, spinning her so her back is to me. Peppering her shoulder blades with kisses, I smile against her skin when her body shivers in response.

I squeeze some of her shower gel on a sponge before rubbing her back in small, circular motions.

"Ah, that's nice," she says, her shoulders relaxing.

I wash every inch of her bare flesh before turning her to face me. Water trickles down her face, her eyes squeezing closed. I repeat the same course of action on her front and savour every moment, committing her to memory, my erection becoming more pronounced as I do.

Her fingers reach out, and she grabs me, pulling me closer to her as she works the length of me in her palm. Losing grip of the sponge, I slide my hand between her thighs and stroke her soft mound. When I slip a finger inside, her pupils dilate, her lips parting.

Unable to resist, I kiss her with abandonment. Her movements become jerky as her hand continues to work me into submission. I insert another finger, and then twist my hand so my thumb can circle her clit. It's not long before she's panting into my mouth, and I feel the friction between us building. I move faster as she does, and then together we find a release.

She bends down for the sponge I dropped, then lathers it up before wiping it all over my body. I return the favour, taking my time to wash her hair, massage her scalp. Every noise escaping her lips is pure torture.

"I think we're clean," she says, biting her bottom lip.

"All I can think about is getting you dirty again." I nibble her chin. At that moment, her stomach growls, and she bursts out laughing. "Okay, maybe after we've eaten," I say, turning off the shower.

I wrap her in the nearest towel before grabbing one for myself. She steps out and rummages in a cupboard for another, tipping her head upside down as she bundles it over her hair.

"Why don't you go dry your hair while I order dinner?"

She smiles and kisses me on the lips before slipping into the bedroom.

While she's busy, I place an order for Chinese, then enter the box room to see what it was she was painting before I arrived.

My jaw drops.

The eyes staring back at me from the canvas are so familiar, I'm momentarily mesmerised. They're mine. The flecks of colour are vibrant, and I'm totally blown away with it. I can't believe she painted this. I let out a whistle in awe of just how talented my girl is.

I hear the hairdryer switch off and return to the kitchen just as she's coming out of Molly's bedroom.

"Sorry, I wanted to see what you'd painted," I say, embarrassed she caught me.

She bites the inside of her cheek. "I hope you don't mind. It was hard to paint from memory..."

"Rachel, do you honestly not know how gifted you are?" I take her hand, pulling her toward the doorway where I point at the canvas. "It's like looking in a mirror—you captured part of my soul."

And she has. Whether she realises it or not, part of my soul is now in her possession.

I glance at my watch and see it's almost ten-thirty. Time always seems to go by too fast when we're together. "I need to get back for Buster," I say as I stack the plates and walk them over to the kitchen sink.

"Of course," she replies, but I hear the disappointment in her voice.

"Fancy coming to spend the night?"

Her eyelids flutter as she stares back at me, and I see her visibly swallow, but then she straightens her shoulders, nodding. "Yeah, I'd like that."

"Great—go grab an overnight bag, and I'll quickly wash these."

She heads to the bedroom. I'm excited to get her back to my house.

Chapter Twenty-Nine

Olly

It's just after eleven when we arrive back at mine. Rachel nibbled on her bottom lip the whole way here—I know because when my eyes weren't on the road, they were flicking to her. Unlocking the door, I usher her inside and whistle for Buster who comes bounding out with his latest toy in his mouth.

I crouch down and give him a good pat and stroke behind the ears. "Was you a good boy?" I say in my dog-dad voice. When I look up at Rachel, she's watching with a smirk on her face.

I shrug, trying to hide my embarrassment, but then she crouches down to join me, giving Buster a quick stroke. "Come on, Buster, out."

After I've let him outside to the back garden, I turn back to Rachel. "Do you want a drink?"

"Just water, please."

I pass her a bottle from the fridge and watch as she takes a small sip. I can't take my eyes off of her. When Buster scratches to come in, I open the glass door and lock it before ushering him to his bed.

"I love his little nook," she says, her head tilted.

I nod. "Me too. I didn't want to put him in a crate, but I also wanted him to have somewhere to feel safe when I'm not here."

"I would never have taken you for a dog man," she says, smiling.

"Really? What did you take me for then?" I ask, stepping closer to her.

"I don't know…a fish or two, maybe a hamster," she replies, a soft giggle rumbling from her lips.

"Is that so?" I reply, sneaking my knees between her legs.

"Yep." Her voice is playful. I grip her chin between my thumb and forefinger, angling her face before leaning down, my lips so close to her.

Her soft breath floats over my mouth, and I hold back my desire to devour her, waiting until she closes the gap between us with a soft murmur. Pulling back, I rest my forehead on hers. "Ready for bed?" I ask.

I watch her throat contract as she swallows before nodding. I lift her off the stool and slide her down my body until her feet touch the floor.

Grabbing her small holdall, I keep her hand securely in mine as we make our way upstairs and towards my room, my excitement palpable. But the truth is that even if all we do is sleep, it would be good enough for me.

I walk over to the lamp on the other side of my room to switch it on, and when I turn back, Rachel's just standing in the doorway.

I beckon her towards me with my finger; she shuffles over to me slowly, then stops when she's in front of me. I lean down, my lips grazing her ear as I whisper, "I just made you come with one finger."

I expect her to laugh at my comment, but instead, she gasps and damn if I don't go rock hard. My teeth nip on her earlobe; her breathing speeds up, the air crackling with anticipation and want.

She steadies herself with her palms against my chest. Her fingers grip the oversized, neon pink hoody she leant me. "Off," she grunts.

I am quick to oblige, pulling it over my head, tossing it onto the floor. She scans my chest, fingers working over my skin excruciatingly slow. And then her hot mouth covers my pierced nipple, tongue languishing, and I let out an uncontrolled moan as she applies suction before nipping on it gently.

Her eyes flutter up to meet mine and I see the want and lust reflected there. I can't hold back any longer.

I push her towards my bed, dipping her backwards until she's laying on the mattress.

My fingers are at the waist of her leggings. "May I?" I ask, flicking my eyes to hers.

She gives me a quick nod, and I pull them down along with her knickers and toss them aside. I kiss my way up her feet, to her inner thigh, and when I blow on her clit, she arches towards the sensation. I smirk before my mouth travels to her pulsing entrance.

"Olly," she sighs when my tongue dips inside, and I lap up her arousal. I insert a finger while my thumb rubs over her clit. Her thighs clench on either side of my head, her climax building. I pump my finger into her harder and faster, my mouth covering her clit to suck on her soft mound.

"Yes," she cries out, her hot channel pulsating around my finger, her body shaking as she comes. When her thighs relax, and she releases her hold, I get to my feet, strip out of my jeans.

Taking myself in my hand, I squeeze my length from base

to tip, watching her; she stares at me, unable to look away as she bites down on her bottom lip. It turns me on more.

"You're wearing too many clothes." My words come out more like a grunt, hoarse with need.

She shuffles to pull her top off, followed quickly by her bra. Her nipples sit proud and hard, begging me to suck them. The mattress dips as I kneel between her legs. My body hovers over hers as my lips slowly cascade kisses down her throat, to her chest, until I take her erect nipple into my mouth.

My dick brushes against her stomach. Her trembling hand reaches for me, and she squeezes it so hard, I think I might come just from her touch alone.

Groaning, I sit back on my knees to reach for my bedside drawer, searching for a foil packet.

After ripping it open with my teeth, I roll the condom on and squeeze the base of my dick, hard, in warning not to let myself come too soon. I don't want this to be over before it's even begun.

"Do you want me, Rachel?" I ask, voice cracking.

"Yes, Olly, I want you." She guides my body back to hers. Desire flows through me, her touch so tender.

I lock eyes with hers. This moment so intimate, the air around us is charged, prickling our naked skin with unbridled anticipation. I align myself with her entrance, our stares still tethered. I pause just for a beat before I bury myself deep inside her.

We both groan in unison as our bodies move together. I have this fervent need to go harder, faster, and when she urges me on, I don't hold back. She meets each thrust with earnest.

Over-zealous from the sensation of being buried deep inside her, my body shakes from the exertion. It's the first time, but I know this won't be the last. I will never get enough of her, of this.

It's not long before we're both sweating, our breathing heavy and erratic.

And I know I won't last much longer.

"I'm going to come," I grunt out.

She grips me tighter with her thighs, the heels of her feet pushing me deeper, and I know she's right there with me. Our movements are uncontrolled, animalistic as we find a drawn-out release together.

Chapter Thirty

Rachel

Something warm and heavy covers me from behind. It's still early, and it takes a moment for last night to catch up with me. I'm sated and satisfied, and for some unknown reason, I can't stop the giggle that rises from my throat.

"What's so funny?" Olly grumbles into my neck his hardness pushes into my back.

"Nothing," I reply, trying to shake off the imminent giggle-fit working its way out.

His grip over my stomach tightens. "Really? Because you could give a guy a complex laughing like that," he says.

"Believe me, Olly, you have nothing to worry about," I say, trying to stifle my laughter.

His teeth drag softly over my skin, my breathing hitches. "Maybe I need to impress you some more just to be sure," he says.

The heat from his body leaves me, and I peek over my shoulder to see him searching his drawer. He pulls out a condom, and then all I can hear is the sound of our breathing along with the ripping of the foil packet before he sheathes himself.

"Now, where was I?" he whispers, kissing me between my shoulder blades.

My breathing increases in anticipation when he lifts my leg, his fingers finding me wet and ready. I need the bathroom—my bladder heavy—but somehow, the sensation is heightened. I'm too turned on to stop, so I wait as he adjusts us and slides into me from behind.

"Fuck," I gasp.

He stills. "Did I hurt you?" he asks, genuine concern in his voice.

"No, it's good, don't stop."

And he doesn't until he has me climaxing and screaming his name.

I wake to the sound of a dog barking and stretch with a blissful sigh. Before I open my eyes, I already know Olly isn't next to me; I can't feel his body heat. I pull the cover over my chest as I sit up and look to the clock on the bedside table. It's almost nine am. I reach for my t-shirt on the floor, then slip it on before grabbing my bag slipping into the bathroom, locking the door behind me.

I comb through my hair with my fingers as I stare at my reflection. My lips are swollen from his kisses, my body aches, and warmth pools between my legs as I have a flashback of him waking me with his face between my legs.

He fucked me with his tongue until I was screaming out his name. And when he climbed back up the length of my body, as it quaked from the aftermath of my orgasm, he grinned at me wickedly. I couldn't hold back—I pulled his mouth to mine for a searing kiss. And as much as I would love to have repaid the favour, my body was well and truly spent. I pulled his head to my chest, my fingers working through his scalp as I drifted off into a euphoric sleep. I can't remember the last time I slept so well.

I tie my hair in a knot on the top of my head and take it upon myself to hop in the shower. Using his body wash, I make quick work of it. When I finally pull myself away from the hot spray, I dress quickly, forgoing make-up.

Padding downstairs, I hear him talking, and when I walk into the kitchen, he is standing there, his back to me while he talks on the phone.

"Love you, too," he says, and my heart lurches into my throat, my ears ringing.

He turns to me and smiles, but it drops when he sees my expression. "Sorry Mum, I need to go. I'll see you tomorrow."

He hangs up, and I almost want to sink to the floor and put my head between my legs to work on my breathing. *His mum.*

"Are you okay?"

I nod, and then I shake my head. "I'm sorry, I heard you saying *I love you,* and I jumped to conclusions." I cover my face, my skin hot against my palms.

He tugs them away and crouches a little, so we are eye level. "I'm sure that would have been a little confusing to hear," he says, laughing. I chew the inside of my cheek—what kind of person does that make me? "Just so you know, I wouldn't do that. Not ever."

"Olly, you don't owe me any explanations," I say, wanting to wipe away the last couple of minutes.

"No, I don't, but I *do* want to make it abundantly clear that I'm not seeing other people."

I exhale. "Good to know."

"Now, how about I make you some breakfast?"

I pull back to look at him. "You cook?"

"Amongst other things," he says, his eyes roaming the

length of my body. I can't help but laugh as he pulls me into him, kissing me softly. "Omelette?"

"Yes, please."

He flicks the kettle on and begins moving around the kitchen as I slide on a kitchen stool. I watch him pad around barefoot, and can't help but appreciate a half-naked Olly in only his jeans.

He peeks over his shoulder. "Are you perving on me?"

I cough and sit up straight. "Of course not." He turns back to the pan. "I was ogling, if you must know."

His shoulders move up and down, then he turns to me, pointing the spatula in my direction. "You are trouble with a capital T."

"What can I say? You make me want to be bad."

He quickly turns off the stove and struts over to me. Grabbing my face between his hands, he sucks my bottom lip into his mouth and bites it softly before pulling away. An instant want pools in my lower stomach.

"I'll hold you to that, but first, breakfast." He returns to the task at hand, and I can't remember the last time I felt like this—if ever.

Chapter Thirty-One

Rachel

I can't stop humming to myself as I ready the tables for opening.

"Someone's chirpy this morning," says Sophie, leaning against the counter, watching me. "Anything you want to divulge?"

"Maybe," I reply.

She stands up straight. "Rachel-Mae, did you and Olly have some sexy time?"

I laugh out loud and nod, unable to prevent the grin that splits across my face. "Yep, we had a *lot* of sexy time," I say, wriggling my eyebrows.

"About time you got some." I throw the dish towel at her. "I mean, you look happy, or happi*er*. It's nice to see," she says, catching it in her hand, the diamonds of her engagement ring sparkling in the light.

I can't control the blush that spreads over my cheeks.

"Thank you," I reply, not sure what to say in response but understanding what she means nonetheless.

My phone pings with a vibration in my pocket and I pull it out. *Have a nice day xo*

I quickly type back. *And you xo*

"Awe, that was him, wasn't it?"

I nod and sigh, slipping my phone back into my jeans, aware I'm already counting down the days to when I'll see him again.

But to my surprise, I don't have to wait days because about an hour before closing time, Olly makes an appearance.

"Sophie," he says in greeting.

"Olly," she replies, giving him one of those *I-know-what-you-did* smirks.

"Hi," I breathe out.

He beckons me forward until I'm leaning over the counter to meet his lips for a chaste kiss. "Hi beautiful."

I can't hide my blush. Without him asking, I cut a slice of lemon drizzle cake and load it into a takeaway box. I know he has a shift tonight—he told me when he dropped me off at home. "You know, I mainly come in here for the view rather than the cake," he says with a cheeky wink.

Coughing from the kitchen catches our attention. "I heard that," says Sophie, but I hear the smile in her voice.

"The cakes are a bonus," he calls back.

"Smooth," I say and pass him the box.

After he pays, he graces me with a soft smile. "Thank you, I'll text you later."

I nod, biting on my bottom lip. "Okay, have a good shift."

"I will *now*," he says over his shoulder, the door chiming on his way out.

"Now, there is a man who is smitten."

I almost choke, spinning to Soph. "Don't be daft—he'll get bored in no time." He never asked for a ready-made family, but for just a little while, I want to enjoy his touch, how he always manages to make me laugh. The way he looks at me in a way that makes me feel."

Sophie shakes her head. "I can't see it myself," she says.

"I'm enjoying the attention. And being wanted is something I don't feel I've ever had before… But I'm a single mum, and he's a hot-as-hell bachelor. He's not lacking in the personality department, either. He wouldn't struggle to find someone more suited."

Soph crosses her arms and frowns. "Then why are you with him?"

I trace an invisible mark on the counter. "Because I like him, and I want to live in this bubble for as long as possible," I reply, honestly.

"Rachel, you don't give yourself enough credit. I wish you could see what we all see. You deserve to be doted on and have someone love you. You'd want that for Molly, wouldn't you?'

I straighten up and stare at her. "Of course."

"Then do yourself a favour and start leading by example."

I understand what she's saying, but self-doubt and self-sabotage are hard habits to break. I guess I'm used to being let down emotionally—by my parents and then Marcus. It just became more comfortable to be as independent as possible, to not rely on anyone else. That way they can't hurt me.

"I don't mean to be all preachy," she says. "I want the best for you."

I nod. I honestly feel so lucky both she and Felicity accepted me as a friend and into their circle—warts and all. I've made mistakes, but they didn't judge me on those. "Thank you. I know I'm a little hard to swallow at times, but I do appreciate your friendship."

She laughs. "You are *not* hard to swallow. I see the walls you've built… It's easy to see when I've been there myself. But we are all just trying to take it one day a time. We're all a work in progress."

I digest her words, knowing she's right. So maybe, for now, I can enjoy whatever this is between Olly and me. Maybe I can allow myself to have hope again.

Chapter Thirty-Two

Olly

I haven't been able to see Rachel much—only small, stolen moments when I stop by the deli—but we've talked on the phone every night, laughing about and discussing everything and nothing.

Hearing a commotion, I look up from restocking the bottles. "What the fuck?" I mumble. Marcus is supposed to have Molly tonight. He already appears half-cut, and I'm sure he's going to be as arrogant as ever.

"Marcus," I say, approaching him from behind the bar.

He double-takes, then smirks—yeah, he knows who I am all right. "Well, if it isn't the flavour of the month," he says.

I ignore his jab and cross my arms. "Aren't you meant to be with your daughter?"

"It's none of your fucking business."

I clench my fists. "Well, that's where you're wrong."

He leans on the bar, and I can smell the alcohol oozing from his breath. "No, I'm not. Because whatever you may think is going on between you and Rach—you are sorely mistaken. We have a past, we're just going through stuff right now, but it's only a matter of time before she takes me back."

I cock an eyebrow. He believes the shit that is coming out of his mouth. "I doubt you shirking your duties as a parent is going to win her back," I retort.

His nostrils flare. "Why would you want some ready-made family anyway? What's wrong with you? You some kind of perv?"

I lunge forward, grabbing the arsehole by the collar of his shirt. "I'll let that slide because you're drunk. Next time, I won't be so amicable." I release my hold, and he wobbles onto his feet. I stand on the rail on the inside of the bar—giving me a little extra height—and signal for Jase.

"You're just a fuck to her, you'll see."

"Jase, show him the door."

He nods. "You got it." His hand cups Marcus's elbow, but he shrugs him off.

"Oh, and Marcus?" His eyes stare daggers at me. "You're barred. Stay the fuck out of this bar."

"Fuck you," he spits as he ambles to the exit, shoving people as he goes.

"Everything all right, mate?"

I turn to Charlie. "Fine," I reply, but my body is pumping with adrenaline. I clench my fists tight, needing to calm down.

"I thought I was going to have to hold you back." I nod, not sure what to say. I never lose my cool like that. "I heard what he said. He doesn't know shit." He fist-bumps me and squeezes my shoulder. "You good? Or do you need a minute?"

"I should take a minute." I step around him and make my way into the back office to pace the length of the room. What the fuck will Rachel say when she finds out? I don't want her hearing it from him.

I pull out my phone; she answers on the second ring. "Hello?"

"Hi," I say.

"I thought you were working. Is everything okay?"

"Yes and no," I reply. I sit on the edge of the sofa in the office and stare at the floor.

"What's wrong?" she asks, sounding concerned.

"Marcus was here," I say.

A loud sigh escapes her. "I'm not surprised," she replies, almost resigned to the fact.

"Does he let Molly down a lot?"

"Lately more so, yeah."

It goes quiet for a beat, our breaths the only sounds.

"I don't want you to hear it from anyone else, but I barred him and kicked him out." I squeeze my eyes closed, ready for her comeback.

"I'm sorry," she says.

Why the fuck is she apologising? "Don't be, he was the one drunk."

I hear her let out a sigh. "He wasn't always like this," she says, almost wistful, and I wonder if she does want him to sort himself out so they can be together as a family.

"Well, it's done now. I just don't want you getting any repercussions from it."

"Olly, it's fine—nothing I can't handle. Thank you for letting me know."

"You busy tomorrow?" I ask, hoping she'll say no.

"Laundry, housework, that kind of stuff."

"Do you fancy coming with me to my mum and dad's for lunch?"

I chew my lip as I wait for her answer. "I can't. I have Molly, sorry."

I let out a laugh. "Yeah, I know, she's invited."

"Oh…well okay, yeah. If you're sure?"

I nod and then remember she can't see me. "Absolutely. My mum has been asking about you, and I know she's falling over herself to get to meet Molly."

"Then we'd love to." I hear the smile in her voice.

I don't want to stop talking to her, but I have to get back out to the bar. "Goodnight, Rachel," I say, after we settle the specifics.

The sooner this shift finishes, the faster tomorrow comes. I can't wait to see her.

Chapter Thirty-Three

Olly

I don't know why I'm nervous about Rachel coming to my parents today; she's been here before. Maybe it's because we are together now, and this is all very real.

"Okay, let's go eat," I say as I park in front of the drive. I meet Rachel on the passenger side as she unclips Molly from her booster seat. Maybe I should get one as a spare for my car?

"You okay?" Rachel asks with a frown.

"Yeah, why wouldn't I be?"

She laughs and shakes her head. "Because I just asked you a question and you zoned out."

"Sorry," I reply, reaching for Molly's hand. "What did you say?"

She closes the car door and grabs Molly's rucksack. "Are you sure you don't mind us coming?"

I wrap my arm around her waist and pull her into my side

where I place a soft kiss on her temple. "Of course, it's just... I've never brought a girlfriend home before."

Turning into me, she goes up on tiptoes and gives me a chaste kiss. "Am I your girlfriend, then?" she asks, biting her lip. "I don't recall you asking me out."

I tickle her, and she lets out a squeal. "Well, I'm asking now."

She blushes, her eyes sparkle. "In that case, I'd love to be your girlfriend." Her lips meet mine, and everything else evaporates.

"Does that mean you're getting married?" Molly asks, pulling on my hand.

I pull back from Rachel and cough. "Pardon?"

"You kissed Mummy," she says.

Shit.

"Molly, do you want to come and meet Olly's parent's dog, Max?"

Molly pulls on my hand and darts up the path. "I'll take that as a yes."

"That was close," Rachel says, her cheeks scarlet. I look over my shoulder and wink.

The back garden is swarming with family where I've spent most of the day being interrogated over Rachel.

"I swear to God, Martin, if you hit on my girl once more," I say under my breath.

"Awe, is Olly getting worried?" he asks in a sing-song voice, bouncing on the spot, fake punching me.

Rachel wraps her arm around my waist. "Ignore him, he's winding you up," she says.

I roll my eyes. I know—but it's annoying. Martin leans in and kisses Rachel on the cheek before sprinting off. "That's it!" I launch after him.

The whole time he's running, his cocky laugh echoes around the garden. When I finally catch him, I grab him in a headlock and scruff up his hair before letting go.

"You like her then?" he asks, nodding his head at Rachel, who I'm grateful is occupied by my mum.

"I do. She's special," I admit.

"It's about time you settled down, brother," he says, slapping me on the back.

"Easy tiger, no one is settling anywhere," I reply.

"You keep telling yourself that. Want another beer?"

I shake my head. "No, thanks. I'm driving."

My eyes follow Rachel as she talks to my dad. She's at ease in my space, and I love that, but I also worry about getting too comfortable. I don't want to be another disappointment. She holds in so much, her walls built so high, but it's not hard to see why. I keep replaying the question she asked me.

"What is your biggest fear?"

It was becoming no better than my biological father. A real-life monster, he had no empathy; he was a narcissist. Years of therapy have taught me this. But it's an ugly thing when fear takes root—wondering if it's in my genetic makeup. My mum used to say he wasn't always that way. It didn't make what he did to her, or *us*, any easier to accept.

"Oliver?"

I turn. "Mum?"

"What's the matter?"

She's always seen right through me, even from the first day they brought me home from the hospital. I tried to pretend everything was all right. Even though I spent over a year in pain every day, I acted as though it was nothing. She knew differently. It's why I won't lie to her now. "I'm worried about getting in too deep. I don't want to hurt her—or Molly. But I can't stay away, either."

She takes me by my arm and leads me into the kitchen. "Olly, you've always been so melancholy. Even when you found a group of friends at school…you always held back a fraction."

"It's not intentional." It's not.

I sit on a barstool, and she sits opposite, reaching for my hands. "I know. The first time you called me *mum*—do you remember that?"

How could I not? I felt so guilty afterwards, I didn't utter another word for three days. "Yes."

"You always felt too much. It's why you are so hard on yourself. Why you over-analyse everything you do. It's why you do what you do, with your charity and at the gym."

She taps the back of my hand, and I glance down at the tattoos along my forearm—the ones which were intended to camouflage my scars—but even *they* don't make them invisible. "You can't save everyone, Olly. Sometimes you have to save yourself."

I know she means well, but there are things she doesn't know about that night—something I've never admitted to anyone. "I'm not trying to, and besides, you saved me by never giving up on me."

It's the truth. I know my life would be very different if it weren't for her and my foster family.

"And I never will, no matter what." She stands up. "Now come and give me a hug."

I do as she asks, towering over her, but in her arms, I still feel like the little boy who was bullied because of my burns. "Let's get back out there before dad does something to embarrass me." She laughs into my chest, knowing it's likely already too late.

I scan my family until I find Rachel. Her blush is evident, and I know my brother is likely coming on to her. She looks up, and relief floods her when she spots me. I walk over, reach for her hand. "Mine," I growl.

He lets out a soft chuckle and fake pouts. "Whatever you say, brother."

He turns and walks away. I pull her into my body, oblivious to everyone else around us. "Was he hitting on you?" I ask.

"He was harmless," she replies.

"Yeah, well, I didn't like it."

Cupping my cheek, she stares up at me. It's like she knows how I need to be touched. "Well, as you said, I'm *yours*."

I lean down and give her a chaste kiss, unable to suppress my smile.

Hers.

Chapter Thirty-Four

Olly

Molly is having a small birthday party today at Sophie's deli. Rachel invited the children from Molly's class. I arrive early to help set up, and I smile when I find she's already here. "I would've come earlier."

She looks over her shoulder and smiles. "It's okay. I just wanted everything to be perfect."

I walk over to her and reach for her hand, pulling her towards me. "It will be," I reply and lean down, grazing her lips with mine. She lets out a small hum of satisfaction, and I deepen what was meant to be a chaste kiss.

"Do I need to call the fire brigade?" asks Sophie. Rachel lets out a small snort and steps back.

"Where's Molly?" I ask.

"With Charlie and Selene."

I place the box on the table with the other presents and rub my hands together. "Where do you want me?"

Sophie laughs before heading back to the kitchen. I watch

as Rachel's teeth dig into her bottom lip. I wiggle my eyebrows and wink. She throws a bag at me. "Any good with balloons?"

I look inside and laugh. Then I spend the next half hour using a hand pump to blow up the balloons. My fingers and thumbs are sore by the time I finish tying the last knot.

"Done," I say and sneak up behind Rachel, pulling her into my chest. I eye all the face paint and sponges lined up on the table.

"Thank you." She spins in my arms and kisses my chin. I've never had this with a woman before—the public displays of affection—but with her, it's as natural as breathing, and I wonder why I kept her at arm's length for as long as I did.

"You're so beautiful." I lean in to kiss her, this time keeping it PG-thirteen, pulling back just as the door chimes to the arrival and squeals of Molly and Selene.

Charlie's hair is all dishevelled, but his smile is one of joy. I shake my head and laugh. "All right, boss?"

I hold out my fist, and he bumps it with his. "Dude, why do you always call me boss?"

I chuckle. "Because it pi—winds you up."

Molly bounds over, holding up her arms. I swoop her up and tickle her side. "Happy Birthday." I tap the tip of her nose.

"Thank you. Will you have your face painted, too?" she asks, and everyone busts out laughing.

"Maybe for you, I will," I reply, putting her back on her feet as she rushes to Rachel.

"Mummy, Olly wants face paint, too."

Rachel smiles and tucks her hair behind her ear. "How about I do yours first?"

Molly quickly sits in the chair, head poised and waiting. I check my watch—the other kids should be arriving in the next half hour. Sophie walks out with a tray full of cupcakes, and I take it from her.

"Thank you, just put it over there next to the cartons of juice."

I comply and slip one when I do. Bringing the cupcake to my lips, I take a bite and close my eyes to savour the taste.

When I open them, Rachel is watching me, the sponge frozen in her hand, her eyes heated. I cock an eyebrow. I kneel to offer her some, and she leans back, taking a small bite before licking her lips free from the icing. She missed a spot in the corner. Before I have time to stop myself, I wipe it away with the pad of my thumb and lick it clean.

Her eyes go wide, and I have to remind myself Molly is right there.

"Here you go, Molly." I offer her the last piece, and she looks to her mum for permission. No sooner has Rachel nodded, Molly is shovelling it into her mouth, and we all burst out laughing.

"What time is it again?" Rachel asks.

I turn my wrist to see the face of my watch. "Almost six." She's been waiting on Marcus to light the cake. He was meant to be here at two and hasn't answered Rachel's texts. Molly doesn't even seem bothered, but that's not the point.

I hear the door open behind me and turn to see him, sunglasses on, keys in hand—walking in without a care in the world.

She rushes past me. "*Finally*. Quick, I want to sing happy birthday and cut the cake so her friends can take some home."

He only nods, not even an apology for being late. I step forwards and offer my hand. I'm not surprised when he chooses to ignore it.

Dick.

"Anything to drink at this shindig?" he asks. I tilt my head towards the table, to the bottles of soft drink and water. "What —no booze?"

Shaking my head, I clench my fists. "It's a kids' party, man."

He shrugs—that's when I smell it, the alcohol on his breath. Charlie comes over and says hi; Marcus is just as obtuse with him as he was with me.

"Can you get Molly ready while I go sort the cake?" Rachel asks Marcus.

"Sure," he replies.

When Molly spots her dad, she rushes over and throws her arms around his legs. Her face paint rubs off on his jeans. "Flipping heck, Molly," he says, annoyance in his voice.

She pulls back and looks up at him, her little eyes wide. "Sorry," she says, a quiver in her voice.

What the fuck.

He lets out a sigh and crouches down, a bit off balance, but now eye level with her. "It's okay. Come here," he says, his voice softening. But she doesn't move, her lip trembling ever so slightly. "*Molly*. I said, come *here*."

It takes everything in me not to punch him. I hold out my hand. "Molly." She takes it and stays close to my leg.

He stands to his full height and pulls off his glasses, the dark circles under his eyes on full display, his pupils dilated. "What? You trying to be her stepdaddy or something?" he asks.

I shake my head and grind my jaw just as gasps ring out. I see Rachel from my peripheral vision, cake in hand.

His phone rings, and then Marcus steps outside to take the call right as the intro to *Happy Birthday* spills from the lips of the guests.

I reach down and pull Molly up onto my hip, then step through the opening towards Rachel as she carries the cake to the centre, her eyes seeking Marcus. I see the hurt and anger in her gaze until her eyes catch mine, and I give her a heartfelt smile.

Her eyes soften on the final notes of the song, and everyone applauds. I set Molly down so she can help her mum cut the cake, and while everyone is busy, I step outside to find Marcus leaning against a post box.

"Hey man, you missed the cake," I say.

He slides his sunglasses onto his head, watching me as I approach. "And who the hell are you again?"

"Someone who happens to give a shit about that little girl in there—and her mum." I point my thumb over my shoulder.

"Yeah, well, being a dad ain't all it's cracked up to be."

He did not just say that.

I take a menacing step forwards, but a gasp of air behind me catches my attention—Rachel.

"Are you fucking kidding me?" she seethes, rushing past me.

He rubs his palm over his chin. "I didn't mean it like that, Rach." I hate how he says *Rach* with so much familiarity.

"Yeah, then how did you mean it?" But she doesn't give him a chance to answer. "I don't ask you for *anything*, Marcus —no maintenance, nursery fees, *not a damn thing*. All I ask is that you spend time with our daughter and *show up*. That's all. And you have the cheek to say, *it ain't all it's cracked up to be*. Give me a fucking *break*. *I* was the one who took care of all the night feeds—alone. *I* was the one who had to go to all the appointments—alone. I've never asked you for anything, Marcus. You said you wanted to be part of her life. But you don't get to be an arsehole about it because you've been on a *three-day bender*."

She turns away from him, towards me, when he clutches her shoulder. "How the fuck do you know that?"

"Social media, you prick. Now come and say bye to Molly. She's not staying with you tonight."

She leaves no room for argument. We all head back inside.

Chapter Thirty-Five

Olly

As soon as everyone has left and everything has been tidied up, I help Rachel load her boot with Molly's presents.

"We going to stay with Buster?" asks Molly, her tone pleading.

I look to Rachel. I can see she's about to say otherwise, so I jump in. "Yes, he would love that." Molly squeals and jumps in the car.

Once Rachel has fastened her in, she closes the door and crosses her arms. "Olly, we can't impose on you like that."

I love it when she calls me *Olly*. I pull her into my body. "You're a package deal, Rachel, and I wouldn't have said yes if I didn't mean it."

She stares up and nods, a small smile passing her lips. "Okay, but I need to go home first—grab some overnight stuff. And I promised I'd let her have a Happy Meal."

I kiss the tip of her nose. "Okay, I'll see you at mine in a bit." I step away and tap on the window to Molly. "See you later, alligator."

"In a while, crocodile," she replies with a toothy grin.

Rachel pulls up about an hour later and ushers Molly from the car, dressed in her unicorn onesie. I pull open the front door and Buster comes to greet them, tail going crazy. As soon as Molly walks in, he rolls onto his back for a belly rub.

We all go to the kitchen where Molly sits at the table to finish off her dinner. I pass Rachel a glass of wine. "Thank you," she says before taking a satisfying sip.

"I put a lasagne in—thought you'd be hungry."

Her dimple shows as her eyes bore into mine. "Why, Oliver… Are you trying to seduce me?" she says quietly with a wink.

I lean over the counter and tap the tip of her nose. "Maybe."

A soft laugh escapes her lips, and we stand together, watching Molly as she plays tug of rope with Buster. When she yawns wide, Rachel puts her glass down. "You tired, baby?"

Molly nods and reaches for my hand. "Olly, read to me?"

How can I say no to that pout? I take her hand, Rachel grabs the flamingo rucksack, and then we all head upstairs.

"Teeth first," Rachel says, leading her into the bathroom. I switch on the lamp and pull out the only book in her bag. The Jungle Book.

Molly runs in and jumps on the bed.

"Sorry," Rachel says to me, and I shake my head.

"It's fine."

Molly pats the bed. "I want Olly to sit, too."

Sitting up against the headboard, I open the book and

start reading. Ten minutes in, soft snores notify me she's already in the land of nod.

I close the book and peer over to Rachel, who is looking down at Molly, a soft smile on her lips.

"Looks like today wore her out," I whisper.

"Makes two of us," she replies, her eyes darting to mine.

"Come on, you, there's a glass of wine waiting for you."

We quietly shuffle off the bed, and then Rachel plugs in the monitor, bringing the other one downstairs. "In case she wakes up," she explains.

I take her hand and pull her towards me. "It's fine, you don't have to explain to me," I say, brushing my thumb over her cheek. Her eyes flutter closed, and a soft breath escapes her.

Unable to resist, I lean down and brush my lips over hers. The kiss escalates quickly, and I move until her back is pressed up against the wall.

When the buzzer from the oven interrupts us, I let out a groan and pull back. "Hungry?" She nods, and reluctantly, I head to the kitchen, Rachel on my heels.

We eat in a comfortable silence until I bring up what's been eating at me since the party. "Is that true? Marcus doesn't contribute towards Molly?"

She inhales a deep breath, her chest expanding as she does. "He doesn't give me child maintenance, no. But he does buy her clothes and stuff."

I put my fork down and stare at her. "Yeah, but it costs money to raise a child."

She pushes her plate away, the cutlery clinking against the china from the force, her posture now rigid. "Don't you think I bloody well know that?" She fixes me with a stare.

"Of course, that's not what I meant."

"Then what did you mean?" She jerks her hand between us. "I've been raising Molly for four fucking years, Olly. You've been in the picture a pin prick in comparison." Her voice hardens. "How many kids have you raised?"

I flinch and hold up my hand, palm facing her. "None, but believe it or not, I do have both your interests at heart." Slipping off my stool, I grab our dishes and walk towards the kitchen counter.

"Olly," her voice softens.

I take a deep breath to expel my annoyance—not with her, but the situation with Marcus. She wraps her arms around my waist from behind. I spin in her arms, pull her into my body. "You both deserve better, that's all."

"Thank you," she says, lifting her chin, eyes gazing up at mine.

I lean down. My lips stroke hers, they part, and my tongue seeks hers. I lift her, and she wraps her legs around my waist. I walk her over to the island, rest her on the edge. My lips skim her throat, down to her breasts, her chest heaving.

She grips my hair.

I make my way down her body, kissing her reverently, lifting her enough to pull her free from her leggings and knickers. And then my mouth is all over her—sucking, nipping, licking.

"Ah, Olly," she groans, and my dick strains uncomfortably in my jeans. "Yes," she says, as I continue to fuck her with my tongue. "Please, Olly, I want you," she whines. I suck her hard one last time before pulling back.

I make quick work of ridding my clothes. Her eyes go wide, my dick at attention. "We can't do it here," she says, her gaze darting towards the door.

"Yes, we can," I say and pull her towards me.

She bites her bottom lip. "What about Molly?"

"You'll hear the monitor," I say, and turn up the volume to full.

I lift her off the counter and position her until she's sliding down my dick. We both let out a satisfied groan, and then I walk until her back is flush with the patio door before thrusting into her hard against the glass. The whole structure rattles.

I pull back and slide it open, one arm securely holding her in place. Stepping onto the patio, I walk us over to the padded furniture to lay her down.

And then I continue my ministrations, my balls slapping wildly against her arse as I thrust into her hot centre. Her nails dig into my flesh, her sounds getting louder.

Though my garden is entirely enclosed, the neighbours might hear her. I reach up, cover her mouth with my hand; her eyes go wide and her tongue darts out, licking my palm. And suddenly, I don't give a flying fuck about the noise. I move it away and cup her breast then pinch her nipple.

A feral sound escapes her, driving me harder, faster. Sex has never been this good. She sits up on her elbows, increasing the sensation. I almost let go—until reality settles in. "Shit, condom."

"I have the implant," she says.

"I've always been careful. Are you sure?" I grunt, still thrusting inside her.

"Yes," she says on a plea, her channel pulsating around me like a vice as her orgasm hits. Something builds at the base of my spine. Two more deep thrusts is all it takes, and then ice and fire ignite deep within me as I give over to the blissful pleasure of release.

Chapter Thirty-Six

Rachel

We lay cocooned on the couch, his fingers tracing patterns over the bare skin of my thigh just below the hem of his t-shirt.

"Tell me about when Molly was born?"

I lean back and look at his face. "What do you want to know?" I ask, lacing my fingers with his.

"Anything you're prepared to share."

I peer up, his intense gaze holds firm, and I give over to his request. "It was about four am when my water broke. I remember thinking I'd wet myself." My cheeks heat, but his grin urges me on. "I ordered a cab and was at the hospital by five am."

"A cab?" he asks, raising an eyebrow.

I glance down and pick at the flint on my bottoms. "Yeah. I was in labour all day—and so scared. The midwives were great, but being on your own… Having your first baby is overwhelming. Anyway, she was born at eleven forty-five pm."

He takes hold of my hand, tracing the heart-shaped birthmark below my wrist.

"Marcus didn't put you at ease?"

I shake my head, biting my lip. "No, he wasn't there."

He balks, his eyes landing on mine. "Who was with you?"

I shrug. "The midwives." His jaw ticks as he grinds his teeth. "My nan was away. She tried to get back for me. It is what it is." In all honesty, it was one of the hardest things I've ever done. When I let Marcus know I was in labour, he said he'd come to the hospital, and I'd believed him.

Olly's hand comes up and cradles my cheek. "Why wasn't he there?"

I clear my throat. Embarrassment spreads through me like it always does when I think about why. "He was at a grand opening of a new nightclub in the city."

His eyes go wide. "What a fucking arsehole."

"He hasn't always made the best choices, but he's her dad, so..." I take his hand in mine and pull it into my lap.

"Hell or high water, I'd be there for the birth of my child." Olly's statement full of conviction and I don't doubt him.

But it also stings, because as beautiful as it was bringing Molly into this world, I wish more than anything I could have shared it with her dad. Marcus tries, but his best isn't always good enough. I make sacrifices for Molly; it's not even a question. But Marcus is sometimes removed. I wonder if by him not being present when she was born...maybe that bond isn't there for him the way it is for me. Or all the sleepless nights that followed when I first brought her home. If he were there, too, would he be different?

"What about when you went home?"

Why is he so interested?

"Oliver, you're full of questions today."

He leans close, his lips centimetres away. "I want to know everything about you," he says before brushing them softly over mine.

"It's only ever been Molly and me. I mean, we have dinner with my parents every fortnight, but it's mostly the two of us," I say when he pulls away.

He shakes his head in wonder, his eyes scanning my face. The thing is, when I held her the first time…I never understood unconditional love until that day. It's a feeling I can't explain. I never knew I wanted to be a mum, and then she happened, and I knew it wasn't my choice to make—I was always meant to be her mum. "You never cease to amaze me, Rachel."

My breath catches in my throat, and my stomach somersaults when he reaches for me, then pulls me into his lap. I can't suppress my giggle. He is so tactile; I've never had anyone touch me the way he does—carefree and without restraint. His lips work their way down my neck, causing me to shiver.

"Is it wrong how much I want you?" he says, his tongue trailing over the crest of my breast.

And then he shifts and pulls my legs on either side of his lap, so I'm straddling him.

The cold air hits my bare flesh as his hands work up the back of my t-shirt, and I break out in goosebumps. But when he kisses the tip of my nose before meeting my mouth with a slow, deliberate kiss, heat rushes through me in waves, the temperature in the room spiking. I grip his hair between my fingers and tug.

His dick strains at the opening of his unbuttoned jeans, and I use the tip of my finger to wipe the trace of pre-cum there.

He stands, and I tighten my legs around him as he walks us towards the door. I nip his throat before I pull his earlobe into my mouth and suck. He pushes me up against the wall, lowers me to my feet.

"I can't make it to my room. I need to taste you." His eyes

are dark, full of desire. He lowers himself in front of me, hooks my leg in the crook of his arm. And without another word, his mouth is on me. My head knocks against the wall, hard, but I don't care.

The way his tongue and fingers know what I want and where I need him is almost too much. I want to push him away and pull him closer. And then without warning, I come quickly, almost violently, and I have to bite my lip to stop myself from screaming.

I'm barely coherent when he slides up my body. "This will be hard and fast, but I promise I'll make it up to you."

I didn't even see him drop his trousers. Before I can catch my breath, he rears up and inside me. His thrusts are fast and deep—a man on a mission—and I'm there to take everything he has to give.

Again, a sweet ache detonates, and I come even harder than before with him buried deep inside me. It's a throbbing pleasure that has me digging my nails into his flesh as the orgasm catapults through me.

"Rachel—fuck—" He goes rigid, suspended right there on the edge of release.

Overwhelmed by the emotions and sensations vying for my attention, I hold onto him tighter, giving him everything I have as he arches up into me. Tremors course through him as he climaxes long and hard.

Sated and trembling, he slips out of me, then we're sliding down the length of the wall, our bodies entangled, our breathing ragged. Unable to find the words, I hold his head to my chest until my heart rate slows and my breathing calms.

Quietly, he gets to his feet before reaching for my hand to pull me to mine. He pauses to grab the monitor, and a pang hits my chest, and I wonder why I never saw it before—how amazing this man is.

I follow him upstairs, releasing his hand to check in on

Molly before joining him in his room. He leads me to his bed. When we lay down, he pulls me into him and wraps me in his arms. The beating of his heart lulls me into oblivion.

Chapter Thirty-Seven

Rachel

I wake in the early morning hours, unable to fall back to sleep. Olly is sprawled out on his stomach, one leg hitched over mine, his arm around my waist. I stare at him in wonder for a few silent moments. His breathing is heavy, but I'm still careful as I free myself from him.

I creep in to check on Molly, who is now sprawled at the opposite end of the bed. I pull the duvet back over her, and then I grab my bag before slipping out.

Once I've relieved myself in the bathroom across the hall, I turn on the shower and strip out of my t-shirt. Under the spray and the steam, I allow my mind to wander.

Before I had Molly, I was only ever concerned about what I could get for myself. That all changed when I had her. I want her to have the best of everything, of course, but not at the same cost as me. I want her to understand the difference between wanting and needing something. To wait for something worth having. Not to be bombarded with material items and hoards of toys. It's why whenever she gets a new toy, we always donate one to a charity shop. My parents probably still have a loft full of toys they pacified me with over the years, and truth be told, if any of them held any sentimental meaning, I would've swallowed my pride and asked for them to pass it down to Molly.

Sometimes nostalgia overcomes me when I think of my grandmother and how she was the best of us. It fills me with longing, grief that Molly will likely never know that kind of love and affection from my parents. Maybe they'll be different for her, kinder, offer her more of their time rather than their money.

But I don't want her to suffer the emotional neglect I did. And it's only now—being a mother myself—that I see how my childhood was unhealthy. It's why Nan said no to my frivolous requests. And it's why, even in her absence, I still feel her presence. I want to make her proud.

And then there's Olly. I'm not blind—I've often thought him handsome in a *you-can't-touch-me* kind of way. Like one of those gifts Nan denied me for my own good. Yet here we are.

He broke down my barriers effortlessly and without mercy. I've never known anyone like him. And yet I see him at war with a past, a childhood I could never understand. It's not lost on me, as close as we are becoming, that there are things he keeps buried. And I think it's what's stopping me from falling for him completely. It's not only my heart in his hands now—it's Molly's, too.

Olly

Before I even open my eyes, I know Rachel isn't in my bed. I stretch and blink, checking the time. It's still early.

She shattered me last night when she admitted to being alone for Molly's birth. My dislike for Marcus is growing, and I hate that he has that power over me. Rachel puts on a good front that *it is what it is*, but I saw the hurt in her eyes—even if she tried to play it off.

Marcus has issues, but then, don't we all? I'm no saint. I've done things I'm not proud of, but when Rachel looks at me, she sees me without judgment, and I don't want that to change. I have things from my past I haven't opened up about—not to anyone, not even in therapy.

I don't know what good talking about it will do; it won't change what happened. It won't bring me redemption for what I didn't do. Other than family and my therapist, she's the only other person who knows about me pulling Lottie from the house fire.

I had a carnal need for her last night. It was beyond anything I've experienced before, and I know where she's concerned, I'm already a lost cause.

I check the guest room first. Molly is still fast asleep. How can someone so little take up so much space? The sound of the shower beckons me to the bathroom. I knock on it once upon entering, not wanting to scare Rachel.

She looks through the glass partition and smiles when she sees me. "Morning," she says.

"Morning. Do you want me to wash your back?"

She looks at the door and then back to me. "Lock the door, though. Molly will be up any minute."

I obey, drop my bottoms, then climb into the shower with her. Taking the sponge from her hand, I wash her back and kiss her neck. We swap places, and she does the same to me. "Are you okay? Did I hurt you last night?" I ask.

"Not at all. It was epic," she says, kissing my shoulder.

I turn, kiss her forehead, pull her into my arms. "I don't have to be at the gym until later this afternoon. How about we go for a walk with Buster along the river? They have swans—would Molly like to go feed them?"

"Yes, she'd love that. Olly, you are too good to be true."

I'm glad she can't see my face because there's one thing I know—I'm not worthy of her, especially when she makes comments like that.

Chapter Thirty-Eight

Rachel

Olly has been spending more time training at the gym with his charity fight coming up. We see one another whenever we can, and we're making it work for the most part. But I wonder why he puts up with us, with me.

Molly is staying with Sophie, who wouldn't take no for an answer. Said there was too much sexual frustration and was concerned we were both ready to combust.

Olly told me to dress up, said we were going out in the city, but refused to tell me where. He arrived at mine with a bouquet and a box of chocolates. I've never been wooed before, not like this. He even opened the passenger car door for me. You see these kinds of things in the movies, but to have it play out in real life is even better.

"Where are we going?" I ask for the umpteenth time.

He laughs and squeezes my thigh. "You'll see. We're almost there," he says, turning onto another back street before entering a car park. As soon as the barrier raises, he drives in and around into an open space, marked *reserved*.

"Did you book the space?" I ask, eying the sign again.

Unclipping his seatbelt, he leans over the centre console and gives me a chaste kiss. "Yes. I didn't want to be searching for a parking space all night."

Okay, so he put some thought into tonight. I unclip my seatbelt and reach for the door handle, but he grabs my arm to stop me.

"Wait, let me get the door for you," he says, and my insides melt. Seconds later, he's opening the door and holding out his hand. "You ready?" he asks.

"Well, depends. Are you telling me where we're going?"

"You are impatient. You'll see—it's just a five-minute walk." I can't help but admire him in his black jeans and dress shoes. The light blue shirt he's donning causes the violet hues of his eyes to pop, making him even more irresistible.

I'm grateful—these heels are not designed for long-distance. I bought them on sale, but the great price didn't diminish the guilt of indulgence. I shake my head, cutting those thoughts off. Because tonight, for the first time in a long time, I don't feel like a single mum. I feel…sexy. Confident. Young. I hook my arm in his as he leads the way through throngs of people who are bustling all over.

"Here we are," he says.

I pause and look up. *No way?* "The Shard?" My adrenaline spikes, and I know my face must be beaming.

"Yeah—is that okay?"

"Yes, of course. I've always wanted to come. The view is meant to be amazing." A lightness in my chest has me struggling not to giggle like a schoolgirl.

"Come on," he says, leading me into the lobby. After he gives his name, we bypass the queues and go through security before proceeding to the escalators.

We take an elevator and soar upwards through the London skyline. He pulls out his phone.

"Smile," he says into my ear, and my stomach flutters wildly as he snaps a couple selfies of us.

"I thought we could go to the viewing gallery and have a drink before dinner," he says.

I squeeze his hand. "Sounds perfect."

After another elevator and a small flight of steps, we walk out onto an indoor viewing gallery. An orchestral soundtrack plays overhead as he orders us both a glass of champagne. When they arrive, he tilts his towards mine with a clink. "Cheers," he says, taking a small sip, his eyes penetrating.

"This is breathtaking," I say as he guides me over to the vast windows, the sun setting over the city of London—swirled in yellows, oranges, and reds.

"Not as breathtaking as you in this little black dress," he says into my ear, my insides fluttering from his compliment.

"It's amazing, look." I point out the Tower of London.

"Bet you want to paint now, don't you?"

I nod. The colours dance over the water and the cityscape below in glorious hews of vibrancy. "I can't believe you brought me here," I say as he wraps his arm around my waist.

"I heard a customer telling you about it once at the deli, and I remember the way your eyes lit up."

I lean back to stare up at him, my lips parting in surprise. "That was ages ago." I point between the two of us with my glass. "It was before you and me," I say.

"Maybe I paid more attention to you than I led you to believe," he replies in a soft baritone. My thoughts are scattered from his admission as warmth radiates through my body. "Don't worry, my intentions are all good, I promise," he says, leaning in for a kiss.

"Good to know," I reply before his lips meet mine. It's a soft kiss, tender and sweet. When I draw back, his eyes roam over my face when he should be focused on the view. I'm not complaining. It's nice to have someone look at me the way he does. I turn my face towards the River Thames.

"It's stunning," I say, gazing at the sight before us.

"Yes, you are." My cheeks heat, and I struggle to keep a small giggle from erupting at his compliment.

"Let's take some photos." He takes my glass from me so I can capture some on my phone and he joins me for some selfies, too.

We sip our champagne as we walk the length of the gallery hand-in-hand, the view growing even more spectacular as the sun disappears over the horizon.

"Ready to eat?" he asks.

I nod, reluctant to leave. Darkness has fallen across the River Thames and it takes on a new persona—the twists and the turns of the river merging with the night sky. Tower Bridge and nearby buildings are lit up in all their splendid glory. "Where are we eating?"

He takes our empty glasses and leaves them on the bar, giving his thanks to one of the bartenders. He takes my hand in his, kissing my knuckles. "It's not far," he says, smirking.

I poke him in the ribs. "You're enjoying this, aren't you?"

He laughs. "Yes."

We take the elevators down, but when we stop at level 35, he nudges me out. I stare at him, confused for a moment until we walk towards a reception area leading to a restaurant. He gives them his name, and then they lead us to a table overlooking The River Thames and The Tower of London, the magnificent stone structure surrounded by floodlights, making it impossible to ignore.

"Told you it wasn't that far," he says, reaching for my hand.

Heat radiates through my chest. "This is perfect," I say, unable to believe this is happening.

He shrugs, holding my stare. "I wanted to show you how special you are to me."

"It's lovely, but you didn't have to do all this," I say, waving my hand towards the lights below, the sparkling city life reflected in the river.

"Yes, I did."

I feel weightless under his gaze. I can't remember a time before having Molly, and I definitely don't miss my nights of clubbing and drinking. But this…I've never had this.

I pick up the menu, my stomach dips; these prices are ridiculous.

"What are you thinking?" he asks, a worry line etched on his forehead.

"How different my life is since having Molly." I lay the menu flat. "I don't miss it, the nights out partying, or days spent shopping for frivolous things," I reply honestly.

"I think you fell into those things, but they weren't what you care about."

How does he see me so vividly when I hardly see myself at all? "Maybe. It was easy to get caught up in all the hype, the grandeur of it all."

A waiter interrupts, asking if we're ready to order. I stare back at the menu.

"Can we have a little longer?"

The waiter nods. "Would you like drinks in the meantime?" he asks, pouring us a glass of water each.

"Can I have a beer? Whatever you have on tap."

"Of course, and for the lady?" he asks, turning to me.

"I'll have a small glass of Rosé please."

Olly takes my hand. "Can we have a bottle?" he asks.

Once the waiter is out of earshot, I lean closer to Olly. "I didn't need a whole bottle."

"I'm treating my girl. You don't have to drink it all, but I want you to let your hair down," he says, wrapping his finger around some of the hair hanging over my shoulder.

"The view and the glass of champagne was perfect. We could have had a drive-thru, and it would have been enough."

He sighs. "I know, but I wanted to do this. Let me spoil you for a change. Everything you do is for Molly, but you deserve to be treated like a princess, too." His words are sincere.

"I guess," I reply, biting my lower lip. It's hard not to think this is money wasted.

"Please—let go for tonight. This isn't about the cost; it's about making memories."

"Okay," I reply. I don't want him to think I'm not grateful for the effort and more importantly, the thought he's put into this. "Thank you," I say on a whisper and kiss the corner of his upturned lip.

I could see how exhausted he was when we returned to his. I gave him a back massage, and it wasn't long before he succumbed to sleep. I've been tossing and turning for a few hours now. Marcus and his behaviour are becoming more volatile, and I'm struggling to reconcile the man with the boy I grew up with. It breaks my heart for Molly.

Olly stirs beside me. On other occasions, I've woken to him thrashing around, mumbling, having some kind of bad dream but then they subside. But tonight, his mumbles are louder than I've ever heard him and a cry breaks free from his lips. He jerks awake, sitting upright.

He blinks, his chest rising and falling in quick succession. I reach for his hand. "Are you okay?" I whisper.

He turns his head towards me. The room is coated in darkness but I can still see his tortured face. His hand trembles as he pulls mine to his lips then kisses my palm. "A bad dream. Sorry, I didn't mean to wake you."

I tug on his wrist, pull him down beside me. He lays facing me, our hands entwined between us. "You didn't." He leans in and kisses the tip of my nose. "Do you always have nightmares?" I ask.

He shakes his head. "No, they come and go. I can have months without a single one and then have a week where they are consecutive."

I pull his hand closer to my chest. "Do you want to talk about it?"

"No, that's what I have counselling for."

His words sting, and I pull back. He notices, makes up the distance. "Sorry, I didn't mean to sound like a jerk." He lets go of my hand to trail his fingers over my upper thigh, pulling my leg over his.

"It's okay, but I'm a good listener. I want to know about you, Olly—the good and the bad."

His teeth show when he smiles, and I can't help but mirror him. "I'm beginning to learn there are a lot of things you're good at."

I know he's trying to deflect. "I was trying to have a moment with you then," I say, trying not to sound too defensive.

His fingers trail over my skin softly. "I don't mean to hurt you, Princess. I worry something I say or do will ruin it. I've just never had this kind of connection with someone before." He pulls my centre into him, and I try to ignore the want that builds at my core.

"And what kind of connection would that be?" I ask. I already know our physical connection is undeniable.

"One where I never want to let you go."

I gasp, and before I can utter a response, his lips are on mine—demanding, seeking, pleading.

I open up to him, allow his words to settle over me like a comfort blanket. But what if it frays? Would he fight for me? If push came to shove, would he choose Molly and me?

His lips lift from mine enough for him to speak. "Don't. Don't do that." He caresses my cheek.

"Do what?"

"Question my sincerity."

"It's hard to trust something you've never had before," I reply, feeling emotionally naked.

"You can't see air, but you know it's there, right?"

I roll my eyes, but the corners of my mouth turn up into a smile. "Well, yes, but—"

"No, buts. You and me, what we have—it's like breathing."

His words have the power to steal the breath from my lungs. When I'm with him, when he's like this with me, I feel things I've never experienced before, and suddenly, fairy tales don't seem so far-fetched.

Then he's kissing me again, and all my anxiety and self-doubt are lifted. I no longer want to fly. I want to soar. Olly is everything I've been missing in a friend, in a partner, in a significant other.

Chapter Thirty-Nine

Olly

The closer I get to this charity event, the less time I have to spend with Rachel. Being without her is an ache I can't explain. I know Molly comes first, and I'm pleased about that—Rachel is a damn good mother—but I've noticed how much shit she silently puts up with where Marcus is concerned. His lack of timekeeping, commitment. And I am pretty sure he has some deep-rooted issues of his own, too. I haven't been able to forget the state he was in when he turned up for Molly's party.

As soon as I leave the gym, I dial Rachel.

"Hello?" she answers on the first ring.

"Hi, you okay?" I ask.

"Yeah, fine."

She doesn't sound too convincing. "What are you up to?"

I hear shuffling around, and it takes a second for her to respond. "Nothing, why?"

"I thought I could bring us some take-away."

I hear a door close. And the sound of her feet padding across the floor. "Um, I'm not feeling too great. Rain check?"

Disappointed, I agree and hang up.

Something in her voice didn't sound right; she was hiding something. Before I can think better of it, I swing past the fish and chip shop and grab us a large portion of both.

When I get to her flat, one of her neighbours is just coming out and holds the door for me. "Thanks," I say.

"No problem," she says, a little in my personal space. I breathe in to keep from touching her body with mine, and then race up the stairs two at a time.

I only allow myself one breath before knocking on Rachel's door.

There's a large sigh right before she pulls open the door. "Olly?"

I hold up the bag. "I know you said you didn't feel well, but you sounded off," I say in the way of explanation.

And that's when I hear another voice. "Who is it?" Marcus appears in the hallway, wearing only his boxers, his hair damp. My eyes travel to Rachel who is in her yoga pants and a baggy t-shirt, sans bra.

She wipes her palm over her face. "For fuck's sake, Marcus, go put some clothes on," she says, exasperated.

He comes up behind her, leans his chin on her shoulder. I am ready to rip into him, but Rachel elbows him hard, and he holds up his hands, feigning ignorance. "I mean it, Marcus." He gives me a shit-eating grin before disappearing into the bathroom.

Her face falls, and I take her hand. "What's going on?"

She shakes her head. Looking back over her shoulder, she pulls the door just shy of being closed and steps into the hallway.

"He turned up early hours this morning in an absolute state. I couldn't turn him away," she says. "Nothing happened, if that's what you're worried about."

I take a step back "What?"

"Between Marcus and me," she says, biting her lip.

"Did I say that?"

Her face is crestfallen, and she dips her chin. "No, but I'd never do that to you, Olly."

I kiss her forehead. "I know." And I do. When I saw him, I never thought she had been with him.

"Well, isn't this cosy," says Marcus.

She sighs and pulls away from me. "Don't be like that," she says facing him.

"Whatever, I have to go."

She steps forward, touching his arm. "We need to talk about last night," she says.

"Nothing to talk about," he replies, typing away at his phone. It rings. He turns, answers it. "Cool, man, I'll be there in an hour," he says and then hangs up.

Turning back towards Rachel, he leans down and kisses her smack-bang on the lips, and then just as quickly, pulls back, waves, saunters off. She wipes her lips with the back of her hand, shuddering. It takes everything in me not to go after him, but I'd be giving him exactly what he wants.

I hold up the bag. "I also brought wine."

Her shoulders relax a fraction. I reach for her hand. She wraps her fingers with mine and pulls me into the flat, closing the door behind us before bolting the chain.

When she turns back around, I pull her into my body and hold her until the tension eases.

"Where's Molly?"

"Sleeping," she's says. The bedroom door is closed.

We head into the living room, and I see the sofa made up with a cover and pillows…and a blanket on the chair. She quickly strips off the cover and pillowcases, then tosses them into the washing machine.

"Did you sleep in the chair?" I ask her while she's grabbing plates and cutlery.

Nodding, she sits at the table, and I join her to dish out the food. Thankfully, it was double wrapped and still warm.

After we've eaten, I pop to the bathroom and that's when I see it—on top of the small vanity. "Rachel," I call out but not loud enough to wake Molly.

"Yeah?" she says, pausing in the doorway. I point to the vanity, and her eyes grow large. "That arsehole. He's using again, and *in my flat.*"

She reaches for the rolled-up note and the mirror. With swift, angry motions, she washes it under the tap to rid it of the remnant of what is likely cocaine. "I wouldn't have let him in if I knew he had shit on him," she says. "I don't want that shit around Molly."

It takes everything in me to keep my anger at bay.

Chapter Forty

Olly

I grew up around parents with addictions—that's the last thing I want for Molly or Rachel. I know they have a bond that will forever bind them to Marcus. But I sure as hell won't sit idly by and watch him destroy himself. I saw first-hand what damage it can do. Whether they are together or not…he is their family.

Taking Rachel by the hand, I sit on the edge of the bath and pull her into my lap. "Talk to me," I say, tucking loose hair behind her ear.

"I don't even know where to begin," she says, exhaling.

I lean down and kiss her softly, her warm lips inviting. She opens up to me without hesitation. We kiss until her body moulds to mine and my butt starts to go numb. I pick her up; she wraps her legs around my waist.

Walking into the living room, I make a beeline for the chair, then sit down with her straddling me. Her eyes pierce mine, her fingers delicately tracing the lines of my face.

"One day, I'd love to paint you," she says.

"Like one of your French girls?" I ask with a smirk.

She leans back, hand on my chest. "You've seen Titanic?"

I shrug. "Only about a hundred times. My foster sister, Melissa, was obsessed with it growing up."

Her eyes crinkle at the corners. "So, you'll know exactly how I want you when I do." She kisses my chin. I stifle my groan. My body reacts to her in a way only she has the power to evoke.

I pull her into my ever-growing erection, and she moans. Colour taints her beautiful cheeks. Sliding off my lap, she goes to her knees, her hands fiddling with the fly of my jeans.

I still her with my hand, but she swats it away, her eyes darting up to mine. I raise my hands, watching as she undoes my zipper and pulls it open just enough to gain access.

"Up," she says. I lift my arse, and she pulls my jeans and my boxers down to my thighs.

And then her mouth is on me.

I tilt my head back and close my eyes as her tongue and lips work the length of me, her fingers playing with my balls. It's not long before I'm staring down at her, my fingers in her hair, urging her to go faster, deeper.

"Fuck," I hiss through my teeth. "Stop, I'm going to come." But she doesn't—if anything, it urges her on, and she takes me deeper. I come fast; she milks me for every drop.

I pull my jeans back up but leave the buttons undone, and then pull her back into my lap. "You didn't have to do that," I say before kissing her.

"I know, but I wanted to."

We sit silently for a bit—the only sounds our combined breathing and the creaking, sulking of the fridge in the kitchen.

"He wasn't always that way," she says in the darkness. Her fingers paint a pattern across my chest. "Marcus—he never touched drugs until he got a new job in the city." I play with her hair as she continues. "It's part of the reason we split up. I was never in love with him or him with me. But when he found out I was pregnant, he said he wanted to be part of her life, and that he would quit. He did...I thought."

She looks up, her eyes meeting mine. "I know he's been drinking again, but I didn't know about the coke. I don't want it anywhere near my daughter. I can't trust him to take care of her if he'll do it in my home and not even hide his indiscretions."

"Do you want me to talk to him?" I ask.

Her eyes go wide. "No. I'm only telling you this in confidence. I'll talk to him," she says.

But I don't like the thought of her having to. I know how volatile a vice like this can make someone, and I don't want her being any part of it.

"I don't like the idea of that," I reply, honestly.

"And I love that you care, but I can handle this."

I nod and kiss her forehead. Seeing the sacrifices she makes for Molly leaves me no doubt she can handle it.

But I don't like it.

Rachel

Olly doesn't like the idea—I can tell by the tick of his jaw. But what else can I do? If Marcus doesn't get his shit together, how does he expect to be a good father to Molly? She's more aware now. She notices when she hasn't seen him for a while. Or he shows up late.

"I didn't mean to mislead you when you rang," I say.

He grabs my hand and brings it to his lips. Every time he does this, my insides melt. "I understand, Princess." He kisses the tips of my fingers one by one.

I want to roll my eyes. He always calls me *princess*, but the more I hear it from him, the less offensive I find the term.

"It's a lot to take on—all this drama," I say. My stomach revolts at the possibility of him deciding I am more hassle than I'm worth. At the thought of him walking away.

I don't know when he became part of my everyday life. Even when I don't get to see him, he always texts or calls. It's both refreshing and terrifying. The only constant I have ever known was my nan before she died, and Molly, of course. But not even my parents gave me what I needed the most.

"Not drama. Besides, I have a vested interest." His gaze holds mine. There's so much truth and strength behind his words, that I want to look away, but he holds me captive, those violet orbs a weapon all of their own.

"I see you, Olly. When you try to hide who you are, I see you."

He smiles. "Is that so? And what do you see?"

"Everything I never knew I was missing," I reply, omitting that I also believe maybe…in a small or even perhaps a profound way, that we are the same, that he is my soul mate.

Chapter Forty-One

Rachel

I don't have the heart to tell Olly how Marcus got on his hands and knees, begging me to take him back when he arrived here half-cut last night. As much as Olly bites his tongue, I see how much Marcus pisses him off. If I would have arrived at his place and his ex was half-naked when he opened the door, I doubt I would have been as calm and collected as he was just now.

Marcus can be manipulative, pushy. Lately, he's only been showing these negative traits, and it's building into a much larger problem. Something's got to give. I know this, and yet, I feel powerless to do anything about it.

I never wanted to be one of those women who used their child as a weapon, and I never will, but I have a duty of care to our daughter, and if that means protecting her from her father as he destroys himself…then so be it.

Maybe I should speak to his parents, perhaps they can talk

some sense into him. He will need to be the one to fix this, but he needs a support system, too.

Olly is staring at the floor, elbows on his knees, head down.

I lied—feigned an illness—and he came to check on me. Who even does that? "I am sorry," I say, walking towards him.

He meets my stare, then pulls me towards him and down onto his lap so I'm straddling him. "Don't be—it's not your fault." He kisses my neck softly, and my body warms from his touch. I wish he didn't have to leave, but I know he has to get home.

"You should go," I say.

"You want me to leave?" he asks, hurt in his voice.

"No, but I know it's not fair to Buster."

He tilts his head back so he can see my face. "He's at my mum's." He squeezes my hips; tingles break out over my body. "I tend to do it every now and again when I have late shifts and leading up to fight nights. It's good for their dog, Max, too."

I smile at that. "In that case, stay as long as you want."

He lets out a contented sigh. "How about all night?" he asks, his eyes probing. I glance over my shoulder towards Molly's closed bedroom door. "Hey, it's fine, ignore me."

I reach for his face. "If you don't mind sharing a lumpy sofa with me, I'd love to have you stay the night," I say, kissing him on each cheek before meeting his soft, warm lips.

"As long as I get to hold you, I'm down."

He stands, and I slip down the front of his body. He holds me, swaying on the spot. I close my eyes, savouring his smell, my ear pressed against his chest, his heartbeat my favourite melody.

"Let me go grab the clean bedding set."

Once the sofa is made, I change into a long t-shirt and a pair of sleep shorts. I hear a hum of appreciation from him.

"Are you sleeping like that?" I ask, eying him still fully clothed.

He looks down at himself with a laugh. He pulls his shirt over his head and removes his jeans and socks, now only in a pair of tight briefs.

Now I'm the one trying to suppress a groan. "Go lay down," I say.

He cocks an eyebrow, but does as he's told, turning on his side. I switch off the lamp and lay down so my back is to him. After some fidgeting, he wraps his arm around my waist and pulls me against his chest.

"What did you want to be when you grew up?" he whispers in my ear.

I stroke my fingers over the back his hand. "A teacher. I wanted to be an Art teacher," I reply.

"You would be amazing."

I shake my head. "It was just a dream."

He shuffles us so he's staring down at me, tucking my stray hair behind my ears.

"Rachel, it's not just a dream. You have the talent, you could do it."

I find myself holding my breath. Though it's dark in here, I can see the conviction in his eyes. I turn my head and suck in a deep breath. "It's not that simple."

I think of the cost of getting a teacher's degree or taking a teaching assistant course…not to mention the amount of time it would take.

"You know, there are grants," he says.

"Maybe," I say, hoping he will drop the subject for now. I'll be coming into my inheritance soon, but I don't want to get into that.

"I can help you search online. I believe in you, Rachel, even if you don't believe in yourself."

I nibble my bottom lip, my throat going dry. Apart from my nan, no one else has ever said that to me before. My nose tingles as my eyes begin to water. *Damnit, don't cry.*

His thumb wipes at a stray tear. I sniff loudly, hoping I can dislodge the urge to full-on cry. "I'm sorry, I didn't mean to upset you."

I grab his hand and kiss the pad of his thumb. "You didn't. It's just nice having someone believe in me again."

He leans forward, kissing the tip of my nose, my cheeks, pausing a breath away from my mouth. "I do, and I want to be witness when you start believing in yourself, too," he whispers.

And then his lips meet mine—a kiss so powerful, it's almost suffocating. I grip the back of his head, wanting him closer; the weight of his body on top of me is intoxicating. He pours his words into this kiss. When he pulls away, we are both breathless and he winks at me before pulling me back into his chest. Secure in his arms, I close my eyes and allow the sound of his breathing to lull me to sleep. For the first time in a long time, I have a thread of hope.

Chapter Forty-Two

Olly

I blink awake, hold back my groan. *How the fuck does Rachel sleep on this sofa every night?* She's snuggled into my chest. A soft snore escapes her lips, letting me know she is still in a deep sleep.

The sound of a door creaking causes me to sit up slightly, and I see Molly-Mae walking in with her flamingo blanket tucked under her arm, thumb in mouth. Her big-blue eyes find me and widen. Her thumb pops out of her mouth, then she starts running over.

I hold up my hand for her to *wait* and press a finger to my lips to *be quiet.* "Let mummy sleep," I whisper.

"Okay, Olly." She turns away, and I wonder where she's going—bathroom.

I manage to scoot off the torture device of a sofa without waking Rachel. I reach for my jeans and quickly pull them on. I hear the sound of a flush and water running before Molly comes back out. "You had a sleepover?" she asks.

I nod. "Yeah. You want breakfast?"

She reaches out to me, and I pick her up, popping her on my hip before making our way into the kitchen.

"What do you want to eat?" I ask.

"Chocolate."

I shake my head. "Nice try, Molly-Mae, but your mumma would tell me off."

"Hmm…what today?"

"It's Sunday," I reply, hoping I understood her correctly.

"Pancakes." She wriggles, and I put her on her feet. She grabs her small blue chair and drags it over to the counter to stand on it.

"Whoa, kid," I say.

"It's okay—Mummy lets me," she says as she opens the cupboard, then points to something.

I lean over her and have a look—pancake mix. "Pancakes it is." She giggles and claps her hands excitedly. "You want to help?"

Her eyes go wide. "Mummy says I can't touch oven, it's hot."

I nod. "She's right, but you can help me mix the pancakes, can't you?" Her smile nearly kills me. You would think I just gave her a pony or something.

We get busy making the batter—she drops half an eggshell in the bowl; I dig it out. She tells me exactly what to do, and if I do something different than her mummy, she's not shy to tell me so.

"Ready?" I ask her. She watches as I flip the pancake in the air and catch it in the pan.

"Again, again," she screams.

I cringe, wanting to ask her to be quiet, but it's too late. Rachel clears her throat from the doorway. "Sorry," I say, sliding the pancake onto a plate.

Arms wrap around me, and the side of her face rests against my back. "I'm sorry, did she wake you?" I turn so she's in my arms.

"No, I was already awake."

"I want my pancake, please," says Molly, sitting patiently on her chair. I kiss Rachel on the top of her head before taking the plate to Molly. "What do you want on it, kid?"

A toothy grin appears on Molly's face. "Chocolate spread," she says.

"Chocolate spread?" I ask.

"Yes, that's what I say."

"Molly," Rachel says, trying to sound firm. "Don't be rude."

"Sorry, Olly."

I ruffle her hair, take the jar from Rachel, then get to work spreading it on the pancake.

She takes a huge bite and smiles, chocolate covering her teeth. Rachel and I turn away to hide our laughter. "You didn't have to get up with her—you should have woken me," she says, reaching for two mugs.

I trap her in front of the counter—her back against my chest—and whisper into her ear, "I didn't mind, and you looked so peaceful, except for your snoring."

She jabs me gently with her elbow. "I do not."

I nod my head and nip her ear. "You do, and it's like a tiny baby pig snore—cute as fuck."

Colour spreads over her cheeks, causing me to strain in my jeans. I pull my lower body away from her to let it calm down.

She giggles, throwing me a knowing look. Turning her head, she beckons me forward, then gifts me a swift kiss before shifting back to making tea. "I was thinking… If my mum can keep Buster until tonight, do you fancy taking Molly to the zoo?"

Rachel pauses pouring water into mugs, and I know she's mentally calculating the cost. "My treat—please say yes," I whisper, nipping her neck.

She bites her lower lip. "I can't let you do that, Olly."

"I want to, and why can't you let me?"

She shrugs. "Because—"

I cut her off. "Because nothing. *Please*, I want to, you'll offend me if you say no."

"Molly, do you want to go to the zoo with Olly and me?" she asks, smirking.

An excited squeal emanates from behind us, and I can't hide my smile. "It's settled then. Get ready, and then we'll stop at mine on the way so I can get changed."

"Okay, can I have my tea first?" she asks, giggling.

"Of course."

I pull her into my side, and we stand together, sipping our tea as we watch Molly swinging her legs and eating her breakfast—eager as I to get to the zoo.

Rachel

It's not long before Molly's legs are hurting. We've been walking around for hours; I'm surprised she's lasted this long.

"Shall we take a turn on the train?" Olly suggests, pointing over his shoulder.

I look past him. It's one of the mini railways that goes around the zoo, the name applying to the size of the actual train, too. "Good idea. Do you want to wait here?" I ask.

He shakes his head. "No, I'm coming."

"Are you sure? It might be a tight squeeze," I say as we walk in that direction, each holding one of Molly's hands between us. She goes heavy in our grasps, and I adjust my grip right as she swings between us with a squeal. "Careful, Molly."

She gives me a toothy grin, and I can't hide my smile.

We join the queue, Molly clapping her hands with excitement. Days like this are far and few between. Day trips like these are expensive, but Olly insisted, and I couldn't let my pride get in the way—not when it comes to my baby girl.

"Have you had a nice day?" Olly asks her while we wait for the train to arrive.

"It's the best day ever," she declares, spinning in a small circle, the flamingo tutu she insisted on wearing floating in the breeze.

"Yeah, and what did you enjoy seeing most?" he asks.

"The flamingos," she all but squeals. I couldn't even tell you where her fascination for them came about—maybe it's because pink is her favourite colour—but she wouldn't take her eyes off them. We stayed there for almost half an hour as she ran up and down the path, pointing them out.

The train arrives, and we move along the line until we enter a tiny carriage. The three of us have one to ourselves, which is good. Olly folds himself inside to make it work though his arm hangs over the side of the open window.

"I said it might be a bit snug."

He only shrugs. "It's not for long, besides, I didn't want to miss out on seeing this with my girls," he says, so matter of fact.

My heart misses a beat. *My girls.*

Heat radiates through my chest.

Does he have any idea how much those two words mean?

To anyone looking in this quaint little carriage, they might think we're a family on a day out. We're not…are we? No, no. Not yet, anyway. But him saying that—*my girls*—warms me.

Wining and dining me in London was exquisite, but this—nothing can top this. I've always wanted days like this with someone special, the thought both exhilarating and intimidating. Olly doesn't realise how much it means to me, and I struggle to tamper down the wave of emotion.

"You okay?" he asks, his tilting head almost touching the ceiling.

"Yes. Just thinking about what a lovely day we've had," I say, hoping he can hear the gratitude in my voice.

"Well, it's not over yet." Noticing the penguin enclosure, he grabs Molly's attention, pointing them out. And she begins tapping her feet like in Happy Feet, the movie.

Once we get off the train and begin walking again, Molly asks for a carry. My arms already feel like limp noodles.

"How about you get on my shoulders?" Olly asks, looking between the two of us.

"Okay," she says before I even open my mouth.

He kneels, and I lift her onto his shoulders. He holds her knees in place, and when he stands, she lets out a whoosh of air, grabbing his forehead, covering his eyes with one hand as she holds on for dear life.

"I got you," he says, gently prying her fingers from his eyes.

"It's so high," she declares, a slight quiver in her voice.

"Do you want me to give you a piggyback instead?" I ask.

"You won't drop me, will you, Olly?" she asks, her voice so, *so* vulnerable, and yet…full of quiet, reverent hope. Tears spring to my eyes unbidden.

He lets out a soft chuckle, but his voice cracks when he says, "Of course not, Molly-Mae. I got you."

She relaxes, and before I know it, her chin is resting on the top of his head as we continue walking. I snap a few shots of them together—neither of them noticing—while they study the Meerkats. They have the biggest grins, and I'm not sure which of them is enjoying this more.

After another half hour, Molly starts with a few bouts of yawning, and I know it's time to call it a day.

"Okay, it's time to get going," I say. Home, dinner, bath,

bed. They give me matching pouts, and I can't help but laugh. "Hey, don't look at me like that," I say, crossing my arms.

"Fine, but I want to stop by the gift shop on the way out," Olly says, taking my hand in his.

"Molly, do you want to pick out a sweet for tomorrow?" I ask when he sets her on her feet. She nods, eagerly pulling me over to the stand with different kinds of sweets.

"I'll meet you outside," Olly says, and I nod over my shoulder.

Molly eyes the assortment in front of her. It doesn't take her long to pick a giant lollypop, and we make our way to the tills to pay.

I can't see Olly when we get outside, so we wait by the exit. When his palm touches my lower back, I relax. "There you both are," he says, kissing my temple.

"Thought we'd lost you," I say.

"Molly, I got you something—close your eyes." She doesn't miss a beat, squeezing her eyes closed. "Olly," I reprimand.

"Oh, hush yourself, woman," he says, teasing, causing Molly to let out a nervous giggle. He pulls a flamingo that's wearing a tutu from behind his back, and I cover my mouth. "Okay, open," he says.

Her eyes widen when she spots the fluffy pinkness in front of her. She slowly raises her hand. "It's all yours, Princess," he says.

Pulling it into her chest, she looks up at him with a tender expression that melts my heart, and without me even having to prompt her, she says, "Thank you." Molly gently strokes the flamingo's fur, in complete awe of her gift.

I put my arm around his waist and squeeze his hip. He kisses the top of my head. I hold out my hand for Molly, but she reaches for his instead.

Chapter Forty-Three

Olly

Today I'll be meeting Rachel's parents at the annual Help for Heroes charity day. She doesn't talk about them much—well at all, if I'm honest.

"We only have to stay awhile, and then we can get out of here," she says, pushing her shoulders back and taking a deep breath before we exit the car.

I join her outside, push her up against the door with my body.

"It will be fine, and you look beautiful," I say, inching closer to her delectable lips, which I am dying to kiss, but I don't want to ruin her lip gloss.

"Thank you. But no doubt my mother will say something about my appearance."

I slide my hands down to her hips and give them a gentle squeeze. "Believe me, there is nothing wrong with how you look." I move my lips to her throat and flick my tongue out, licking a tiny path to her ear lobe before sucking it into my mouth. She gasps, and her hands grab my waist, pulling me flush into her body. My erection strains against the material of my trousers.

"I don't want to go in now—I'd rather you took me somewhere and did naughty things to me with your tongue," she purrs, exposing her throat, and I can't hold back my groan.

I pull away from her, cupping her face in my hands, her eyes searching my face. "I promise I can do that for you later." I keep staring at her lips.

"Are you going to at least kiss me?" she asks.

"What about your lip gloss?"

She rolls her eyes. Instead of answering, she pulls my face down to hers and kisses me without restraint until I'm ready to throw her in the car, take her somewhere to do wicked things to her with my tongue.

I pull back, breathless, to calm myself. She wipes my lips with her finger, then pulls out a wet wipe from her tiny clutch. I raise an eyebrow, and she laughs. "It's a mum thing." She cleans off the remaining gloss from her lips, still a little red from our kiss, but doesn't bother to re-apply the gloss.

"So, this is what was taking you so long?" a familiar male voice calls out from behind, causing me to let out a small growl.

"What are you, my timekeeper?" Rachel asks Marcus, looking over my shoulder.

I turn around and force a smile. "Marcus." I nod my head but he just looks me up and down.

"Where's Molly?"

"Out back with my parents," he replies. Rachel crosses her arms. He stares up and down the length of her body, and I want to punch him in the face. "Come on, we hardly ever get to spend time together as a family," he says, stepping towards her.

I tense, ready to put him on his arse, when Rachel holds her hand up to stop him from getting any closer. "Marcus,

Olly is standing right here. And for the record, we were never a family. Even before Molly was born, you couldn't keep your dick in your pants."

I almost want to high-five her for giving it to him straight, but I keep my mouth shut. His nostrils flare as he stares daggers at me.

"Yeah, well, that was then, and this is now. Does he know you're only using him until we get back together?"

Yep, that's all I can take. "Mate, you need to back the fuck off."

"Listen, we aren't at your crummy bar right now, so how about you mind your own business and *piss off*?"

Rachel pushes Marcus away from me, and I'm grateful, but also fuming that she's touching him. How can that piece of shit be related to that sweet baby girl in there? "Marcus, stop it. You only want me when you can't have me. But I told you I don't want to be like that—and I won't."

It's not what I'd like her to have said. It makes me wonder if, deep down, she would still want to be a family if she and Molly were his priority.

"Neither do I. What I want is for you, me, and Molly to try and be a family. Won't you always wonder about how good we could have been? You won't even give it a try…"

"Seriously, man, you need to stop." I take a menacing step towards him.

Rachel grabs my arm. "Come on, Olly, let's get this over with," she says, not entertaining what he just said.

I wrap my arm around her shoulder but not before looking back at Marcus who stands there, watching us, a shit-eating grin plastered on his face. *What the fuck is he playing at?*

"Olly!" I look around the sea of people until I see Molly bouncing up and down while she runs over, her flamingo hanging from her hand. She wraps her arms around my legs, looks up, and smiles. "I missed you," she says, and those three words almost bring me to my knees.

"Don't mind me, Molly. I'm just your mummy."

Molly sighs, then lets go when Rachel kneels down to pull her in for a hug. I see her breathe Molly in, and I wonder what our children would look like. I hope they'd take after their mum. I have to cough to stop from choking on my saliva. I've never thought about having children before.

"Rachel, you're tardy." I look up to see a woman walking towards us. She clicks her tongue, stopping in front of us. "And you couldn't find anything else to wear? Something more flattering?"

Rachel's mouth forms a straight line, but she doesn't respond. *Fuck no.* "She looks perfect as she is," I say, pulling Rachel into my side. She doesn't hesitate to wrap her arm around my waist, and I'm grateful for that.

The woman looks at me head to toe and then back up again like she's just walked through dog shit. "So, this is the boy you're friends with?"

Rachel lets out a frustrated sigh. "No, this is the *man* I'm *dating*, Mum."

"Hmm. What about you and Marcus?"

"There is no 'me and Marcus.' You're making a scene," Rachel says, exasperated.

Her mum's eyes dart around the people mingling about, her lips forming a straight line, and then, shit you not, she raises her nose in the air. "Come, let's go find your father." Without waiting for a response, she turns on her heel and saunters off.

"I am so sorry," Rachel whispers into my ear, her fingers squeezing my hips.

"It's fine," I reply, but the truth is, I am ready to be anywhere but here.

Molly tugs on the leg of my trousers and without a word, I reach down and pick her up so she's resting on the opposite hip her mother is leaning on. She leans her little head against my chest and whispers, "I love you, Olly."

My eyes spring to Rachel, who is looking on in shock, and I can't hold back my smile. "I love you, too, kid," I reply, kissing the top of her head.

When I look back to Rachel, her eyes are glassy, but she smiles, and it's one I've never seen directed at me—adoration. I grab her hand and squeeze, and then look to see where her mother is—she's stopped right in front of Marcus. *Great.*

Chapter Forty-Four

Rachel

Uncomfortable doesn't even begin to describe this whole situation right now. Per usual, my mother is all about keeping up pretences. Marcus isn't helping, either, and the more he behaves like this, the less tolerable he is.

I see my father and decide to steer us towards him, away from my mother. I have a feeling the three of them together is a recipe for disaster.

When he sees us approaching, he smiles at me, and it appears genuine. "There's my girl," he says, greeting me with a kiss on the cheek.

"Hi dad, this is Olly. Olly, this is my dad, Edmund."

Olly holds out his hand, and to my relief, my dad reciprocates the gesture, eying Molly still secure to Olly's hip.

"So, you're the one my daughter is dating?"

Olly clears his throat and nods. "That would be correct."

Dad's eyes peruse Olly but in a more subtle way than my mother just did. "You have a few tattoos, I see."

My cheeks heat and I'm about ready to step in when Olly answers, "I do. Let's just say I have an appreciation for all kinds of art."

"I have a scorpion," Dad begins, and I almost choke. "Not the best decision I ever made, but we live and learn." There's a smile in his voice. And all the while, I'm still trying to process his admission to having a tattoo. "Oh, don't look like that, Rachel. I told *you* never to get one—not that I didn't have any."

"Any—as in plural? Does that mean you have more than one?"

He taps the side of his nose and discreetly clears his throat. "Here comes the Wicked Witch," he whispers under his breath, and now I think I've heard it all.

"There you all are," Mum says in her annoying nasally manner as she joins us, Marcus glued to her side. "Edmund, what were you all gossiping about?" she asks, utterly ignoring Olly's presence.

"Just speaking to Olly, here, about art," he replies, giving me a wink. Who is this man, and what has he done with my father?

"Oh, well, we should go make the rounds, bid on a few items," she says, reaching out for my father's arm who obliges dutifully.

"Make sure you find me before you leave," he says. I nod, still trying to process what just happened.

"Marcus, there you are." A woman joins his side, running her hand up to his shoulder, claiming him. Have at him, love, been there, done that. "I was looking for you," she says sultry, and I almost want to cover my daughter's eyes at the way she's pushing herself into him.

I clear my throat. "And on that note, Olly, shall we?" I reach for his hand.

"Oh, Rach, I can't have Molly tonight," Marcus says before I walk away.

"What?" I tense and squeeze Olly's hand.

"Yeah, something's come up," he replies, winking at the woman glued to his side.

"And when you say *come up*, you mean your latest piece of skirt?" I feel like a bitch referring to the woman that way, but I can't seem to stop myself.

"Who do you think you're talking to?" she says, moving towards me.

I shake my head and step into her space. "This isn't personal, sweetheart, but before you go there, our daughter is right here, so be careful what you say next."

Her eyes widen, and she looks at Molly and back to Marcus. "She's your daughter?" she asks Marcus, confused.

I cross my arms. "Please, tell me you didn't say she was your niece again?"

The girl lets go of his arm. "He did, I'm so sorry," she replies, looking uncomfortable.

"Sara, I'll explain it later—don't look like that," he says, grabbing her around the waist.

"*Marcus*, tonight?" I seethe.

"Oh, yeah, sorry, something's come up—work."

"Olly, would you do me a favour and take Molly to get a drink?"

He eyes me for a beat then nods. "Come, Molly, let's go get a milkshake." He tickles her side, and she giggles, not even throwing a backwards glance towards her father.

"Marcus, you don't just get to dump her whenever the mood takes you. She's your daughter, for crying out loud." How I manage to keep my voice to a respectable level is beyond me.

"I know, but it's networking. Come on, Rach, I need to earn a living," he says, holding up his palms.

"No, Marcus, it's not."

He rolls his eyes. "If we were together, you'd look after her anyway. There's no difference."

I let out a howl of laughter. Is he fucking kidding me right now? "I take care of her because that's what a parent *does*. The way you think it's acceptable to palm her off like you have no responsibilities isn't acceptable."

His eyes dart around. What, is he worried I'm drawing attention to us? I couldn't give a shit. "Whatever, Rach. You never used to be such a bitch."

I have to clench my fists to refrain from doing something I'll regret.

"Now, I'm sure I must have misheard you," says a familiar male voice from behind me. I turn my head as Charlie comes to stand beside me.

"Come on, let's go," Marcus says to Sara, grabbing her hand and pulling her with him.

"Wait, Marcus, I need her booster seat. Mine is in my car."

He looks over his shoulder, and I'm expecting him to be difficult, but he nods.

"Thanks," I say, turning to Charlie.

"I didn't do anything," he replies, smiling.

"You did enough. Where's Soph?"

He points her out—standing beside Olly while Felicity and Nate make a fuss of Molly and Selene. "He sent you over, didn't he?"

"Yeah, it was either that, or he was going to come back over himself." I kick at the grass. "Is everything all right?" he asks, cupping my upper arm.

"Marcus is more difficult than usual."

He nods and stares back in the direction of Olly. "Funny how that happens when your interest lay elsewhere, isn't it?"

I smile and catch Olly's attention. His eyes roam over my body, and I can't hide the blush working its way into my cheeks.

"Just don't let him come between you two—you've got a good thing going on. Don't let him ruin it." I tuck my arm in the crook of Charlie's elbow and go to join our friends, annoyed that, yet again, Marcus has put his selfish needs before our daughter. And now I have to let down Olly and cancel any plans he had for tonight.

When we reach the group, Olly doesn't hesitate in pulling me into his body. "Will you and Molly stay over?"

I look up, ready to say no, but the way his eyes hold mine makes it difficult for me to refuse. "We'd love to," I reply going on tip-toes to kiss him on his lips.

It lasts longer than it probably should, but right now, I don't care. When I pull back and turn to our group, there's a booster seat on the grass with Molly's ruck-sack on top. I glance around, searching for Marcus. "He said he'd call you in the week," Charlie says, trying to hide his amusement.

"Let me go put this in the car." Olly kisses my temple, then grabs it before I can object.

"That boy is smitten," says Felicity, coming to my side, twisting her hair around her finger, watching him walk away.

"He's not the only one," I reply, honestly, and she gives me a knowing smile, linking her arm with mine.

Chapter Forty-Five

Rachel

Other than the situation with my mum and Marcus earlier, today has turned out to be one of the best days I've had in a long time. Nate and Felicity took over hosting the annual Help for Heroes charity day from his Nan, and this year has exceeded every year since.

I wasn't in a position of being able to bid on the auction, but I was able to offer a painting instead.

"I still can't believe you paint." Sophie's eyes trace over the canvas. "It's beautiful." I shrug, still self-conscious about my work. "I better win it," she says squiggling on the clipboard on the table.

I try to stop her, but she shakes me off. "Soph, I'll paint you something else—I have some extra materials."

She holds up her palm. "It's for charity, and besides I want *this* one. But I will be commissioning you to do some pieces for the shop. I think with Felicity's photographs and some paintings of yours, it will help showcase local talent."

I'm stunned, *local talent*.

I'm grabbed from behind and pulled into a hard body. I squeal and laugh when Olly whispers into my ear, "I told you, you were talented."

"You're biased," I say, giggling as his teeth scrape over my earlobe.

I'm so caught up in how he makes me feel, I don't even notice my mum standing beside us until she speaks a greeting. I startle, tensing in Olly's arms. He goes to pull away, but my hands close over his that are wrapped around my waist.

Mum eyes the work, reads the description. A small sound escapes her, but she's quick to cover it up.

"It's beautiful, isn't it?" Soph says, standing on her other side.

"Yes," she replies with a smile. I let out a breath, not sure what I expected her to say. Her voice sounded like admiration. It's a recreation of a day trip I took to the beach with my parents. A rare occurrence, but one I always remembered so vividly—the way the sea breathed in and out, the waves lapping against the shore. My father and I made a dozen sand castles as my mum watched on, contentment in her expression.

I turn in Olly's arms. "Let's go look at the other stalls."

He obliges, and we walk off, not saying anything as we leave. I glance at random items, but I'm paying no attention to what's in front of me. I try to recall if my mum has ever said she's proud of me or congratulated me for any of my achievements.

"Your dad is different than I had imagined," Olly says, drawing my attention back to him.

I frown. "Yeah, totally unlike him...maybe he's having a mid-life crisis." I shrug, and he lets out a laugh.

"Did you not know he had a tattoo, or *tattoos*, as the case might be?"

I shake my head. "No. I had no idea. He's always been so…bland," I reply.

Olly chuckles and the sound makes my lady parts clench. "Well, he's coming this way."

"Hey Rachel, do you have a moment? I'm leaving but wanted to have a quick word before I do."

"I'll go see if Felicity needs a hand trying to pry Molly off the bouncy castle," Olly says. I laugh with a nod.

"Walk with me?" My dad holds out his arm, and we walk away from the milling crowds and stalls and towards the treehouse. "I'm just going to get straight to the point."

"Okay," I reply, apprehensive, as he stops and faces me.

"It's about your mother." He takes my hands in his, totally out of character for him, and my palms sweat at the contact. "She won't say it, Rachel, but she needs you." I roll my eyes and try to pull my hands free. "There's things you don't know —things you don't understand."

"Like what?"

"I wanted your mum to be the one to tell you, but it's difficult for her to express her feelings. You of all people know this. She's been seeing some specialists."

My heart pounds in my ears as my pulse races. I cut him off, my voice scratchy. "Is she sick?" The thought scares me. I might not be close with her the way I was with my Nan, but she's my mother.

He shakes his head. "No, but she has been diagnosed with Adult Autism."

I blink a few times, not sure if I believe him or not. "You're serious?" He nods. "When?"

"About six months ago."

I pull my hands free. "Why hasn't she told me?"

"She's still dealing with it, but it explains a lot. I've always supported her, and I realise now that might not have always been the best thing for you, and I apologise." My jaw drops. "She hides her feelings well, but she does love you."

I'm still not sure how to process what he's saying. "I'm familiar with autism and aware there's different spectrums. She's always been a certain way, but I would never have guessed."

He nods, then his face falls. "I know. She's always been so set in her ways, with routines amongst other things, and I thought it was just her being obsessive-compulsive, but it turns out there is more to it than that."

I shake my head, feeling an overwhelming sadness for her. "And so now what?"

"She's attending a group, which is helping. But I just wanted you to know so you could maybe understand things a little better."

I plop myself down on the grass, and my dad sits beside me.

"She loves you. I know she doesn't show it conventionally, but give her a chance okay?" I nod and turn my face towards him. "I just always thought you were both disappointed in me," I reply. My throat constricts as I try to swallow my emotion.

"Not at all. We get annoyed you're so dead set on doing everything on your own. We didn't like the idea of you splitting up with Marcus when you were pregnant. We know how hard it is—raising a child. You're so independent. You've always been that way. We are proud of you and the mother you are to Molly. And we both love you very much."

I bite my lip and sniff back my tears. I never realised how much I needed to hear that affirmation from him until now. "Thank you. I love you, too."

He stands and offers me his hands before pulling me to my feet and into a hug. "I just wish this is something we could have discovered sooner," he says.

"Me, too," I reply. It would have helped to explain a lot.

Chapter Forty-Six

Rachel

I spent the week researching on the internet after work. I wanted to understand my mum's diagnosis a little better before visiting. I learned so much, things that should be more widely known. Growing up, I genuinely thought she didn't love me, that I wasn't enough. And she was so focused on my father, she lost sight of herself at times. I hated her for these things…so many of which I now know she couldn't help.

I take a deep breath, knock, then wait for her to answer the door. I have a key, but I've never felt comfortable using it, not even when Molly and I come for dinner.

"Hello," she says in greeting.

"Hi."

"Well come in, don't just stand there." It's hard for me not to get defensive.

I follow her through to the living room, where she already has afternoon tea set out meticulously. She takes her usual seat; I follow suit. "Where's Molly-Mae?" she asks, pouring me a cup of tea.

"She's with Marcus."

Mum hands me the cup and saucer, the delicate china rattling as I take it from her. I have the urge to set it down for fear of spilling it. She clucks her tongue, barely loud enough to notice, and I want to roll my eyes. "And you're sure the two of you can't make it work?" she asks, stirring her tea.

"No, we weren't right for each other." I take a sip of my tea, pausing when I see what's hung above the fireplace. She turns her head to see what has my attention. "You were the one who won the bid?"

"Yes. I wanted it, and your father likes it, too."

I cough to cover my emotion, a little choked up by the gesture. "I didn't think you liked art."

"I liked *that*, and besides, my daughter painted it," she replies, her lips twitching into an almost-smile as she hands me a small plate of cucumber sandwiches. I wonder if she remembers the day as well as I do.

"Thank you." I don't know if I'm thanking her for the compliment or the sandwiches, but at this moment, I don't think it's important. She's never shown much interest in my art before, and I'm taken aback that she even wanted it in the first place.

"So, Dad told me—"

She cuts me off mid-sentence. "Napkin." She holds out the napkin, and I lay it over my lap. Her facial expression remains stoic. "About my diagnosis?"

"Yeah, it explained a lot."

"I was meaning to tell you, I just kept putting it off." She places her plate back down and fiddles with her napkin as she continues. "I've always struggled with anxiety and depression. I hid it well, but your father has always known."

I nibble on the sandwich, contemplating my words before I speak.

"You have questions?"

I nod and swallow. "Yes."

"I'm listening."

"I found some articles on the internet, and I wondered how you've always acted in a socially neurological way, for the most part?"

She fidgets. "I was always quiet growing up and knew from watching other people I was different. But I didn't want to be, so I learned how to act more sociably. It doesn't come without effort, and it can be exhausting. It's also known as camouflaging, or so I'm told."

"How did the diagnosis come about?"

"Your father and I were having issues—my anxiety and depression was spiralling—and he threatened to leave me if I didn't go to the doctor. I was referred to several different specialists, and that's when I was diagnosed."

"I'm so sorry, Mum." And I mean it.

"You have nothing to apologise for." She reaches for my hand, the gesture unfamiliar. "I'm aware of how hard I've always been on you, and for that, I'm the one who is sorry. I never wanted you to turn out like me."

I shake my head. She makes it sound like she's a bad person. "You never left me starving. I never went without…"

"But you needed a mum—one more like my mother and the kind of mum you are to Molly. And I'm sorry I couldn't be the mum you deserved."

"You didn't do anything wrong," I say. She can't be held accountable for something which is out of her control any more than I can. "What happens now?"

"I'm learning to share my experiences with other women. The group meetings help, and your father has been very understanding."

We talk for another hour, and it's only when I need to go that I realise I've never spoken to her for this length of time, not ever.

She stands up, straightening her loose-fitting trousers. "You'll come again soon and bring Molly-Mae?"

"Yes, of course. Dinner next Thursday," I reply as she walks me to the door.

"Yes, or sooner if you'd like—just call us to let me prepare." I'm shocked when she pulls me in for a hug. Just as quickly, she lets go, but I can't hide the urge to cry.

"Bye," I choke out and rush from the house towards Betty.

Inside the confines of my car, I let the tears fall, wondering how many people go undiagnosed every day. My dad always told me she judged herself harshly, but I couldn't understand why she always seemed so well put together. To think, those social situations took considerable effort on her part… It makes me admire her in a way I never have before.

I want to make a point of learning more about Adult Autism. Perhaps we can do something to help raise awareness. Perhaps it's this diagnosis that will finally bring us together as a family.

Chapter Forty-Seven

Rachel

Olly is far more than I deserve.

He never signed up for this, for us. Before me, he was a carefree bachelor. And there I go again stereotyping him—he was and is so much more. But how long will it be before he realises this isn't worth the trouble?

"Penny for your thoughts?"

I startle at the sound of Sophie's voice. "Oh, I was thinking about Olly."

She joins me at the counter, takes the cloth from my hands. "It's clean." She tosses it to the side. "Fancy a tea before we close up?"

I go to check the time on my wrist, sigh, and then look at the clock on the wall. "Yeah, sounds good." I still have another hour before I need to collect Molly.

After Sophie makes a pot of tea, she grabs the last two slices of carrot cake, nodding towards the table. I sit with a satisfied sigh. It's nice to be off my feet.

"So, tell me about Olly," she says with a warm smile.

I shrug, not because I don't know what to say, but because I don't know where to begin. "I just...well, he crept up on me, you know? One minute, he was just Olly, who worked for Charlie, and then I get to know him, and he's...so much more."

She takes a bite of cake, nodding her head for me to continue like this is the best thing to happen to her all week.

"Marcus is going through some stuff, and Olly has been understanding—maybe even too understanding." I take a sip of my tea before continuing. "It's just—I have never felt like this about anyone before, and I have Molly to consider. What if it gets to be too much for him and he breaks her heart?"

And mine.

She reaches over, taking my hand in hers. "Rachel, I'm not going to lie. When I first met you, I was dubious, but now that I know you, I see how much you deserve someone like Olly. If he's with you, it's because he *wants* to be. I doubt that boy does anything he doesn't want to." She's right, but honestly, I don't know what he sees in me. "You don't think you're good enough for him, do you?"

I shake my head. "No. Not really."

"Why?"

A humourless laugh escapes me. "I'm a mess, in debt up to my eyeballs. Olly deserves better than me."

Sophie grabs hold of my hand. "Don't let your insecurities ruin a good thing. Talk to him."

I know she's right, but by admitting my fears to him, I'll be exposing myself. And that terrifies me—I'm already in too deep.

Olly

Today has dragged; it might as well be going backwards.

"Hey, mate. What's up with you?" Charlie asks, tossing a tea towel at my face.

I catch it, drop it on the bar. "I'm good," I reply, stacking the glasses.

"I doubt that. You haven't been your usual flirty-self with the patrons of late."

I cross my arms and lean back against the bar, raising an eyebrow. "I'm still professional."

"Yes, but you're— How do I word this? You're not carefree as you once were."

I smile, knowing he's right. "It's Rachel," I say.

He faces me, giving me his full attention, eyes sparkling. "Spill?"

"I like her. And I'd never want to do anything to disrespect her."

He punches me in the arm. "Well, damn. Mate, you are well and truly whipped."

I shake my head, unable to hide my smile. "Yeah, she has me tied in knots…and that's the problem."

He plays the top of the bar with his fingers. "And why is that?"

I need to say it out loud; the more I try to ignore it, the more it's beginning to fester. "She doesn't need my shit to add to her already hectic life."

He raises his eyebrows. "And how do you figure that?"

I don't want to talk about her business with people, but Charlie is a friend. "You know every penny she earns goes on Molly?"

He nods. "Yeah, kids are expensive," he says with a blissful smile.

"No, I mean—Marcus doesn't contribute fuck all."

His eyes turn into slits. "Are you shitting me? There is no way the money she earns is enough to keep her afloat."

"Nope, and she even pawned her Rolex." I only know this

because I found the receipt from the pawnbroker in her kitchen drawer.

"She, what?"

I nod. "I've never known a woman as tenacious as her. She blows my mind. Come on, you saw her painting at the charity day. She's so fucking talented." I already feel as though I've said too much. "Anyway, that's only between you and me. But yeah...she's pretty mesmerising."

His shit-eating grin forms. "Damn. You're in love with her, aren't you?"

I stand up straighter. His words echo. "Well, I mean, I care about her."

He laughs. "Mate, you are. You're in love with her."

I swipe my palm over my face. If I am, she'll be the one to hear it first. I grab a bottle of coke off the side and pop the cap, downing it in one go. The bubbles tickle my nose.

"Listen, it's a minefield. Just be honest with her. She's probably just as scared as you are."

I toss the tea towel at his face. "Who said anything about being scared?"

"You don't have to, mate. I've been there."

I am terrified. Opening up to her won't be easy, and I hate the thought of her having the power to hurt me. It wouldn't be just her, I'd lose Molly, too. Growing up as a foster kid, I know how important family is—whether you're bound by blood or not.

When my shift is finished, I slide out my phone from my back pocket. *Are you busy?*

Bubbles appear, and I bite my lip, waiting for her reply. *If you mean is Molly in bed and have I finished adulting for the day? Then the answer is yes. So, in answer to your question, no I'm not busy xo*

I can't hide my smile. *Can I drop by on my way back from work?*

I wave bye to Charlie and Jase. Not having to lock up and getting out early works for me.

Sounds good xo

I stop at the supermarket to grab a bottle of wine. At the checkout counter, there's a multicoloured orchid that reminds me of her painting. I smile, pay, then make a beeline for my girl.

When she buzzes me up, I suddenly feel nervous. What if she thinks this was a booty call?

She opens the front door, hair piled on top of her head in a messy array, her lips curved into a wide smile. She's never been more beautiful. And it hits me in the gut—what I wouldn't give to come home to her and that smile every day.

I hold out the orchid, words suddenly failing me.

"What's this?" she asks.

"I saw it and thought of you. I know, it's stupid."

She pulls on my hand, closes the door behind us. She ushers me further into the small hallway, the orchid in the crook of her elbow. "No, it's beautiful. I saw one similar the other day," she says, trailing off.

"Oh, and I got you this." I hold up the wine bottle.

Her eyes crease. "Has something happened?"

I shake my head. "No, of course not. I just wanted to stop by. I couldn't stop thinking about you."

Her shoulders relax, and I follow her to the kitchen. She sets the plant on the small windowsill, where it fits perfectly, then puts the wine in the fridge.

Turning back towards me, she walks straight into my body and wraps her arms around my back. And just like that, I can breathe again.

"I missed you," she says.

I kiss the top of her head and pull her closer. "I missed you, too."

I hold her, reluctant to let go when she pulls back. "Do you want a drink or something to eat? I have leftover cottage pie—if you're hungry?"

"I could eat," I reply.

She smiles, then makes me sit at the table while she heats it in the microwave. "Drink?"

"Water, please."

"It's only tap water."

I let out a laugh. "Perfect, thanks."

I get up to try to help, but she *shoos* me away. Being with her eases any doubts I have when we're apart. I am right where I want to be.

Chapter Forty-Eight

Olly

Rachel would likely kill me if she knew I was here.

I snuck the receipt for the pawnbroker out of her kitchen drawer when she was in the bathroom. The fees are astronomical in these places, especially for a watch like hers. But it's not the physical value, it's the sentimental value that makes it priceless. I can't sit there knowing she doesn't have the one possession, other than her car, which means the most to her.

It was only by chance I came across it in the first place when I was hunting for a corkscrew. She wasn't lying when she said it was in the shop, however, didn't elaborate either.

I can't say I'm surprised. She'd starve if it meant providing for Molly, of that much I am sure. It infuriates me she even has to do it alone. Marcus is a real fucking piece of work, and I still struggle to comprehend how he had a part in making such a beautiful daughter like Molly. But then, I'm also not. With a mother like Rachel, what child wouldn't flourish? If I were to have children of my own, I couldn't think of anyone more suitable than her.

But fuck if the thought doesn't scare the shit out of me.

I have more than enough to cover the cost. I know she's too proud not to pay me back so I won't even insult her by rebutting her. She's independent, and part of me knows this could cross a line with her, but I'm prepared to take the chance.

"Thank you," I say to the man behind the counter. He's been a great help. He was suspicious at first, but when I explained what I was doing, his demeanour softened.

"You know, that young lady has sold everything she had of value except the shirt off her own back…and *that* watch."

I nod in understanding. Sometimes I take for granted how fortunate I am, but I'm not oblivious to how quickly it can all be gone in a heartbeat. If anything, it makes my resolve to help her even stronger.

"Well, I'm just glad she has someone to help her carry the load." He shakes my hand with a quick nod.

"Me too, and thank you," I reply before making my way to the door to wait for him to buzz me out.

It's a heavy weight as I turn up at her flat. She doesn't even know I'm stopping by, but I didn't want to hold off giving it back to her. Quite frankly, my nerves couldn't take it. I don't even feel this wound up before a fight. I have to wipe my brow before I buzz and wait for an answer.

Rachel

Finally, I sit down. My feet are killing me. *What a bloody day.* I turn my wrist out of habit to check the time, then berate myself before checking my phone. Maybe I'll have an early night. It might only be eight o'clock, but I've been up since six and haven't stopped all day.

The intercom sounds and I groan. If it's the neighbour's kids again, I'll be pissed. They keep playing buzz down fucking ginger. I wouldn't mind, but Molly is in bed.

I jump up and rush to pick up the handset. "Hello?"

"Rachel, it's me."

"Olly?"

"The one and only," he replies, but he sounds off.

"Buzzing you up."

Weird. He usually texts before stopping by. Fuck, I hope everything is all right.

I open the door and cross my arms as I wait. When he comes round the top of the stairs, I smile, but it drops when I notice his unease. "Is everything okay? What's wrong?" I ask, stepping into the hallway.

He takes my hand and leads me inside, closing the door behind him.

"Oliver?"

He smiles when he turns to face me, crowding me against the coats hanging on coat pegs. "Everything is fine," he says, pulling me into his arms, and I let out a sigh of relief. He leans down and kisses me, slow and deliberate enough for me to almost forget my name. It's only when something heavy hits my leg that I peer down at the bag in his hand.

I quirk an eyebrow, and he tilts his head. "Let's go sit in the living room," he suggests, and I nod. His fingers lace with mine as we head to the sofa, and I smile—I love how he touches me.

"Okay, I'm going to get straight to the point, and I don't want you to be mad or freak out."

I tense. "What? Why would I get mad? And you say you don't want me to freak out, but now I'm freaking out," I rush, not even sure if I'm making any sense.

He places the bag on my lap. I peer down at it, then back to his face. "Did you buy me something?"

Shaking his head, he squirms in his seat—something I've never seen him do before. "Not exactly, just open it, please," he says quietly.

I reach into the bag and pull out a box—a familiar box.

My eyes shoot to his face and then back down to my shaking hands. I'm completely thrown.

I lift the lid and gasp—my watch. I don't even need to take it out to know it's mine.

My lips tremble—they actually fucking *quiver*—as I pull it from its padding. I slip it over my wrist and clip it in place, giving it a shake to adjust the weight.

"I don't understand." I keep my eyes on the strap and finger the links—afraid if I look at him, I'll cry.

"I found the receipt in your drawer the other week and put two and two together when you mentioned it was in the shop." He hooks his finger under my chin, lifting my face until his eyes lock with mine. "I'm sorry, but I couldn't stand the thought of you being without it, and I know if I offered to get it back, you'd refuse."

I bite my lip. He's right, I probably would have.

"Are you mad?"

Somehow, I find my voice and shake my head. "No, I'm kind of speechless, to be honest."

He smiles. "In a good or bad way?" he asks, all confidence missing.

"Good, I think." And it's the truth. I'm blown away. He *did this* for me. "I can't believe you would do this. I'll pay you back," I add as an afterthought.

Olly looks to the ceiling and then back to me. "I wouldn't have expected you'd have it any other way." He cups my cheek, and when his eyes pierce mine, my entire world tilts.

"I can't believe you'd do this for me," I say again, my voice raspy.

"Well, believe it," he replies, wiping the tears from under my eyes.

"Thank you." I lean in and kiss his lips softly before pulling back. "Honestly, Olly, this means more than you'll ever know."

He nods before his lips find mine, and I allow myself to get swept away in his kiss. I've only ever cried happy tears once before—when I had Molly.

I've seen women happy, with honest-to-good men, but I knew they were few and far between.

Unknowingly, I found a good man in Olly—who has me believing in the impossible.

Chapter Forty-Nine

Rachel

My stomach is full of nervous energy as I walk in the arena with Charlie and Sophie. He insisted I leave my car at theirs where Molly and Selene are having a sleepover. It took a bit of convincing from Sophie, but I agreed to let Charlie's dad watch Molly tonight since he was already sitting Selene. And this charity event means a lot to Olly, so I wanted to be here.

"There, over there," Charlie says, pointing out our table. The palm of his hand is on Sophie's back as we weave through all the people, his protective gaze finding me every couple seconds to make sure I'm still with them.

"You made it," Felicity squeals when we get to our table. She gives me a quick hug before moving onto Sophie.

"How's Betty?" Nate asks.

"As good as new," I reply. She's never run so well.

"Good, good. So, you here to support your man?" he asks. Felicity swats his shoulder and pushes him to sit down. I take a seat beside her.

I look at the caged ring a couple of feet away, the sound of laughter and excitement echoing through the hall. I see Henry among the swarming masses. When he approaches, I stand, and he greets me with a kiss on the cheek.

"You made it," he says, smiling. "Olly will be stoked." My face heats. "He's just finishing up with an interview, but he'd love to see you. Want to come round back?"

Interview? "Oh, no, I don't want to get in the way."

He loops his arm with mine. He's a big guy—solid. "I'll bring her back soon," he says to everyone and spins us around.

"What do you mean—the interview?"

He lets out a soft chuckle. "I take it he's been keeping low-key how big these events are?"

I'd bring us to a stop if I thought I was strong enough. Taking in all the people as we pass, I notice several paparazzi and wonder just how much he hasn't told me.

Coming to a large door, Henry knocks twice. A guy opens the door, and damn if he isn't bigger than Henry. He gives Henry one curt nod, then steps aside to let us in.

"Thank you, yeah, it's a cause close to my heart," Olly says to a smartly dressed woman in front of him.

"Well, best of luck for the fight tonight, and we hope you exceed last year's donations."

A flash goes off from the camera before she shakes Olly's hand, her crew in tow as they exit.

"Rachel?"

I don't say anything as I take him in. He looks cage fight ready, and I think my baby makers just somersaulted.

"We'll be just outside and give you both a minute," says Henry.

Olly approaches me, his brow furrowed. "You okay? I thought you couldn't make it."

"Molly is with Selene. Charlie's dad is babysitting."

He wraps his arms around me and leans in for a quick kiss. "Well, I'm glad you could make it."

I gaze up at him. "Olly, you never told me how much of a big deal this all was," I say.

He squeezes me a little tighter. "It's just a charity fight. But I'm glad you made it," he replies.

"Olly, this is so much more than *a little charity fight*, as you called it. There's paparazzi out there," I say, pointing over my shoulder.

He laughs. "Good. The more exposure we get, the better."

Taking me by my shoulders, he recedes a step to appraise me. "Damn, you look stunning," he says.

I couldn't hide my blush even if I wanted to. "And you look hot," I reply, trying to sound sultry, but my voice cracks, making me sound like an idiot instead.

"Oh, do I now?"

I nod. He keeps his eyes fixed on me as his lips meet mine. A moan escapes my throat. "Please tell me you're coming home with me tonight?" His tongue sweeps down my neck towards my cleavage.

"I might be able to," I reply, trying not to sound utterly enamoured by him.

"I'll make it worth your while," he says, eyes dark with desire. He presses into me.

"Oh, is that so?"

He's about to reply, but a knock at the door interrupts us.

Henry pokes his head around. "Ready to escort your lady back to her table."

Olly nods, giving me a warm smile. Leaning down to my ear, he whispers, "It's a promise. Don't you dare leave without me." He kisses just below my ear. It sends a shockwave of pleasure through my entire body.

He gives me a chaste kiss, then walks me to the door. I turn before crossing the threshold, going up on tip toes.

"Good luck," I say and kiss him one last time before I take Henry's arm and return to my table.

A few minutes later, Henry is at the table next to us, Meghan on the other side. She continues to try and gain his attention, but he's doing everything in his power to ignore her, and the more he does, the more it seems to rile her up.

He drags his chair over and positions himself next to me, not leaving much room between us, but I don't feel uncomfortable.

"You don't mind if I join you guys, do you?" he asks.

Everyone says it's okay. Charlie knows him from the gym, and everyone is just at ease by his presence as am I.

He begins to regale me with past charity fights and the line-up for tonight when a shadow falls over us. "Henry," says a timid voice.

His shoulders tense, and for a second, I think he may ignore her, but he turns his face towards her. "Meghan," he responds.

She looks gorgeous in her floor-length dress, the slit up to her thigh. Her legs go on for days.

"Can we talk?" she asks, quickly looking around at our table, everyone now quiet since her approach.

"Not now, no. I'm talking to Rachel," he replies.

I suddenly feel awful for her, and I'm about to say it's not a problem, but she replies, "Oh, okay, sorry, maybe later?"

He nods once and turns his attention back to me. But she's still standing there, squeezing the life out of her clutch.

"I love your dress; you look stunning," I say.

Her eyes go wide at my compliment, and she looks down at herself. "Oh, thank you. You look lovely, too," she says. "Well, I'll catch you later—enjoy the fights."

"You too," I say as she turns in the direction of the toilets.

Henry's gaze follows her until she disappears behind the door. His shoulders relax a fraction. "I would have given you a minute," I say.

He shakes his head. "No, honestly, it's fine. You were doing me a favour."

Someone takes the mic to introduce the first fighters and his attention focuses on the ring. Unable to get Meghan's crestfallen face out of my mind, I quickly excuse myself and head towards the ladies'.

Chapter Fifty

Rachel

I don't know why I felt the need to follow her. I hardly even know her. She seems to get on with Olly... Well, up until she accidentally knocked me out, that is, but he'll get over it. I did.

She resonates with me, a younger version of myself. She tries to hide her vulnerabilities, but I see them. I push open the door to find her facing the mirror, wiping her cheeks.

"Are you okay?" I ask, stepping up beside her.

She gazes at me from her reflection, shaking her head once. "Not really," she replies, sniffing.

I grab a tissue from the box on the sink and hand it to her.

"Thanks." She wipes under her eyes, trying to clear up the smudged eyeliner.

"If you need someone to talk to, I'm a good listener," I say.

Cautious eyes hold mine as she contemplates my words. "It's just Henry and me. It's complicated," she says, throwing her hands up into the air.

"When isn't it? Men are nothing but trouble," I reply.

This makes her smile. "He thinks I did something, and now he can barely look at me. We have history—me, him, his brother. But I'd never intentionally want to hurt either of them," she says, wiping her eyelashes and drying off the excess tears.

"Listen, I don't know what's happened, but I can assure you, he sees you. His eyes never left you once when you walked away from our table."

"Really?"

I nod and cup her shoulder. "Really," I reply. "I'm sure you'll figure it out."

"I hope so."

Just then, two women burst through the door, giggling, and when they spot Meghan, they poke their noses up in the air like their shit doesn't stink.

I look at Meghan, and she shrugs.

"She's got a nerve, showing her face here," says a voice from one of the cubicles.

"I don't know why she even bothers. He wouldn't go there and have sloppy seconds."

Meghan's cheeks heat, and I feel uncomfortable. They're talking about her. I cough loudly and call out, "You know, this isn't school. Isn't it about time you two bitches grew the fuck up?"

There's a gasp followed by a ruffle of fabric and the flush of the toilet.

The tallest of the two girls exits first and approaches the sinks, but I do not attempt to move out of her way. I square my shoulders. I've known girls like her my whole life—I used to be one.

Her friend joins her, all her bravado now gone. Maybe because they aren't used to people calling them out on their bullshit. I smirk.

"Do you mind?" asks the girl who seems to have the biggest chip on her shoulder.

"No, not particularly," I reply, crossing my arms and looking her up and down.

"Jess, leave it. Come on, I have hand sanitiser," says the other girl, digging through her bag, already angling towards the door.

Puffing out her chest, she spins on her heels, and they both scurry away.

"You didn't have to do that," says Meghan but her smile is grateful.

"No, but I wanted to. I can't stand bullies, and besides, I know what your right hook can do." I wink.

She cringes but smiles, knowing I don't mean it in a bad way.

"Well, thank you all the same. I've always struggled standing up for myself. I can speak up for others…but never myself." She straightens, giving herself a once over in the mirror.

"Do you have your phone?" She slides it from her clutch. "Let me give you my number. I think we could both use a friend." I quickly enter it and then text myself.

"I'd like that, thank you."

I hand it back to her. "I better go before my friends think I've done a runner."

"I should get back to my table, too."

We walk out together, and she smiles as we part ways. It isn't lost on me how Henry's line of sight found her and didn't waver until I sat down beside him. He's about to ask me something but shakes his head, and instead, we talk amongst ourselves, laughing at something Selene did with an entire box of crayons.

The next half hour goes by in a drama-filled blur—some skirmish with Meghan and another man I've never met had

Henry rushing around, masculine protective anger pulsing around him.

When everything settles back down, Henry takes his seat next to me again. "You ready to see your boy fight?"

"Yes. But he's no boy. He is all man," I say, trying to appear confident. But I'm apprehensive. It's one thing—having Olly teach me, seeing him training, the occasional sparring session. But this is something else. And truth be told, the thought of him getting hit makes my stomach roll.

My mouth goes dry when he is announced, followed by his opponent. I watch on, holding my breath, trying not to cover my face—wanting to both watch and look away at the same time.

I'm lost between rounds. It's only when the fight is called, and Olly is announced the winner that I let myself relax. The room fills with chaotic applause and wolf whistles.

"He's good, isn't he?" Henry says close to my ear.

It's hard to hear him over the crowd. "Yes, but I didn't like seeing him get hit."

"No, but he's trained, and he knows how to take a punch."

I clap along with our table, pleased he won…wondering how much he's hurting right now.

Chapter Fifty-One

Olly

Once I've showered and changed, I hurry out in search of Rachel. Approaching the table, I find Henry sitting considerably close to my girl. I almost falter until she looks up, her smile beaming as she stands before launching herself into my arms.

"Congratulations," she says, going on her toes to give me a quick kiss. I hold her firm, deepen it.

A throat clearing causes me to relinquish my hold on her and acknowledge everyone who's come out to support me and this cause. "Hey, guys! Thanks for coming—it means a lot," I say, greeting all around the table.

I'm met with cheers and fist bumps from all my friends, and it means the world.

"I need to go and thank some of the sponsors and see if I can find my parents," I say to Rachel once I've chatted with her table for about ten minutes. She kisses my cheek in understanding, then sits down.

"Come with me?" I ask, holding out my hand for her. She stares at it before taking it, allowing me to pull her to her feet. "We'll be back in a bit, don't lose our seat," I say to Henry who nods with a warm smile.

"Are you okay?" she whispers as we walk away from our friends.

I turn into her and cup her cheek. "I'm fine, never been better. It felt good having you here."

"It did?"

I trace her bottom lip with my thumb, desperate to take it between my teeth. My body's natural reaction to her strains in my trousers, and I will it to calm down. "Yes, so thank you."

I wrap my arm around her waist, stopping only to talk to the necessary people and to make brief introductions.

I finally spot my parents and some of my foster brothers and sisters in tow.

"Rachel." My mum throws her arms around her.

"Hi, Lily," she says, smiling at Mum's excessive need to hug.

My mum gushes over the bruise breaking out across my cheek, and I try to wave it off, but she makes a point of coddling me in front of Rachel. I let out a groan.

"We need to go back and get ready for the next fight," I say. It's only half true—no one would think badly of me if I didn't stay to watch all the fights, but I do want to support the other fighters.

Before I know it, the evening is already coming to an end.

"Okay, I need to go wrap this shindig up," I say to Rachel before releasing my hold on her hand.

Climbing into the middle of the ring, I take the mic and work my way through the speech I memorised—thanking everyone for attending, recognising the sponsors and all the charity donations.

The giant cheque is handed to me, the amount raised exceeding my expectations. Over five hundred thousand pounds. I couldn't be more humbled than I am at this moment.

Camera flashes go wild in every direction as I hold it up to show all the guests. The cheers are deafening.

This money will make such a difference. It will go towards the shelters and the walk-in centres for abused women and their children. I wonder—if this was a thing back when I was younger, if my mum would have taken the risk. Would she have left my dad?

As soon as we walk through my threshold, I kiss Rachel with vigour. My hands caress the material clinging to her like a second skin.

"Did I tell you how edible you look tonight?" I breathe into her mouth.

Her lips twitch into a smile. "Edible, hey?"

"Yep, and you remember what I said earlier about making it worth your while if you came home with me?"

She giggles, then pulls back, searching the hallway. "Where's Buster?"

"At my mum's. I haven't been here all day, and it wouldn't have been fair on him." I love that she asks after him. To most, he might have been a lost cause, but not to me.

Delicately, I begin to pepper her face with kisses. Sounds of satisfaction escape her as I move to her cheeks, her chin and eventually plant a kiss on her neck. She softens under my touch, and I swoop her into my arms bridal-style.

She gasps. "What are you doing?" she asks, eyes shining with want and lust.

"I'm going to make good on my promise," I say, before sucking her bottom lip between both of mine. A moan of pleasure escapes her mouth, and I know I need to take her to my bed right now so I can worship every inch of her body before sinking myself balls-deep inside her.

Rachel

A noise rouses me from my slumber. I turn to my side to find Olly's spot empty. I stretch, and my joints protest like they always do upon waking. Grabbing my phone, I check for the time—four in the morning. I reach for the nearest item of clothing and slip it over my head.

Going in search of Olly, I follow a metal *tapping* sound and come to a stop when I find him. The patio door is open, and he is sitting on one of the chairs—knitting.

I watch him intently, mesmerised by his ability to continually interlink loops of yarn without even looking. He's fixated on staring out into the expanse of the early morning sky.

Olly peers over his shoulder with a smile; I take it as an invitation to join him. He places the ball of wool and needles beside him. Holding out his hand, he pulls me into his lap. "You caught me," he says, his voice hoarse.

"So, knitting—is that a pastime of yours?" I ask, stroking the back of his neck with my fingertips.

"Something like that. When I was younger, and I suffered from night terrors, we tried all sorts of things. The only thing that seemed to help with my PTSD was knitting." He shrugs off his admission with a shy smile. I know he has nightmares, even now, but he never really talks about them.

"You seem quite the pro. Does that mean you knit for your family?"

His face now takes on a red hue. He clears his throat. "I've been known to knit a scarf or two, but now I knit hats for the premature baby unit at the local hospital."

I am momentarily stunned, blown away by this man. "You do?"

He nods, dipping his face as if to hide his embarrassment. He places his soft lips on my throat, causing my skin to break out in goosebumps. "Damn, Olly. I think I just fell in love with you."

As soon as the words pass my lips, dread settles in my stomach, and my body tenses with the urge to get off his lap, be anywhere but here. The air crackles with the echo of my words.

I know he thinks he's a monster who doesn't deserve to be loved—but if anyone does, it's him.

His hold on me tightens as he begins tickling me, playfully. I wriggle and laugh. It's his way of not making a big deal out of what slipped through my lips, and I've never been more grateful.

"Do you want to try and sleep for another hour?" I ask.

He smiles. "We can give it a go, but I'll be honest, you might be too much of a distraction."

"Oh, really? Is that a promise or a threat?"

His warm lips trace a path over my collar bone and along my throat until he sucks on the skin beneath my ear and my entire body is alive with excitement and need. "Oh, it's a promise." He picks me up, places me on my feet, and then takes my hand in his.

Wordless, he leads us back to his bedroom.

The euphoria of early morning sex with Olly is like nothing I've ever experienced before. It hits me at the same time as my building climax—this isn't just sex, it's making love. I have a moment of panic. Not because I don't have feelings for him—because I do.

As if sensing my inner struggle, Olly's fingers dig into my

hip a little tighter, pulling me closer to him as he whispers into my ear and eases my internal battle, "Let go."

So I do.

Chapter Fifty-Two

Rachel

I stretch out, Olly asleep beside me.

I love these rare moments when he's asleep, and I get to admire him. There wasn't an inch of my body he left unexplored last night, and I have never felt such satisfaction, such pleasure.

I know I can't keep ignoring how I feel about him. And the thought is almost too much to handle. I don't know when I relinquished myself to him. He makes me feel alive with every touch, every look.

I stare at the slight bruising on his cheek and lean over, kissing him softly.

His lips quirk up. "Morning," he groans, then quickly pulls me on top of him.

"Morning," I whisper as his hand traces my spine until he comes to a stop at my arse. If I don't force myself to get up and out of his bed, I might let him keep me here, doing unspeakable things to me all day long. "I need to get ready and go pick up Molly," I say, kissing his nose.

"Shower with me first, and then I'll come with you," he says.

I push myself up to try to get off him, but he holds fast. "Come on, then," I say, wriggling to get myself free.

"Why does it feel like you're trying to run away from me?" he asks, his voice still thick from sleep.

"Because if I stay like this for much longer, I know we won't make it to the shower any time soon," I say, his hard length rubbing against my stomach.

He wriggles his eyebrows, and in one swift movement he's hovering over me, caging me in between his forearms, and I wonder how he does it when planking is the worst thing ever invented.

"I can make it quick," he says with a wink. And I know he's only half-joking, but my body is already thrumming with excitement.

"You're insatiable," I reply, my voice husky.

"Oh, you have no idea," he says, dipping his head and moving down the length of my body until he's at the valley between my legs. I grip the sheets in anticipation.

Olly

Almost two hours later, we arrive at Sophie's. Rachel needed to go home and change. As much as I enjoy her wearing a pair of my joggers rolled at the waist with one of my hoodies, she said she wasn't picking up Molly in my clothes.

"How was she?" Rachel asks Sophie as soon as she opens the door.

"Hi, come in." She ushers us both inside.

"Sorry, hi," Rachel says, her cheeks heating.

"Don't be, she was fine," Sophie replies, smiling at me with a look I can't quite decipher.

"Hey, Rocky," Charlie says when we enter the kitchen. He gets up and greets Rachel with a kiss on her cheek.

And now I get it—why he was so hell-bent on me staying away from Sophie. Even though I have nothing to worry about with him, the only one I want kissing Rachel is me. This feeling is foreign to me, and I find myself pulling her back against my chest.

Charlie snickers, the fucker knowing what he did, and Sophie lets out an *awe* sound.

"Olly," sings Molly as she comes bounding around the kitchen counter. I grab her and tip her upside down, her giggles priceless.

"Oliver, if she's sick, you're clearing it up," says Sophie with a smile.

I quickly right Molly and pop her on my hip.

"Mummy, are we going to Olly's?" she asks.

"Hello to you, too, munchkin." Molly giggles and sticks out her arms for Rachel before giving her a big hug. "We have to go pick up Buster, and then we need to get home," she says.

Molly's bottom lip protrudes, not liking her mum's answer.

"Why don't you come out with us for Sunday lunch?" asks Sophie.

Rachel looks to me, and I nod. "I can see about collecting Buster later," I say, about to pull out my phone.

"You can bring him. There's an adventure playground there, too. What do you think, Molly?" Sophie asks.

Molly squeals excited at the prospect. "Can we, Mummy?"

"Only if it's okay with Olly," she says.

And I realise I'd do anything for this little girl if it meant seeing her smile. "Absolutely, sounds like a plan."

She claps her hands together and then lunges forward. I

manage to catch her, and Rachel covers her chest with her hand. "Careful, Molly."

"Give me the address. We'll go get Buster and then meet you both there," I say to Charlie and Sophie.

"Should we ask Felicity and Nate?" Rachel suggests.

"I like where this is going. Yeah, I'll give them a call," Sophie says.

I can't help but smile to myself at just how very domesticated this all is. Never would I have thought I'd be having joint family days out. My heart stutters at the thought. Rachel and Molly are like my family, and it's a feeling I can't quite decipher…one of joy and fear. I might not be the best guy for the job, but I'm too much of a selfish prick to walk away.

Chapter Fifty-Three

Rachel

Today was spontaneous and unexpected…priceless. Olly never complained once, not even throughout Molly's constant interruptions while we were trying to eat. He dropped Buster home before bringing us back to my flat.

He carries Molly, who is asleep in his arms, up to mine, and it does something to my insides. My heart beats a wild staccato at how wonderful he is with her, with us.

"Let me go get her settled," I say, holding my arms out to take her from him.

I manage to change her into a night-dress and slip her under the covers without rousing her too much. She drifts back into a deep sleep, and I close her door behind me.

I find Olly leaning against the kitchen counter, staring at his feet. He looks up when he sees me and smiles. I stop next to him and he pulls me into his chest.

We sway to the sound of music playing from the kitchen radio.

Contented, I sigh, moulding into his body. "Thank you for today," I say.

"You don't have to thank me, I had fun."

He continues to hold me in his arms for long moments until, reluctantly, he pulls away. "I need to get going," he says.

"I wish you didn't have to."

"Same, but I'll see you Monday?" His fingers caress my cheek, the simple touch warming me all over.

"Definitely." Now that this fight is out of the way, I know he will have a little bit more free time. It's hard juggling our relationship with our shifts and Molly, but we seem to be making it work for the most part.

I walk him to the door, and before he goes, I'm rewarded with a scorching kiss, my body tingling with want and anticipation. I let out a squeak of satisfaction, and he lifts me, wrapping my legs around his waist, my back against the wall.

"Let me take care of you before I leave?" he asks, grinding into me.

I think I nod because he walks us into the bathroom and closes the door behind us with his foot.

He sets me on my feet and spins me so my back is to his chest. Other than our hurried breathing, he doesn't speak as his fingers work their way to the top of my trousers before he slides them down and ushers me to step out of them.

I go to turn around, but he shakes his head, flicking his eyes to the mirror, his reflection full of desire. "Put your hands on the sink," he says.

I do, my heart racing. The sound of him pushing his jeans down has me peering over my shoulder. The cool air caresses my skin as he lifts my top. Goosebumps of anticipation break out as he strokes his length along my lower back.

"Lean forward," he says, his foot spreading my legs slightly.

He takes hold of my hip with one hand and moves until he's positioned himself between my thighs. His hand comes around, and he strokes over my clit as I lean my head back and close my eyes.

"Is this okay?" he asks.

I roll my head to the side until my lips catch his, and I breathe my answer into his mouth. "Yes."

"I'm going to take you from behind," he says, pushing my back away from his chest. My breath catches as a hot, raw need flows through my body at the sound of his commanding voice. "Keep watching me," he says, looking at our reflection in the mirror.

I'm completely exposed to him at this moment. He's in control; I'm at his mercy. All my senses are heightened. The anticipation of knowing he is about to enter me has my pulse raising, my mouth watering. His calloused hands roam over my hips, his fingers digging into my skin.

His eyes hold me captive in the mirror, the blue fierce and intense as he continues to stare at me, his swollen erection pressing closer to my entrance. I inhale his scent, a heady mix of sandalwood and the musk of his arousal.

Heat consumes me when he rolls his hips and thrusts inside. I stifle my groan, biting my lip not to scream out, forcing myself to keep eye contact with him through the mirror.

I clamp around him as he fills me. His soft grunts as he pounds into me, his eyes focused on mine—it's too much. Does he know what he does to me? How he's infiltrated my heart and soul?

My orgasm climbs with every thrust of his hips, and I know it's there, on the precipice.

"Keep watching me," he demands, and with those three words, my climax ricochets through me, tears springing to my eyes. His release follows, hard and fast. He grunts and strains from the force of his own orgasm.

He wraps me in his arms and pulls me into his chest, kissing my neck.

"Rachel, you've ruined me," he says, his hold on me tightening.

"Aha." It's the only response I can articulate at present. He chuckles, and it vibrates through me.

"Thank you," he says before gently sliding out of me and reaching for a flannel. He holds it under the tap until the water is warm, then wrings it out before cleaning me between my legs.

I stop him and turn, taking it from him to wipe his still semi-hard length. He tugs up his jeans and buttons them while I slip on the dressing gown I keep on the back of the door.

"Okay, this time I'm leaving." His gaze is so intense, I can't look away. He opens the bathroom door before either of us cracks and we carry on where we left off.

"Make sure you lock up," he says once he steps out into the hallway.

"I will. Let me know when you get home."

He nods and waves me back inside before walking away.

Those three little words sit heavy on my tongue, trying to break free. I'm desperate to say them out loud, but I won't for fear of rejection. When we are together, I have no doubts at all—he completes me in a way I never could have imagined, but knowing he also has the power to destroy me is too much.

I pull out my duvet and collapse on the sofa, willing my tears away. What am I going to do? I need to tell him how I feel, then if he wants to end this, I can at least be ready for the fallout.

Chapter Fifty-Four

Olly

Rachel has been jittery and short with me for the past few days. As much as I'm trying to be understanding, it's hard when she's taking shit out on me. Molly is with her dad, and yet, she's more wound up than ever.

"What's going on?" I blurt out.

She sinks onto the sofa, unable to meet my eye. "It's Marcus."

Always fucking Marcus. Why doesn't he fuck off to Dubai already? "What about him?" I don't want to know, but at the same time, what choice do I have? Being with her means accepting that he's part of their lives.

"He wants me and Molly to go to Dubai with him."

I already know this.

But she's not finished—there's more. "He keeps asking me to marry him."

My heart thunders in my ears. "What the fuck?" She flinches from the boom of my voice. "Shit, sorry."

She shakes her head. "Don't be. Those were my sentiments exactly."

"Why now? What does he think he'll achieve?"

She shrugs. "I don't know, but he keeps threatening to fight for custody of Molly."

"You have got to be *kidding me.*"

"No, and the thing is, with his money and his connections…I'm worried he'll win."

I shake my head. "No fucking way."

"Olly, I can't put Molly through a custody battle."

I'm listening to what she's saying, but I also hear what she's not. "It's because we're together, isn't it?"

Her eyes fill with tears, and she nods.

I stand and pace the room, trying to sort this all out in my head. "So, what? You marry him, move to Dubai, and play happy family?"

She's in front of me, shaking her head. "What, no!"

"You said you couldn't put Molly through a custody battle. And this is the same guy, I might add, who left drugs in your fucking bathroom."

Her body is tense, her eyes wide. "Don't you think I don't know that, Olly? But he feels threatened, you don't understand."

I clench my fists. "And what exactly don't I understand? Please fucking enlighten me."

She takes a step back, and I feel like a prick—I know this isn't her fault but it's not easy to hear. I pull my fingers roughly through my hair.

"This is why I didn't want to tell you. I hoped he'd come to his senses, see past his own fucking ego. It was eating me up inside, keeping it from you." Her tears fall freely, and it guts me. I reach out for her, wanting to hold her, but drop my arms. This is my fault. I'm selfish for wanting her the way I do.

"I can't do this," I say, the words thundering in my ears.

"Do what?" she asks her voice almost shrill.

"See you hurting like this. Fucking hell, Rachel, I'd sacrifice never seeing you again if it meant you not suffering."

I don't want to be part of the reason she's sad or torn. She shouldn't have to make a choice or sacrifice her happiness. But Molly is her priority, and it's one of the reasons I've fallen irrevocably for her. I take a physical step back. My chest is tight, the air in here suffocating.

"What are you saying?" she asks, trying to control her breathing.

"I don't know. I need to go."

"Olly, please don't leave. Don't let him come between us," she says on a plea.

She reaches out for my hand, hers shaking, and I cave. She pulls me gently towards her, and I wrap her in my arms. Her breathing against my chest calms as I stroke her silky-smooth hair. "Please stay," she whispers.

I pull back, and she stares up at me, her eyes heavy with worry. "He's always going to be part of my life—he's Molly's dad."

She's right, of course she is, and I'm jealous of that fact. "I know, but it worries me, and I don't trust him or his intentions."

Her eyes soften. "Then trust me." Her eyes plead for me to listen.

"I do." I stroke my hands up and down her arms.

"Then you'll stay?"

I lean down. "Of course," I reply before kissing her tenderly.

Tonight, I want to forget about Marcus and his manipulative games. I want to hold her secure in my arms and never let go.

Chapter Fifty-Five

Rachel

I've been even more unsettled ever since I told Olly about Marcus's proposals. Olly was quick to suggest I make it work with Marcus. Does he not feel this as strongly as I do? I still haven't told him how I feel…

The thought of losing him because of Marcus and his selfish antics crushes down on my chest with force. It becomes a physical effort to breathe.

Marcus was meant to be here over an hour ago to pick up Molly. Sophie had her over for a play date with Selene this afternoon, and now she's here at the deli, colouring while we wait for her dad.

I hear the bell ring and look up, ready to give him hell, but it's Olly.

His smile is infectious, and before I can stop myself, I round the counter, colliding with him, wrapping my arms around his waist.

He kisses the top of my head. "You okay?" he asks. I turn

my head in the direction of Molly. "Hey kid," he calls out, then she bounds over to him.

He picks her up. She kisses him on the cheek. I never tell her to kiss or cuddle someone—I want her to feel comfortable—and she always has been with him. "Daddy's late again," she says, and I hate how she's not even deluded by the fact.

"I'm sure he'll be here soon. How about you show me what you're colouring while your mum makes me a nice cup of coffee," he says, giving me a wink.

I mouth the words, *thank you*, as he takes Molly back over to her table.

Coffee and a slice of lemon drizzle cake in hand, I take them over and place them in front of him. "See kid? She's a keeper," he says to Molly.

"What's a keeper?" she asks, and I can't hide my chuckle. Always with the questions.

"It's where I want to keep her and never let her go," he replies, his gaze fixated on me.

"Oliver," Sophie says, coming out from the kitchen.

"Well hello, beautiful," he says with a playful wink.

I shake my head, laughing as the door chimes.

Marcus, *finally*.

He pulls off his glasses as I approach him. The smell of booze hits me first, a sure sign he's either drunk or hungover, and then his bloodshot eyes do.

"Outside, Marcus, *now*," I say, shoving him in the direction of the door. "Olly, I'll be right back. Soph, can you watch her?"

"Of course," she says, her hand going to Molly's shoulder to stop her from coming over. Olly stands, but I shake my head.

Outside, Marcus's speech is slurred. "Desperate to get me alone, were you?" He wobbles, and I grab his arm, pulling him across the road and away from the shop window.

"What the fuck, Marcus?"

He leans in, and I turn my face away from the stench of alcohol—it's almost flammable.

"I miss you," he says in a whiny voice. It's the one I used to cave to when he'd cheat on me and then come running back with his tail between his legs.

I place my palm on his chest to stop him from coming closer and shake my head. "Just stop this, Marcus. There is no *us*. Did you drive here?" I ask, incredulously looking for his car.

He nods just once but winces when he sees my expression.

Hell no. If Marcus can't get his vices under control for the sake of our daughter, then I don't want him around her, not when he's like this.

"I came to pick up Molly," he slurs.

It takes everything in me not to punch him in the face. "You can see her when you've sobered up."

"I'm not drunk," he retorts.

"Okay, then what are you? Because you're drunk or using. For fuck's sake, Marcus, you drove intoxicated to collect our daughter. What is wrong with you?" I whisper-shout as a pedestrian shakes their head, giving us a wide birth.

He looks at me, but he can't focus, and part of me wonders why I'm even trying to have this conversation when he's like this. I reach into his back pocket until I feel his keys and pull them free. "I knew you wanted me," he says.

I wave the keys in his face. "No. I wanted these. I'm going to call you a cab, so you can go home and sleep this off. There is no way I want Molly around you like this." Or anyone else, for that matter.

Something in my peripheral catches my attention, and I turn my head.

My whole body tenses.

Her head bobs up and down as she runs towards us—Molly. She's on the other side of the street, and she's waving to Marcus, calling out, "Daddy."

She steps off the curb and into the road.

My world implodes as I rush towards her.

"NO!" I scream.

My legs are as heavy as cement blocks, not moving quick enough as I try to get to her.

A horn blares—once, twice. The screeching of rubber tyres skids across the tarmac.

She turns to the oncoming car and freezes in place.

I can't breathe. I pump my arms and legs.

I'm not going to get to her in time. "Molly!"

My world implodes.

Impact—bones, crushing against metal. A windscreen cracks and shatters. There is a brief moment of silence, my ears go numb, and then I'm screaming.

Chapter Fifty-Six

Olly

It was clear as day. He arrived out of his face. I see enough people intoxicated to know the signs. The guy needs help—Molly and Rachel don't deserve this. And what happens when she gets older? I have to count back from ten to keep myself from following them.

"Your mummy just needs to talk to your daddy real quick," Sophie says to Molly, who keeps peering out the window.

"Why?"

"Nothing for you to worry about, sweetie. How about a cupcake?" Sophie asks, trying to distract her.

It does the trick; Molly smiles. "Can I have the chocolate, please?"

"Yes, of course." Sophie goes behind the counter, and I walk over to the window to see that they're now across the road.

Rachel has her hand pressed against his chest. She reaches behind him, and then dangles some keys in front of his face.

"Molly," Sophie says, just as the bell chimes and Molly darts out the door.

In the time it takes me to pull it open and follow her, she's already stepping down from the curb and into the road.

I hear Rachel's frantic scream, see the car coming.

I focus solely on Molly, rushing after her and into the road.

I grab her into my arms, probably too harshly, and angle her away from the oncoming car. It cracks against my legs, lifting me off the ground and slamming me into the windscreen. And then we're in the air. Before I can think, I'm falling towards the ground.

I collide with the unforgiving surface at my shoulder. It scrapes and burns as I roll onto my back.

All the air is forced from my lungs as my head ricochets into the ground. My teeth clamp together with such force, I bite the inside of my mouth or my tongue. The taste of blood floods my mouth, my neck jars awkwardly.

I can't hear anything over the sound of my pulse in my ears at first, and then it's replaced by screams and people shouting.

Molly clings to my shirt.

I remember the night of the fire. I can still smell the scorching flames and burnt flesh as I carried Lottie from the house. I wouldn't let her go. I thought she was dead. The paramedic had to pry her from my arms so they could get me treatment.

"It's okay, son. She's crying, let us help you."

"But she's dead," I said.

"No, son, she's crying, she's alive."

I cradle Molly's head beneath my bloody hands. Her sobs vibrate through my chest, and I know she's alive.

Thank God.

I try to breathe, to comfort her, but my limbs are weighted and no longer my own. I can't find my voice to ease her distress.

Dark spots begin to overtake my vision.

Clouds loom and swirl overhead with anger.

But then they're replaced with eyes I recognise—clouded with fear. *Rachel*.

All too soon, she disappears, and darkness follows. She's frantic—I can hear her calling out mine and Molly's name. I want to tell her Molly is okay, but I can't—I'm suffocated by ice-cold darkness.

Rachel

Struggling to breathe through the panic engulfing me, I throw myself to the cold hard ground.

Olly has Molly cradled to his chest. His eyes are unfocused. Her small sobs let me know she's alive.

"Olly?" His eyes roll into the back of his head, his movements still.

Sophie is crouched beside me, phone to her ear. But I can't focus on her, on anyone else. My attention is on my baby and the man who just put himself between her and an oncoming car. I have to swallow down the nausea.

"Molly," I croak, trying not to let my emotions overpower me.

"Mummy," she sniffs into Olly's shirt, his hands stained with blood.

"Come here, baby." I hold out my trembling hands, and she shifts and raises her head, her eyes scrolling over Olly's face.

"Olly, can you hear me?" Sophie asks, her voice trembling when her eyes meet mine.

"Baby, come here please. We need to help Olly, okay?"

She nods and moves away from him, into my open arms.

Gently, I begin tracing her arms, face, head, all the way to her toes. I ask if anything hurts, but she shakes her head.

"I'm sorry," she hiccups. "I didn't stop and look," she says, her lips trembling as tears cascade over her plump little cheeks. I kiss her face, unable to keep my own at bay.

"Paramedics are on their way," Sophie says, her words a distant echo.

I press Molly to my body, her back now to Olly, who is lying motionless on the street. "Is he—" I struggle to find words.

"He's breathing," replies Sophie, pulling me into her side.

I notice the driver of the car sitting on the curb, his head between his legs. I look over my shoulder to see cars backing up down the street.

"Let me run in and get the first aid kit." Sophie dashes back to the shop.

I see Marcus vomiting into the gutter. He straightens, wiping his mouth with the back of his hand before coming over, his face drained of colour. "I'm so sorry, Rach. I'm so fucking sorry." He grips his hair in one hand. His entire body vibrates with shock. "Is she okay—is our baby okay?" he asks, his voice strained, laced with worry and concern I've never heard from him before.

I kiss her hair and breathe her in deep. "I think so. Shaken, maybe a few grazes, and shocked," I reply.

He takes my hand in his and places the other on the small of Molly's back as she clings to me. But I pull my hand from his and into Olly's—it's cold, so cold.

Thankfully, Sophie returns with a foil blanket and covers him.

"I don't want to move him," she says. "Just in case."

I nod.

Molly begins to shiver, and without a word, Marcus strips off his jacket and wraps it over her and me.

Sirens are heard in the distance, a wail of noise into the midst of silent chaos.

This is all my fault.

I bite the inside of my mouth, drawing blood.

I can't lose him—not when we've only just found one another.

Chapter Fifty-Seven

Olly

Disorientated, unfamiliar voices echo around me. It takes a moment for my mind to catch up with me. I attempt to sit up in a rush, but I can't move. I open my eyes and a stranger's face appears in my line of vision. I reach up to my throat.

"It's okay, it's just a neck brace. You're in an ambulance," says the paramedic.

My body is strapped into a gurney. "Molly?"

"It's okay, your little girl is fine."

Mine.

The paramedic continues to ask me questions until we arrive at the hospital, and I'm rushed through to triage.

Everything is foggy, and I keep forgetting where I am when my mum comes crashing through the curtain, terror written all over her face.

"Mum, I'm fine," I say, as she rushes towards me. I try to hold back a groan.

"No, you're in pain. Are they giving you anything?"

My dad pulls her into him. "Lily, let him speak." But worry is etched across his face, too.

"I can't remember, but it's getting worse, the pain. As long as Molly is okay."

She covers her mouth with her hand, eyes filled with tears. "Rachel told us you saved her from an oncoming car. You both could've been killed."

I wince, coming over nauseous. "I couldn't do nothing," I reply. The image of her frozen in the middle of the road will forever haunt me.

"Of course, not."

I didn't know if I'd get to her, but I wouldn't have been able to live with myself if I hadn't. The pain under my ribcage increases, and I let out a hiss between my clenched teeth.

"I'm getting someone." She pushes past my dad and flies out through the curtain. When she returns, a nurse follows close behind her.

He comes around to the other side of the bed.

"Do you have localised pain?" he asks.

I nod. "Left side, under my ribcage."

"Okay, let me go get the doctor."

He rushes out, and when he returns with a doctor in tow, I'm asked more questions, but the pain increases and concentrating on them is becoming increasingly difficult.

"You might have some damage to your spleen."

I hear my mum crying. I want to assure her I'll be fine, but everything else happens too quickly, and I'm being prepped for emergency surgery.

The room is dim when I wake. It's unfamiliar and smells of cleaning products, and it takes me a moment to take note of where I am—the hospital, hooked up to an intravenous drip.

I'm parched. I see the jug of water to my side and attempt to reach for it.

"Olly?" Rachel rushes in and fills the cup with water. "Careful," she says, holding it to my lips.

I take a small sip and lean back against the pillow. I stare at her face, eyes swollen and red. "Are you okay?" I ask, lifting my hand towards her.

She bursts out crying. "You just had surgery and saved my daughter's life, and you're asking if *I'm* okay?" Her voice catches, her sobs are unbearable. Tears cascade down her cheeks.

I take her hand in mine and squeeze. "Is she really okay?" I need to hear it from her.

She wipes her face with her sleeve and takes a deep breath. "She's fine, apart from a couple of scratches and a little shock. She's perfect. Thanks to you."

At her words, I allow myself to relax.

"This is all my fault," she says. A fresh wave of tears assaults her, and the ache in my chest is too much.

"Come here." I tug her hand. She leans closer. "Accidents happen; it's not your fault. I'll be fine." She is about to argue, but I don't give her a chance. "I promise, I'm fine. Nothing a little TLC won't cure," I say with a wink.

A cute snort leaves her lips, and she smiles. "I can do house visits," she says with a smirk. "But right now, I need to get Molly home. I couldn't leave until I knew you were okay and out of surgery."

There's a tap on the door, and my mum enters, holding a sleeping Molly in her arms. My chest tightens.

"Olly, don't you ever scare us like that again," she whisper-shouts.

Rachel leans down and gives me a chaste kiss before standing and holding out her arms for Molly. "Thank you, Lily."

I watch them—my girlfriend with my mum—it's like they've known each other for years.

"You'll message me, and let me know when he's being discharged?" Rachel asks.

"Of course. Go on, get this little angel to bed."

They know I'm right here and perfectly able to tell her myself, *right?* "Wait, hold on, how are you getting home?" I ask.

My mum rolls her eyes. "Your dad is taking her."

I've never been so grateful to have hit the jackpot with my foster parents. Their compassion knows no bounds.

"Thank you again, Olly, I owe you everything," Rachel says.

"Go get Molly home," I say and smile as she leaves me alone with my mum.

"Olly, are you okay?"

I let out a dry laugh. "Aching and sore. Was it my spleen?"

She takes the seat Rachel vacated and holds my hand in hers. "Yes, you had a partial splenectomy. But the doctors said you were fortunate, considering…"

"Do you know how long I have to stay?"

She gives me a stern look. "When the doctors give you the okay. They'll be doing their rounds shortly. Visitation finished hours ago, but they said we could wait until you were out of surgery."

I sigh and squeeze her hand. "You should have gone home."

She cups my cheek. "Don't be ridiculous. I know how much you hate hospitals."

She stays until a stern ward nurse politely asks her to leave, and it's not long before I drift in and out of sleep.

Rachel

I couldn't leave the hospital until I knew Olly was okay. Joshua carries Molly up to my flat. When I get to my front door, Marcus is sitting there, waiting. He jumps to his feet.

"This is Joshua, Olly's dad. Joshua this is Marcus."

Joshua nods, and Marcus reaches out for Molly, taking her in his arms as I unlock the door and push it open. Without a word, Marcus walks in and takes Molly to her room.

I cross my arms over my chest and turn back to Joshua. "Thank you again. Lily will let me know if anything changes, won't she?"

He nods and leans in, kissing my cheek before leaving.

I close the door and go straight to Molly's bedroom. Marcus is on his knees, staring at her, his fingers stroking the hair away from her face.

He hears me approach and peers over his shoulder. "Rachel, I'm so fucking sorry," his words catch, and a lump lodges in my throat.

My nose tickles, on the verge of tears. "I know," I croak out. And I do know, regardless of his faults and his indiscretions, he does love her.

I sit cross-legged next to him, stroking the back of her hand. We both watch her chest rise and fall, whistles of soft, contented snores escaping her mouth.

I'm unsure how long we've been watching her when he turns his head towards me. "I'm getting myself some help. I don't want to be this person anymore," he whispers. I nod, because this version of him isn't who he is, and I want more for our daughter. "How is he?"

I let out a sigh. "He's been better. He had to have surgery—they removed part of his spleen." The thought makes me sick to my stomach.

"How am I meant to compete with that?" he says, half-serious.

"There is never a competition where Molly is involved," I

reply, and it's true—she is the most important person in my life.

He nods. "And you?" His eyes search my face.

"We'll always have a bond, Marcus. We created her," I say, angling my head towards Molly. "But we didn't work as a couple, and I want to be a better example for her."

His face drops. He looks wounded, but he knows I'm right. "I'm going to go see him when he's well enough. Thank him in person." I eye him sceptically. I don't doubt he's genuine. However, he is still Marcus. He holds up his hands. "I'll be a saint, I swear," he says, crossing his fingers over his heart.

"You better. That man is the reason our daughter is safe and well in her bed."

"I know." His fingers seek out mine, and he squeezes it once before I pull my hand away.

"Can I come by in the morning? I'll bring her breakfast."

"Yes, of course." I'm a little surprised he didn't ask to stay, not that I would have allowed it. I have to draw boundaries where he's concerned.

Leaning over Molly, he kisses her forehead before I see him to the door.

I lock up once he's gone, grab myself a glass of water, and then go back to Molly. Kicking my shoes off, I manage to climb in her tiny bed beside her. I don't care if it's cramped. Tonight, I need to hold my baby girl and know she's safe in my arms.

Olly saved her, and in doing so, he saved me in every other way humanly possible. I could have lost them both today. I let my tears fall silently.

I know I need to tell Olly how I feel, but after what happened, I don't want him being with me out of some hero complex. He helps people; he takes something that's shit and turns it into something beautiful. I don't want him to feel obligated, to do that with me.

Chapter Fifty-Eight

Olly

I've been going out of my mind in this hospital room. I know I'd heal just as quickly at home. It's only been two days, but it feels like weeks.

There's a knock on the door, and in walks Marcus. He holds up his palms as he comes into the room. "I just wanted to stop by," he says, hovering by the door.

I nod, and he walks in until he's beside my bed.

"Firstly, I can't thank you enough for what you did for Molly-Mae." He grips the railing of the bed. "It's made me realise now more than ever how much I don't deserve her or Rachel. But I do love them."

It's not lost on me how he says *them*, and honestly, I can't blame him because I'm right there with him. "They're both great, and I'd do it again in a heartbeat."

"I know, and it's part of the reason why I'm here."

Here we go. "Okay."

He looks to the chair. "Do you mind if I sit?"

"Have at it," I reply, trying not to let my irritation show.

"Listen, it's true—I haven't been the best father or role model. But I'm getting help, and I want a chance to remedy my behaviour."

I clear my throat. "And by remedy it, you mean, you're serious about being a family?" I don't see the point of sugar-coating the truth. As much as I can't stand him, I kind of respect the fact he's shown up here.

"Honestly, I can't say I won't stop trying. Rach and I have a history. But I'm also not blind. I see the way she is with you."

"So, what you're saying is, you're not giving up without a fight."

"I'm saying, I will respect her decision and won't stand in your way if she chooses you. But I will give it my best shot."

"You had ample opportunities. You fucked up, man. Your priority should have always been her and Molly. Just do right by Molly."

He gets to his feet and holds out his hand. I shake it once before he turns and leaves. Deep down, I wonder if he will pursue Rachel again… Maybe if he's getting the help, she'll consider what he's offering.

The more I sit here and stew over it, the more anxious I become. I don't do well in this kind of quiet. It messes with my head.

Boredom must have won out because when I open my eyes, a fresh scent washes over me, and I know it's her.

"Hi," she whispers, reaching out and stroking my face.

She looks exhausted. "Is everything okay? Is Molly all right?"

"She's been clingy. I'm not surprised after everything, but otherwise, she's fine. Missing you. How are you feeling?"

I let out an exaggerated sigh. "Ready to go home."

"Not until they give you the all-clear."

For some strange reason, this feels awkward. I shift uncomfortably and flinch. She springs to her feet. "Do you need a nurse? Should I call someone?"

I squeeze her hand. "I'm fine. Honestly, I've been worse." And it's true. The pain from the burns I received from the fire was the worst I've ever felt, and although I probably couldn't put it into words, I know this is slight in comparison.

"I feel so guilty," she says, her eyes glassy.

How many times do we have to go over this? "Don't. Please stop being ridiculous, come here." I tug on her hand, and she moves closer. I've never wanted to hold her more than I do right now.

"I've been selfish thinking I could have you."

I can't help but laugh. "And how is it selfish? You deserve to have someone who'll stand beside you, Rachel."

She wipes at her cheeks, angrily. "Because of me, you could have died, and Molly, could've—" She doesn't finish her sentence.

I pull her close and try to hug her awkwardly. "Will you get on this damn bed so I can hold you?"

Sniffing back her tears, she doesn't fight me, managing to lay on her side, facing me. "It's okay, everything's okay," I repeat, caressing her cheek.

When her breathing calms, and her tears subside, I pull her hand to my lips and kiss her knuckles. "You okay now?"

"Sorry, you're the one in hospital, and I lost it."

"You're allowed to be upset, Rachel."

She locks eyes with mine. "So, you don't hate me?"

I grunt out a response. "Not possible." Her warm smile will be the death of me. "I had a visitor earlier," I say, stroking her hair.

She fidgets and sits up a little. "Marcus?"

"Yeah. Did you know he was going to come by?"

"He mentioned he might."

I'm about to ask her about it when we're interrupted by a nurse. Rachel almost falls off the bed in her haste to sit in the chair, her cheeks rosy with embarrassment. I can't hide my laugh but instantly regret it as a wave of pain shoots through me.

The nurse tuts. Her eyes, however, are kind as she checks my stats before leaving us alone.

"You should've seen your face. It was priceless."

She gently swats my arm. "Oliver."

It's nice to see her smile again, even if its lined with exhaustion. I don't let her stay long. I'd rather she were with Molly, anyway. I also know I need to be honest with her about my past, about the mistakes I've made, and how I can never make them right. It's why I fear deep down that I'm no better than my biological father—a monster.

Chapter Fifty-Nine

Olly

I was glad I only had to stay in the hospital for less than a week. I would've gone stir crazy if it had been any longer. Thankfully, Henry agreed to take over my classes for the next six weeks. I'm not even allowed to drive or take a bath yet, thanks to the laparoscopic splenectomy. But I *will* have a shower as soon as I get home.

My dad insisted on picking me up. After he pulls up outside my house, he grips my shoulder. "I'll let you get some rest. I'll bring your mum by tomorrow."

I nod and say goodbye. I'm halfway up the path when Buster comes bounding out, tail spinning like crazy.

"Sit." He does as he's told, and I carefully kneel to give him a quick stroke. "Missed you, boy."

I grunt when I stand and come face-to-face with Rachel. "He's missed you, too."

"I thought you'd be at work," I say with a warm smile.

She shrugs. "I asked for the day off. Thought I'd help you

out with that little TLC you were going on about," she says with a wink.

I walk towards her. "Does it involve a hello kiss?"

Laughing, she goes up on her tiptoes and kisses me softly, but it's not long enough. "I hope you don't mind me being here. Your mum gave me her spare key."

I take her hand in mine. "No, it's fine. Besides, she seems a little smitten with you."

She rolls her eyes and leads me into the front room. On the table is a plate filled with cookies and a handmade card. She hands it to me—it's from Molly.

"I love it."

Rachel takes it and rests it on the centre of the fireplace. "Sit down," she says.

I don't argue, coming home has already taken it out of me. "Okay, but I'm desperate for a shower," I say.

"Bed baths not your thing?"

I shake my head. "Wouldn't know, didn't have one. Why? Are you offering?" And even though the thought of her hands on me is something I love, I know I'm not good for much right now.

"I might wash your back, if you're lucky. But first, do you want anything to eat or drink?"

"You don't have to wait on me," I say, reaching out for her.

"I want to. Let me help you, Olly."

"Let me go shower first. I need to rid myself of this hospital stench."

She leads me upstairs, where she gets me towels and clean clothes. I don't spend long in there. I already feel knackered.

Dressed, I head back downstairs, the smell of food leading the way.

"It's just a pasta bake," she says, filling two bowls when I join her in the kitchen.

"Smells like heaven."

We eat, but she's subdued. She gets this line in-between her eyes—I've seen it at the gym—when she's overthinking something. "Talk to me, Rachel. What is it? I can tell something is on your mind."

She puts her fork down. Her eyes meet mine. "I worry maybe Marcus was right about you and me."

I put my fork down. "What about us?"

"You're a bachelor, Olly. You shouldn't have to worry about a single mum and her daughter, let alone have to save her life because I can't parent for shit. It's selfish of me."

Pushing my bowl away, no longer hungry, I cross my arms. Since when am I a bachelor? I thought we were together. "You're shitting me, right?" *Fucking Marcus.*

"It's a lot of commitment for anyone. I'm a parent. It's not fair of me to ask it of you," she says, biting her lip.

I can't believe she's playing the single mum card. What the fuck? "You haven't asked me for a damn thing. You're too proud," I snap out.

Now she's the one crossing her arms. "What's that supposed to mean?"

I reach for the pepper and play with the pot. "Come on, Rachel, I've seen you struggling. But you'd rather sell the shirt off your own back than ask for help. You pawned your watch, for Christ's sake."

She stands up, her nostrils flaring. "It's none of your damn business."

I follow suit and round the table until we're toe-to-toe. "Marcus is playing you, Rachel. Manipulating you. And why? Because you found someone else. I've never once had a problem with you being a single mum. And yet, he's the one who should help raise your daughter. You wouldn't have to struggle if he paid his fair share."

"I know what he's like, Oliver. I've known him my whole life. No matter what you think of him, he's Molly's dad—that won't ever change."

I step away from her, putting space between us. "Don't I know it. Fuck it, maybe the two of you should try and make it work. Go to Dubai. Be a family."

She lets out a gasp. "Are you being serious right now?"

I nod and turn my back towards her. "I think I need to go and have a lay down." I hear her moving the bowls and turn to her. "Leave them. I can get those later," I say.

She's angry and hurt. "Are you asking me to leave, Olly?"

I shrug. I don't know what I want or how this even escalated. But she is so damn quick to defend Marcus—after everything. And I am a fucking hypocrite. I'm not a perfect man. If she knew what I did, what I'm capable of, would she stand by me as loyally as she does him? "Yeah, I think I am," I reply finally, my mouth dry.

"Okay, fine."

She walks past me. My heart beats all wrong, and I feel sick. I grab her hand just before she leaves the kitchen. Her eyes are glassy. "I'm just tired, it's been a long week," I say, but I know it's too late, the damage is done.

"Get some sleep, Olly." She reaches up and kisses the corner of my mouth.

I want to take it all back and ask her to stay, but I don't. I stand here like the monster I am and let her walk away.

Chapter Sixty

Olly

I should have at least texted her after the way we left things yesterday, but I think maybe this is for the best in the long run. I have to switch my phone off, the urge to get over myself and contact her is borderline obsessive, but I won't—I can't.

After making myself something to eat, I down my medication and let Buster out before going back to bed. At least when I'm asleep, I can pretend my life isn't a shit storm. But my nightmares are worse than ever when I wake.

I don't get away with blocking out the world for long when my mum shows up. "Oliver?"

I groan and then call out, "up here."

She pulls the curtains, and the room fills with too much light. I cover my eyes with my arm. "Olly, I've been worried. You haven't answered your phone. Rachel came by," she says.

I peek out from my arm. "What?"

"She dropped off your key."

I swallow down my shame and shift so I'm sitting up.

"What happened? She wouldn't say, but I know something was wrong."

Buster comes into the room, wagging his tail, and sits at my mum's feet expectantly. "Have you fed him?" she asks.

"Of course, I have, but he's always hungry."

She nods and takes my hand in hers. "Let me make you something to eat, and you can tell me what's going on."

I don't have a chance to argue because she's already on her way out of my room to head back downstairs. I force myself out of bed and take a quick shower before joining her in the kitchen.

"Well?" she asks and points to one of my breakfast stools.

I take a seat and shrug.

"Oliver?"

"We disagreed, and I told her to leave," I grumble.

"What?" Her back is to me as she finishes making the sandwiches, and I don't need to see her face to hear the disappointment in her voice.

"It's complicated."

She slides me over a plate and a bottle of water before joining me. "I think I can keep up."

"Fine, I may have suggested she work things out with Marcus." I take a bite of my sandwich, hoping it saves me from her barrage of questions.

"You silly man. I saw how upset she was over you being in surgery. She's in love with you. Why would you do something so stupid?"

I push my plate away and fold my arms over the table. "Do you want to know the truth?" It's a stupid question, of course, she does, this woman—my saviour has never suffered fools gladly. "I'm no better than Marcus. I sit there on my high horse, telling her how he should be a better father, and yet, I'm no better than he is. I'm worse."

Her eyes soften, and I think I prefer it when she's angry with me. "And why do you believe you are worse?"

I pick off a piece of crust from my sandwich and toss it in the air for Buster to catch. "Because I'm a monster."

She shakes her head and leans over, reaching for my hand. "You are not a monster. You're not your father."

"There's something about the night of the fire you don't know—things no one knows," I say, but the words get caught in my throat, and my lungs become tight with the effort to breathe.

"Then tell me."

I take a deep breath and try to fill my lungs. Everything comes flooding back, the smell, the pain—all of it. "The fire was my fault."

My mum gets to her feet to round the counter and sit on the stool beside me. "No, it wasn't. It was a cigarette which caused the fire."

I shake my head. "But it was because of me."

My father had been drinking more than usual, and he'd hit Lottie. It was mostly Mum who took the brunt of his anger, or me, but never Lottie. I was so angry, I wanted to kill him. But he was too big, too strong. I swung at him, and he pushed me over like I was nothing. And I got a backhander for my trouble.

I felt worthless. I hated him, and my mum had become numb to it all. She'd polish off a bottle of wine, then go sleep it off while he'd sat up, smoking and drinking until he passed out in the front room.

Usually, when he'd fall asleep, I'd take the cigarette and put it out in the ashtray. I'd wait until I heard him snoring and then sneak out of my room to go get Lottie and me something to eat. There were too many nights we'd go to bed hungry.

I was so mad. I wanted him to burn himself, wanted him to know what it was like to be burnt with one—how he had burnt me. I wanted him to feel the same pain.

So, I left it between his fingers and went back to Lottie with two slices of bread and margarine. It was when I snuck back to my room that the smoke first hit me and then—the hiss and the heat from the flames. I didn't know what to do. It's still hazy, my memory, but I know I tried to put it out. It was wild and out of control—it's how I ended up being burnt.

I ran to my mum's room, but she wouldn't wake up. I picked up Lottie and managed to get her out, but my parents never made it. And all because I wanted my father to suffer as I had.

"I never put his cigarette out. They both died because of me, and in the end, I was no better than him. I became the monster I despised."

My mother is crying, holding my hands in a tight grip. "Oh, Oliver, it wasn't your fault. It wasn't your job to take care of your parents. That burden should never have fallen on you in the first place."

"I disagree. In the end, I was no better than he was, and no matter how much I try to redeem myself, I fear I never will."

She shifts and pulls me into an embrace. "Olly, you already have, don't you see? Nobody is all bad or all good. But you're the best parts of your biological parents. Why do you think I read Frankenstein to you?"

I pull back so I can see her face. "Because I feared I was a monster. Because of all the times I came home from school crying from the name calling?"

"In part, yes, but also because of this quote: 'Life, although it may only be an accumulation of anguish, is dear to me, and I will defend it.' And you always have defended life, Olly. You are not, and never will be the monster you fear."

I cry then, for the little boy who blamed himself for the death of his parents. For all the times I was bullied and taunted—too afraid to defend myself.

Chapter Sixty-One

Olly

I missed the text from Rachel. I had been on the phone for hours, and by the time I saw it, I decided it was too late to text her back. Sleep is the holy grail when you're a mum, and more so when you are a single parent.

There is so much I want to say, so much I need to tell her. I get a cab to the gym so I can go over the self-defence classes for the upcoming weeks. I might not be able to do anything physical, but I want to make sure everything is ready in preparation.

"Man, what are you doing here?"

I smile when I see Henry. "Just wanted to check the rota."

He comes over and holds out his fist. "It's good to see you, but I told you, I got this." He sits in the chair opposite my desk.

"I know, but I still think it's too much with your fight coming up."

He waves his hand. "It's months away, and it's not like the days are booked out solid—it's a couple of classes a week."

I drop the pen and lean back. "Fair enough. Thanks, man, I appreciate it."

"So, where's your girl at?" he asks.

My stomach drops. I need to see her. I can't go another week with things being like this. "Work, I think."

He straightens. "What did you do?"

I cross my arms. "Why do you assume I did anything?"

"Because you are a self-saboteur. I've known you long enough."

He's right, but with Rachel, it's different. I want to be selfish by being with her. "We had a disagreement when I came out of the hospital, but I intend to make it right."

It's a strange sensation—the longing I have for her. It's so intense, it has manifested into a physical ache.

"And yet you're here?" I throw my pen at him; he catches it without effort.

"You're a fine one to talk. What the fuck is going on with you and Meg? I heard about Emilio showing up at the fight and getting in her face?"

He gives me a stiff smile, which is out of character for him. "I don't know, but I plan on getting to the bottom of it." He clenches his fist in his lap. "Has she said anything to you?"

I shake my head. "Not a damn thing. You two ever going to accept you like each other?"

His laughter is subdued. "I think that ship has sailed. Besides, I can't do that to my brother, you know."

He is loyal, it's one of the reasons we all became friends. We were a motley crew, with our quirks and flaws. Maybe it's what brought us together. "Talk to him; he might surprise you."

He shrugs with indifference, but he can't ignore it forever.

There's a knock at the open door, and when I peer over Henry's shoulder, I see Charlie with Simon on his heels.

"Well, damn, look what the cat dragged in." I stand and walk around to greet Simon, Sophie and Felicity's best friend.

"Heard you had a fight with a car and lost," he says, smiling and pulling me in for a quick man-hug.

"Henry, this is Simon, Selene's godfather."

"Hey, man." Henry nods and stands. "I need to get back downstairs," he says and leaves us to it.

"I wasn't sure if you were here, but thought I'd check," says Charlie. "Just picked him up from the airport and thought we'd stop by before going to surprise Sophie at work."

"She's going to lose it when she sees you, man."

He puffs out his chest and then smooths down an eyebrow. "Can you blame her?"

We all laugh. He's been living in New York. He comes back when he can, but Charlie told me how much she and Felicity both miss him when he's not here.

"Ryan not with you?" I ask.

"No, he's coming out in a week or two."

"Cool, we can do a lads' night, then?"

He holds out his hand and shakes mine. "You bet ya."

I look at my wrist and see it's almost eleven. "Don't suppose I can bum a lift off you? I can't drive yet, but I need to clear some shit up with Rachel…"

"Of course, but she's not at work. Soph said something about her needing to take some time off…something about Marcus and Dubai."

"What the fuck? Can you drop me to hers on the way?"

"Yeah, no worries."

Charlie pulls over at the end of the cul-de-sac, and I cut through the bollards on foot. I'm approaching the block of flats when I see Rachel jogging towards the curb. My heart speeds up. She's beautiful.

"Got it," she calls out, waving a passport in her hand.

"Hurry up, Mummy. We'll miss the plane."

I stop walking, my feet rooted to the pavement. *The plane?* The car door slams shut and I hear the rev of the engine as the car pulls away. I have to sit on the wall to catch my breath.

What the fuck?

My mind goes into overdrive. She's taken some time off work... She and Molly were in a car on their way to the airport...

A sudden coldness hits my core. How could she, and not even talk to me first? I rub my temple, my chest tight.

This can't be happening.

"You all right?" I look up to see an older man walking his dog.

"Yeah, fine. Just waiting for a cab," I reply, sliding my phone from my pocket, noticing a missed call from a number I don't recognise. I go to the app and order a cab before listening to the voicemail.

The voice is unfamiliar and yet familiar.

She has a nervous catch to her breathing as she leaves me a message, and when she says her name, I'm grateful to already be sitting. *It can't be.* My hands shake as I end the voice message and my finger roams over the number of the missed call. After taking a deep breath, I dial the number and wait for her to pick up.

Chapter Sixty-Two

Rachel

I'm beyond exhausted.

I've been up since the crack of dawn helping Marcus get ready for his trip to Dubai. We agreed it might be good for him to get away from bad habits here, and he can find out about this job opportunity while he's there, too.

He spent some quality time with Molly, and though she continued to ask after Olly, he didn't seem to be annoyed by the fact. I mean, how can he? Olly saved her life.

I hesitate when I arrive at Olly's house. There's a car parked over his drive. His is parked on the driveway. I get a sinking feeling in the pit of my stomach—maybe this was a bad idea.

Hesitating, I walk with trepidation up his path and to the front door. I pause at the voices floating out through the open window. His is distinct—I would sound it out in a crowd—but it's the female one which is unfamiliar.

And instead of knocking like any sane person, I step

towards the bay windows. The blinds are open, his living room visible.

My breath catches when I see him embrace another woman. He is holding her by the shoulders, and her face is tilted towards his. But what crucifies me is the way he's gazing at her with so much admiration and love.

And suddenly, I can barely get air into my lungs. I step back and try to breathe. Who is she? Was he playing me this whole time?

I stagger back down the path and towards Betty, needing to be anywhere but here.

Molly has a sleepover tonight with Sophie, but I can't bear going home. I know there is one place he won't be, so I drive towards the bar.

Olly

I should be sitting down. I know pacing like this is not doing my body any good, but I'm a ball of nervous energy. How did she even find me?

When she said she wanted to see me, I was floored.

When she called herself *Charlotte*, I almost thought I mistook her voice for someone else, but as soon as she corrected herself and said, Lottie, I knew it was her.

I'm sweating profusely, so I go to the bathroom to rinse my face. I don't want the first time I see her to be dripping with sweat.

God, what if she blames me for our parents' death? What if she hates me and she's coming here for answers?

The sound of the doorbell echoes through my house like a final curtain call, and I know it's now or never. Buster is out with the dog walker which means it will be just the two of us.

I inhale a deep breath before I open the door, and the air is knocked right out of me.

"Olly," she says on a small exhale.

"Lottie," I reply, struggling not to get choked up.

We stare at one another for a brief moment. She is so much like our mother, whereas I look like my father, but we both have the same eye colour.

I reach out my hand towards her, and she takes it without hesitation before stepping into the doorway and wrapping her arms around my neck.

I hold onto her, probably too tight.

"You're so grown up," I say when I let go. I close the door behind us and lead her into the living room.

"So are you," she replies, wiping moisture from her eyes.

"I can't believe you found me."

"I've been trying for years. And then I saw an article in the paper, and I knew it was you."

"I'm so sorry, Lottie, about everything…about that night."

She touches my shoulders and stares up at me. "What? Why are you sorry?"

"Because I never put out his cigarette—the fire started because of me."

Her eyes turn to slits. "And him hitting us…was that your fault?" she asks.

"Of course, not," I reply, frowning.

"Exactly. We were innocent, Olly. You saved me. I remember everything about that night," she says. "If it weren't for you, I'd be dead. I never forgot you—not once."

I can't believe she's here. "My parents—I mean, my foster parents tried to help me find you. But we were both wards of the court, and our records were sealed."

She nods in understanding as I reach out and cup her face, still unable to process she's here, in my home. My sister. "Were you okay? Were you fostered or adopted? Did they treat you well?" I ask. I always worried about where she ended up. Not able to protect her, some of my nightmares were of the Lottie I knew screaming, but I could never reach her.

"My foster parents adopted, and they are wonderful."

I let out a breath. "I always worried."

"I missed you," she says.

"I missed you more," I say, and it's the truth. When we were separated, I thought I was being punished for the part I played in the fire—not the physical scars but the emotional ones, of not knowing if she was being taken care of, whether she was loved.

"Impossible," she says with a laugh—one so much like our birth mother's.

"Come sit down, we have so much to talk about," I say and lead her to the sofa, keeping her hand in mine, not ready to let go quite yet.

Rachel

I order a double gin and tonic. *What the hell*. I'll get a cab home and get my car tomorrow before collecting Molly. I only recognise Mavis who served me when I arrived here, so I find a small table in the corner where I decide to plant myself.

It's the vision of the way he was staring at her like she was everything I'm not that has me downing my first drink and ordering another. I never imagined pain like this. Why does loving someone hurt so much?

"Rachel?"

I peer up over my (third or fourth, who can count?) glass and make eye contact with Charlie. "Oh hey," I reply, heat seeping into my face.

I must look a right state in my ripped jeans and the baggy t-shirt I usually only wear when painting. I didn't change after dropping off Molly because I needed to see Olly. That went fucking swimmingly.

"You alone?" he asks.

"Would seem so," I reply, trying not to sound rude.

"No hot date?" He smiles, but I know he's curious as to why I am at his bar this early, drinking alone.

Right now, I don't care about other people's opinions of me—it's none of my business—and those who don't care, don't matter.

"I thought Olly was more than a stereotype, but boy, did he have me fooled."

He takes a seat opposite me with a frown. "What do you mean?"

I down the rest of my drink and get to my feet. I need another. He touches my hand to stop me, then signals Mavis. She nods and minutes later, a fresh drink is in front of me. I take a huge swig. "Thanks."

"Why does he have you fooled?"

"Isn't this against guy code—me talking to you about him?"

He shakes his head. "No code, not when you seem so frazzled."

That's a polite way of putting it. I bite the inside of my cheek and thumb the condensation on the glass between my palms. "I saw him earlier with another woman."

Charlie leans away, crossing his arms. "Are you sure?"

"Yes."

He scrubs his hand over his face. "I'm not sure what to say, except, I know he more than likes you Rachel. I've never known him to be anything but transparent with his intentions."

I pick at the cardboard coaster in front of me, the urge to cry coming to the forefront. I push it away. "Oh, he was transparent, all right."

Charlie stands, seeming at a loss. "Listen, I need to get

behind the bar. You'll be okay? Do you want me to call anyone?"

I shake my head.

I lose count of what time it is or how many drinks I've had. I don't even fully comprehend Felicity showing up with Nate until she's joining me in the ladies' toilet.

My head spins as I pee and rest my temple against the cold, tiled wall.

"Are you okay?" she calls out.

"Fine. When did you get here?" I ask, my words slur.

She chuckles, low. "About an hour ago."

I flush when I'm finished and join her at the sink. She looks over me with pity. "Want to talk about it?"

I tilt my head back, a wave of dizziness assaulting me, so I stare at my reflection that's slightly blurred, instead. "Does it bother you? That I slept with Nate?" I ask her.

She bites back her grin. "I wasn't with him when you did. So no, it's a moot point. Anyway, don't change the subject—what happened with you and Olly?"

I groan and slump against the sink. "I thought he cared about me. I went to see him, to apologise. To tell him how I feel…and he was with someone else."

She nods and eyes me. "Charlie said something like that in his text."

My shoulders sag. "It's why you came. Are you my search and rescue?"

Laughing, Felicity grabs hold of my hand. "No, I'm your friend." And that's when the torrent of tears come. She pulls me into her and hugs me.

"The worst part is, I've never felt like this about anyone else before," I say, pulling back and wiping my nose.

"What did he say when you saw him?"

I shake my head. "Nothing. I was peeking in his window."

Felicity tries to cover her smile. "You were spying on him?"

"God, no. I was going to apologise. I heard him, and I

peeked through his window." Saying it out loud, I sound like a fucking crazy bitch.

"You need to talk to him."

I know she's right, but right now, he is the last person I want to see. "Fancy having a shot with me?"

"Why not? Nate drove," she replies, linking her arm through mine as I exit the restrooms, a little wobbly on my feet.

Chapter Sixty-Three

Olly

I've been leaning against the wall outside the toilets for the past twenty minutes. *How long does it take a girl to pee?*

Suddenly, the door flies open and surprised eyes meet mine. Rachel steps back, almost knocking over Felicity in the process, but she manages to right herself, her arm securely tucked into Rachel's.

"Oliver. What are you doing?"

"Waiting to talk to you," I say, nodding to Felicity in greeting.

"Shall I give you two a minute?" she asks.

Ignoring Felicity's question, Rachel speaks, "I have nothing to say to you." Her bottom lip trembles and she bites her lip nervously.

"Well, I have plenty to say to you."

She huffs out a sigh. "Just leave me alone, Oliver."

I take hold of her elbow and pull her towards me, her

pupils dilated. How much has she had to drink? "Felicity, can you give us a minute?"

She nods, slips her arm free, and then quickly walks to the door leading back into the main bar.

I pull her gently with me, then scan my pass to open the office door and take her inside.

"Really?"

"Yes."

She crosses her arms, albeit sloppy, and I usher her to the small couch where she reluctantly sits. I study her face. She looks like she's been crying and I fucking hate it. "Why are you here bad-mouthing me?" I ask.

Her eyes pin me to where I'm standing. "You are a jerk," she replies.

I point to myself. "I'm a jerk."

"Yes. Why did you even make a big deal about us being together when you were already messing around with someone else?"

I take a step forward and come to a stop. "What are you even talking about right now?"

She gets to her feet and steps right up to me, her chest practically touching mine. Tilting her head to stare back at me, she pokes me hard in the chest. "You—" She pokes me again, and I grab her hand to still her. "I saw you with someone else. And don't try to deny it, Oliver."

Is she fucking kidding me right now? "I was not, nor have I *ever been* with anyone else whilst I've been with you."

She cocks an eyebrow and leans on her hip. "Then who was the woman I saw you making googley eyes with?"

I almost want to laugh. "What?"

"I came to your house to apologise. I wanted to tell you *I love you*. And I saw you standing in there, staring at another woman the way I wish you would stare at me."

I have to take a tiny step back to catch a breath. "You love me?"

She turns her back on me and heads towards the door, but I grab her elbow and pull her around to face me. "Olly, just let me go."

Is she kidding me? "No, not until you answer my question."

She crosses her arms in defiance, her nose in the air. "No—why should I?"

"Because I love you, too," I say, soft. She shakes her head in disbelief. "It was Lottie—my sister."

A whoosh of air expels from her lips, and her eyes trace my face in search of a lie. Her shoulders droop, and her arms fall to her sides. "Lottie?"

I nod.

Covering her face with her hand, she lets out a groan. "Oh, my God."

"Did you mean what you said? Do you love me?" I ask, my heart beating rapidly in my chest.

"Does it even matter now?" she mumbles through her fingers.

I pull her hand away and tilt her chin. Her eyes meet mine. "Of course, it matters."

A tear leaks from the corner of her eye, and I wipe it away with the pad of my thumb. "Yes… But I thought you were with someone else," she replies, waving her hand around for emphasis.

"Well, I thought you left to go to Dubai with Marcus."

Her eyes go wide. "What? Why?"

"After our argument, I came to see you, but you were jogging to the car holding your passport. I thought you chose him."

A snort of laughter escapes her. "No. Molly and I were seeing him off at the airport."

"So, you aren't going to try again with Marcus?"

She shakes her head. "No, but he is Molly's dad…and a friend."

I didn't know how badly I needed to hear her say those

words to me. "I'm not good enough for you," I say, the thoughts which have plagued me finally passing the confines of my mind.

She goes to step towards me, but I notice she is unsteady on her feet, and then I remember she's likely drunk and direct her back to the couch. "Olly, you're the best man I've ever known."

Her words slice through me, melting my worry and anxiety. "I'm flawed like anyone else."

"We all are," she replies, her trembling hand reaching up to stroke my cheek.

I squeeze my eyes closed. Her touch eases my internal battle. "Could you see yourself with someone as flawed as me, though?"

She leans forward, and I can smell the alcohol on her breath. "Yes."

She seals the word with a scorching kiss, and I can barely think straight. I am lost, drunk on the slide of her tongue and the way she kisses me with determination and purpose.

When we pull apart, I rest my forehead against hers. "Will you stay with me tonight?" She nods. But I clarify, "Just so I can hold you—nothing else."

Her forehead forms a frown.

"I'm still getting over my surgery, and as much as I want to make love to you, I won't while you're intoxicated. I want you to be right there with me."

"Oh," she breathes.

A soft smile forms on her perfect face. She strokes my jaw, and my dick twitches. Damn, she makes it impossible not to want her. I stand and hold out my hand; she takes it without hesitation. I'll do whatever it takes to make this work between us.

Chapter Sixty-Four

Rachel

My head pounds without mercy, my mouth so dry, I can barely swallow. My tongue sweeps over my front teeth. I sit up too fast and have to lay back down, covering my eyes with my forearm, groaning out loud from the effort.

"Morning." Olly's deep baritone voice greets me, and I struggle to remember what the hell happened.

"Why do I feel like death warmed up?" I ask.

"You had a little to drink last night," he replies.

"Why are you shouting?" His laugh echoes around me, and what was once a favourite sound of mine has now reverted to distain. "Sshhh."

"I made you a cup of tea, but in case you aren't ready for caffeine, there is a bottle of water and some paracetamol on the side table." His hand strokes my arm, and a shiver rolls over me, lulling me into almost forgetting how dreadful I feel.

But then I panic and sit bolt upright. "Molly," I squeal.

He grabs my hand. "Calm down. Sophie has taken her to the zoo. You're good."

I clutch my chest and wonder if I might be sick. "I need to use the bathroom."

He shifts off the bed, and I gingerly climb out. "Feel free to have a bath or shower," he says to my retreating back.

I want to curl up and die.

I spend an obnoxious amount of time in the bathroom and end up soaking in the bath for well over half an hour when he taps on the door. "Can I come in?"

"Yeah."

He enters carrying a bottle of water and passes it to me, unscrewing the cap before he does. I drink it slowly at first, then end up finishing it and leaning my head back against the tub. "I'm so sorry, Olly."

His hand dips into the water, and he swirls it around. "Me, too." I was such a foolish idiot. "Do you remember what you said last night?" he asks.

I let out a deep breath and turn my face towards him. "Yes."

"And now?"

I reach into the water for his hand and grip it in mine. "I love you, Olly," I whisper.

He leans towards me, and his nose strokes mine. "I love you, too," he replies just before his mouth brushes against mine.

I squirm and deepen the kiss, pulling him closer, the water sloshing over the sides. He laughs against my lips, and I'm grateful for his spare toothbrush I used. Otherwise, I wouldn't be kissing him right now.

When we come up for air, he sits back. "How about you get dressed and we'll make some breakfast?"

I nod, and he passes me a towel. The water drips off my skin as his eyes soak me in. "On second thought…" His hand cups me between my legs, causing me to gasp. "I think I'd like to start with you."

He slides a finger inside me, which is quickly joined by another as his thumb circles my clit.

"Fuck," I curse.

Gripping his shoulder, I rest my wet forehead over his chest. He drops his head against my neck and lets out a growl as his fingers hook inside me, hitting the spot I needed them to be so badly.

Olly

After I manage to get her to eat, we go and sit on the sofa. She's wearing a pair of my joggers and a t-shirt. Damn, I hate my body for not being up to the task of ravishing her right now. I can't keep my hands from roaming over her body though, needing to touch her.

"So, Lottie, how did she find you?"

I shake my head. "She saw an article in the paper and called the gym. The rest is history, can you believe she lives less than half an hour from me?"

"It's fate."

I kiss her temple. "I still can't believe she wanted to. She'd been looking for me, too."

Rachel strokes circles over my tattooed arm. "Well, believe it."

"You'll love her. She's so down to earth."

Rachel leans up and nibbles my jaw. "If she's anything like you, I don't doubt it." I tense beside her. "Don't, Olly. You're a good man." She caresses my face. Her fingers work up and into my scalp, my eyes drifting closed.

"But I'm not perfect. I need to tell you something about

my past. And I'll understand if this changes things between us."

Her hand falls away from my scalp and into my lap where she grips my hand. "I doubt it," she replies, sounding so sure of herself.

I take a deep breath.

And then I tell her about the night of the fire—how I never put out my father's cigarette.

"Look at me?" I do as she asks, completely exposed and bare at this moment. "You're a good man. You were a *boy*. It wasn't your job to be the parent, it was theirs. Oliver, you knit hats for a baby ward, for Christ's sake. You give self-defence classes to show women how to protect themselves. You saved my daughter." Her words are determined and passionate. She cups my face. "I don't care if I have to tell you every day what a good man you are, I will until you believe it. Olly. You. Are. Not. A. Monster."

And then she kisses me.

With every stroke of her tongue, hope seeps in, the fear no longer holding me prisoner, and I know it's partly to do with this exceptional woman who I already know I want to spend the rest of my life proving I'm worthy of her love.

Chapter Sixty-Five

Olly

The room is almost finished, and I'm doubting myself. But then, I know if we're going to make this work, I want Molly to have a space to call her own—and not just at weekends.

Simon was the one who gave me the idea, so here we are, at my house, making the finishing touches.

"I haven't told Felicity or Sophie yet, but we're thinking of adopting," says Simon.

I drop the paintbrush into the tray and look up. He's focused on the stencil he's painting but pauses to look over his shoulder. "We want to come home—start a family," he says.

I'm a little humbled he would share this with me first instead of his best friends. "I think it's awesome. man. But why haven't you told them yet?"

He stops what he's doing and climbs back down the ladder. "I don't know. It's a long process, and we might not even be eligible. I wanted to hear what you thought—Soph mentioned you were fostered as a child."

I smile. "I was. My foster parents *are* my parents. And I think it's great, there are a lot of children out there looking for a forever home."

"So, you don't think it's wrong to have same-sex parents?"

I let out a rough laugh. "Hell no. The fact you're even worried shows you are serious about this. If you didn't have concerns or questions, then I'd be worried. But what I do know is you'll make a great dad. Your sexual orientation doesn't determine what a good parent makes."

"I'm ready to settle down, and we've talked about it for the past two years. Seeing Sophie with Selene has solidified it for me—this is what I want."

I take him by the shoulder and hold his stare. "Then you go for it, man. When will you be moving back?"

He smirks. "I already have. I'm renting a short term let, while we wait for our house to be finalised with the solicitors. Ryan is tying up everything else in New York, and he'll be leaving and coming over with the dogs next week."

"Damn, man. I can't wait to see Sophie's face when she hears you're coming back."

"Same, and it'll be nice being closer to my god-daughter."

"Yeah, they grow up so fast, don't they?"

He laughs. "They do, I mean look at Molly-Mae."

"She's a sweetheart." I get back to my stencil. I want this finished before Rachel gets here.

"You love her like a father, don't you?"

I do. I couldn't love her more if she were my own. "Yes, hence this," I say, waving around the room.

"Well, if this doesn't seal the deal and have Rachel's baby makers ready for more, I don't know what will."

I shake my head. "Slow down. I don't want to scare her away."

"Scare *who* away?"

I squeeze my eyes closed and take a deep breath before standing and turning towards the door. "You're early."

Rachel points over her shoulder. "Do you want me to leave and come back later?"

Simon laughs. "There, all done. I need to get going. I'll catch you both soon?"

"Yeah." He pats my back as he walks past. "Thanks again for your help and good luck."

"Likewise," he says, giving me a wink. He turns to Rachel, kisses her cheek, and dashes off.

"What's going on?" she asks, looking around the room. Her eyes go wide as she takes it all in—the Disney sleigh bed covered in a transparent dust sheet, new carpet I had fitted, and the walls painted two days ago. The stencils were the finishing touches.

"It's for Molly," I reply.

"Wow, Olly, it's lovely, but seriously, it's too much."

Shit, not the response I was hoping for. "You don't like it?" I ask, my shoulders sagging.

"No, I love it, but she's never going to want to leave," she replies as her eyes roam over the stencils.

Man up, Olly. Ask her.

"Are these..." She walks over to the wall.

"Molly's baby hand and footprints. It was Simon's suggestion. Your mum gave us her copy so we could create the stencils."

"She did?" I nod and come to stand beside her. "It's the most thoughtful thing you could've done. But like I said, she's going to be a terrorist when it comes to leaving."

I fill my lungs and blurt it out, "I don't want you to leave."

She turns to me slowly. "What?"

"I want you and Molly to move in with me." Silence ripples over the room, her jaw slack. "Sorry, I had a whole speech prepared. I wanted to make it special when I asked you." Now I'm rambling. I wipe my slick palm over my face, not sure what I'm even saying now.

"You've lost me—ask me what?"

Fuck it. It's now or never. I drop to my knee and grab her hand. This was not how I'd planned to do this, but what the heck.

"Rachel Evans, I love you with a passion I never thought existed. You make me want to be the only man you see. Will you and Molly-Mae move in with me…and will you agree to be my wife?"

I'm not sure if it's her hand that's shaking or mine. But it's the lack of response which has my heart stuttering in my chest.

I scramble to my feet and release the grip I have on her hand to begin pacing the room.

Shit!

Chapter Sixty-Six

Olly

"Shit, I blew it, didn't I?" I turn away.

"Olly," she says her voice timid.

"I love you, Rachel." I rack my brain how to fix this.

"Olly," she says, louder this time. Her breath tickles the back of my neck. I turn around, our toes almost touching. "I love you, too, but do you know what you're asking?"

I grab her hips and squeeze. "Of course, I do. I've been planning this for months."

Her eyes sparkle. "You have?"

I nod. "Yes." I cup her face between my palms. "I'll wait if you're not ready. But I want us to be together. And I'd prefer to be living together. If you're not ready to get married, or don't want to then—"

She covers my mouth with her lips, kissing me hard. I'm lost to her touch. When we both come up for air, her eyes meet mine. "We'd love to move in with you, and I'd love to be your wife."

I pick her up, and she wraps her legs around my waist. "You're saying yes?"

She nods. "Of course, I am, but only if you're sure, Olly, I won't do this unless you're sure."

"I've never been more sure of anything in my entire life." I kiss her again, getting lost in the taste of her lips while I carry her out into the hallway. I force myself to stop and put her back on her feet.

Only I could royally fuck up a proposal. "Close your eyes," I say.

"What?"

"Please, close your eyes."

I rush to my bedroom and grab the box from my bedside cabinet and then return to her, her eyes still closed. "Keep them closed." I take her by the elbow and lead her to the other guest room, which was mainly for storage, and push the door open. "Okay, open your eyes."

I watch her intently as she opens one and then the other. She covers her mouth with a loud gasp. Her gaze sweeps across the room, and when she turns to find me, I'm on one knee, holding out the open jewellery box, the ring on display.

"You did this for me?" she asks.

I nod. "I know it's not quite the studio you deserve, but it's a start."

Falling to her knees in front of me, she grabs my face and kisses me, knocking me onto my arse. The box goes flying. "Shit." She scrambles away from me and retrieves it.

"Am I ever going to get this proposal right?" I ask, defeated.

"Are you kidding me, Olly? This is perfect." She throws her arms around my neck and squeezes me hard.

"Can't breathe."

Leaning back, she loosens her grip, her smile radiant.

I take the ring from the box and reach for her hand; it trembles as I slide it onto her ring finger. *Thank fuck it fits.*

"It's beautiful. It must have cost you a fortune."

I stroke her cheek. "You're worth it."

She shakes her head, smiling. The diamonds catch the reflection of the setting sun through the window and dazzle. "I had something made for Molly, too," I say.

Her eyes soften. "You did?"

"I didn't want her to feel left out."

"Olly, you decorated her a room fit for a princess—how could she feel left out?"

"I don't know, but it's a promise from me to her. I love her like a daughter."

Her lips crash against mine, almost feral. She reaches for my jeans. "Off," she says, demanding.

I laugh and oblige, pulling my t-shirt over my head as she strips out of her own clothes. She pushes on my chest until I'm on my back and she straddles me. Gripping my hard length, and without waiting, she lowers herself onto me with a hearty moan.

"So good," she says, throwing back her head as she begins to ride me hard and fast.

I grip her hips, the sensation mouth-watering. I sit up a fraction and then pull her down hard, holding her in place. "So, will you marry me?" I ask, pushing up into her, stilling until she answers me.

"Yes." She's panting, her chest heaving.

"When?"

"Oliver, please make love to me first."

I flip her onto her back. She wraps her legs around me, digging her feet into my arse. "When?" I ask again, pushing into her slowly.

"Deeper," she begs, her nails biting into my flesh.

I hold still again, and she gazes up at me. "As soon as you want, but please, fuck me already."

I drive into her, my balls slapping against her arse. She

reaches between us and touches herself, knowing how much I love it when she lets go of her inhibitions.

It's enough to make me come, but I hold back, wanting her to ride the wave with me. I watch in awe as her climax builds, her hot centre tightening around me like a vice.

"Come on, baby, let go," I grunt, thrusting into her.

She leans up, her teeth bite down on my shoulder, pulling me tightly against her naked flesh, slick with sweat as we find our release together.

Chapter Sixty-Seven

Rachel

Panting heavily, I lay in Olly's arms, our sweat-slick bodies coming down from our ministrations. I gaze over the room, overwhelmed he would do this for me. "It's beautiful. Thank you."

He kisses my shoulder. "I wish it were a real studio, but for now, I think it'll do."

I can't wait to paint. My fingers itch to pick up a paintbrush, to allow my imagination to run wild over the canvas. There is always something magical about a blank canvas right before you start—anything is possible.

"I still want to paint you," I say, stroking up and down his arm.

"Oh, you do, do you?"

I giggle when he nips at the skin below my ear. "Yes, like one of those French girls," I say, teasing.

He pulls me underneath him, hovering, his arms either

side of my head. "Well, I can think of something else I'd rather do," he says, his lips covering mine.

I don't know if I'll ever get enough of this man, of the way he touches me, which I now understand to be his love language. "And what's that?" I whisper into his mouth.

"How about I show you," he says, working his way down my body. It tingles in anticipation, and then a soft breath caresses my most sensitive parts.

With a flick of his tongue, I become lost and found with every stroke, lick and nip. He brings out a wild, lustful side of me I never knew existed. With him, I am insatiable. I trust him with my body and heart. I didn't realise until now how the two go hand in hand.

He kisses his way up my body, back to my face.

"One of my favourite things is to witness how your body reacts to an orgasm. Do you know you flush pink? You get patches here, here and here." He kisses each one for emphasis.

"What can I say? You do things to me."

He laughs and kisses the tip of my nose. Letting out a contented sigh, he lays beside me, and I curl into him, utterly sated.

I hold up my hand and admire the ring, wiggling my fingers. "It's beautiful," I whisper.

"Hmm, hmm."

I peer up, his eyelids close, a contented smile gracing his face. I watch him until he drifts off, one arm under his head.

Slipping his shirt over my head, I find a palette and pull out the paints. I study his sleeping figure, then, positioning the easel, I sit on the stool. Pencil in hand, I trace a quick outline before getting lost in vivid colours with every brushstroke.

I see the moment he begins to wake—he blinks, and his gaze finds me.

"Like what you see?" he asks, his arousal evident.

Biting down on my lip, I drop the palette onto the desk behind me and stalk towards him, holding out my hand. He reaches for it and pulls me swiftly on top of him, playfully kissing my neck.

"Fancy washing my back?" I ask, giving him a sly smile.

He sits up, his hands tracing underneath the fabric of the t-shirt. His fingers seek out my breasts until they find my nipples, and he gives them a quick tweak. "Only if you promise to let me dirty you up again later?"

I let out a laugh. I'd let him dirty me up right now, but I'm also conscious of the fact this room probably reeks of our post-coital ministrations. "Absolutely."

He wraps his hand around the back of my neck, stopping just before our lips meet. "I love you." His violet-blue orbs hold me captive as they always do; his words settle over me in warm waves.

"I love you, too." I make up the distance, my lips connecting with his, warm and accommodating. His thumbs trace the tracks of the tears I'm unable to hold at bay.

"What is it?" he asks, concern in his voice.

"I never thought I could be this happy or that I'd love someone as much as I love you."

He smiles, it's devilishly handsome, and I know I'll never get enough of this man. "Do you remember the fortunes from our first Chinese together?"

I nod. "My stars predicted tall, dark and handsome," I say with a giggle.

"But do you remember mine?"

I shake my head. "No."

His stare is so intense, my body heats from that penetrating gaze. "If you love something, set it free." He leans up to kiss my chin, my cheek, all my nerves alive with every tender kiss. "If it returns, keep it and love it forever." His gaze is sincere, powerful. "I plan to keep you and love you forever," he whispers, just as he positions me above him, and I sink down. He fills me completely. His words pierce my soul. I grip his shoulders as I ride him. We come together as one; only this time, we don't fly, we soar.

In time, the flames may fade, but burning embers will remain. And with him by my side, I believe anything is possible.

Letter to Reader

Thank you for making it this far, and I hope you enjoyed Olly and Rachel's story as much as I did writing it. Please consider recommending Burning Embers to your book friends and leaving a review. It doesn't have to be much—one sentence will do—but I would be forever grateful if you'd consider doing so. Your reviews are extremely important for authors as a way for readers to find out about our books. And we can't make that happen without you, thank you!

Midnight Embers is Book 2 in the Embers standalone series. Available now on Amazon and **FREE** in Kindle Unlimited.

Acknowledgments

Mum—Thank you for being the best friend a daughter could ever have. There isn't anyone else who could put up with me during lockdown. I love you.

Cassie—Soul sister, lobster and best friend. You are my Yoda, thank you for the power of your edits and always pushing me to be better. I wouldn't be able to do this without you. I love You.

Crystal—you are beautiful in so many ways, and your friendship means the world to me. Thank you for proofreading and your endless support. Love you and miss your face.

Amber—You have been such a rock this past year, and the fact you aren't even aware shows how amazing you are. Thank you for beta reading and supporting me. Love you.

Kirsten—Beta Bitch girl you rock, thank you for always being honest and providing your endless support.

Dusti—thank you for always being so beautifully you and beta reading when my novels are at their roughest and loving them anyway.

Julie—I love your guts, always.

PLN authors—especially Ruth, you are pure sunshine and

Kayleigh for always being ready and willing to read my books. Victoria Ellis for always being so supportive, I love you ladies. Lyndsey, Heather, I wish I could name you all, thank you, Tarryn Fisher, for bringing us together.

My famalam—especially Grace, Tam and Dave, love you guys. Jon, we miss you always.

Friends who are family—Victoria, William, Laura, Andy, Evie and Zach, and my mountain goat, Ethel. I love and miss you all.

All the people I've met along the way who continue to support me. I see you, thank you!

My family—I love you to the moon and back.

Harley—my most loyal companion, gone but never forgotten.

Also by L.S. Pullen

Where the Heart Is
Dysfunctional Hearts
Hearts of War
Burning Embers
Midnight Embers
Forever Embers Pre-Order

About the Author

L.S.Pullen, aka Leila, was born and raised in North London, but now resides in Peterborough, England. When she's not walking her adopted pooch Luna, you'll likely find her squirrel spotting or taking care of her two adopted guinea pigs, Caesar, and Maurice.

She is passionate about everything books, lover of photography and art. And in true English cliche fashion, loves afternoon tea. No longer working the corporate life, she is currently writing full time and managing a small craft business Wisteria Handmade Crafts and Indie Author's Book Services.

For more books and updates:
https://lspullen.co.uk